BILLY MCKENZIE

ALSO BY COLIN MACKINNON

FICTION

Finding Hoseyn

Morning Spy, Evening Spy

The Contractor

NONFICTION

William Friedman's Bletchley Park Diary

BILLY McKENZIE
—— *A Story of Love* ——

A NOVEL BY

COLIN MacKINNON

Title: *Billy McKenzie, A Story of Love*/Colin MacKinnon

Identifiers:

LCCN: 2025913928

ISBN: 979-8-9929580-0-3

LCSH: Man-woman relationships—Fiction| Americans--England--London--History--19th century—Fiction| Biographical fiction, English| London (England) Fiction| Voynich manuscript—Fiction|

BISAC: FIC027170|FICTION/Romance/Historical/Victorian| FICTION/biographical| FICTION/literary| FICTION/historical|

www.colinmackinnon.com

Cover and Interior Design: Andrea Purdie

Cover Photograph: Sergei Mikhailovich Prokudin-Gorski, Library of Congress, Prints and Photographs Division, Prokudin-Gorski Photograph Collection

Illustrations on pp. 48, 165, and 209: Cipher Manuscript (Voynich manuscript), General Collection, Beinecke Rare Book and Manuscript Library, Yale University

BILLY McKENZIE

for Diane

Remember me when I am gone away,
Gone far away into the silent land;
When you can no more hold me by the hand,
Nor I half turn to go yet turning stay...

CHRISTINA ROSSETTI, *Remember*, 1862

...I say Live, Live because of the sun,
the dream, the excitable gift.

ANNE SEXTON, *Live*, 1966

PART ONE

PRÉLUDE:

Washington Square, 1918

"It's You!"

She realised who he was a few moments after they had passed one another. Her heart snapped then, and she cried aloud, "My God, Billy, it's you!" A man she had seen in the dimming afternoon light in Washington Square had been Billy McKenzie, who, for a brief, ecstatic period more than twenty years before, had been her lover.

Only Billy was dead.

She walked a few paces further mechanically in a slow-gathering tumble of emotions. When she finally had the wit to turn and look for him amongst the few other pedestrians hurrying by in the falling snow and intense cold, he had vanished. She did not believe in spirits, yet Billy's apparition – striding smartly along, his face set like flint, his hair dusted with snow – had been as vivid as life.

She started to walk in the direction he had seemed to be going, then clasping her drawings portfolio to her chest, she broke into a half-run, loping past the central fountain and down the wide walk as far as the south edge of the park, where she halted, out of breath and feeling foolish.

There had been no Billy, of course. She knew that. She marvelled at the intensity of the experience and wondered what had come over her.

—

Her name was Flora Bowles Lijak, and it was late January 1918. She was fifty-three years old, a tall, slender woman with a plain face and chilly eyes. Her thick russet hair, which had once been her glory and which had impressed Billy greatly – he called her "Divine Fire" and "Goddess" – her hair had thinned and turned grey and was acquiring streaks of white.

She had been born in Ireland to English parents. Her father, William Bowles, who died shortly after she was born, was a mathematician and had taught logic and mathematics at Queen's College, Cork; her mother, Mary Catoe Bowles, also deceased, had been a feminist writer and intellectual. Flora was married to a man named Wilfrid Michael Lijak, who was Polish by birth, British by nationality. She had been married to Lijak and living in London when she and Billy had had their disastrous affair.

Now she and Lijak lived in New York City, where he, once an impoverished fugitive from exile in Siberia, had a lucrative business dealing in rare books and illuminated manuscripts. It was one of those manuscripts, an unimaginably strange codex written in an unknown script and filled with bizarre, erotically charged illustrations, that had brought Flora that afternoon to an herbalist's in Greenwich Village hoping to find help solving its mysteries.

Returning through the park Flora thought on her – she must use the term – hallucination. She would not allow it to upset her. She most certainly would not be frightened. Things of the sort sometimes happened to people. It was singular and queer, but that was all. She was not losing her mind.

In Fifth Avenue she boarded a bus to return to her husband's showroom, a spacious suite on the top floor, the 16th, of the newly-built Aeolian Building, on 42nd Street just west of the Avenue. On the frosted glass window of the office door discreet black lettering read: "Lijak Rare Books and Prints. Incunabula. Woodcuts. Maps. Early Printed Books. W.M. Lijak, Prop."

With its view onto Bryant Park and the New York Public Library and its location at the heart of the city's commercial district, Lijak's office suite was the perfect place to entertain wealthy bibliophiles. He counted amongst his customers Henry Clay Frick, the industrialist, and J.P. "Jack" Morgan, Jr., son of the late financier. Each was known to visit Lijak Rare Books and Prints and sit chatting with its proprietor, a charming and learned raconteur.

The bus was crowded – it had started at the Battery – and hot. It smelt of sweat, tobacco, damp wool, machine oil, and engine fumes. As the bus lumbered north a sweet-faced young man in Army cap and uniform noticed her and her unwieldy drawings portfolio and quickly stood to give Flora his seat. Smiling her gratitude, she took his place.

He looked all of eighteen. He wore no overcoat or gloves, and she wondered how he could have gone out dressed as he was without freezing. Was he stationed here in New York? Would he be off soon for France? Would he be gassed? Blinded? Killed? Would he merely lose a limb? Hanging from the strap, swaying as the bus lurched forward, he seemed so young and innocent.

As Billy had been.

Billy – William Boyd McKenzie of San Francisco – was an Anarchist and Socialist, one of many from all over the world in London in the 1890s. Though personally kind, he professed admiration for revolutionary violence – "propaganda by the deed" as it was called back then – a trait that made Flora, who was pacifist by conviction, uneasy.

When she and McKenzie had become lovers Flora took to calling him "Billy," sometimes "Billy Boy," from the song ("Oh, where have you been, Billy Boy, Billy Boy?"). The name was incongruous. Billy, by turns fisherman, dockworker, and labour agitator, was over six feet tall and powerfully built and could sometimes show a rough manner. Men, sizing him up, took him seriously. As did women. No one other than she thought to call him Billy.

Flora looked out onto the Avenue: automobiles, buses, vans, shops, crowds. At 23rd Street, by the entrance to the Flatiron Building, she noticed a poster affixed to the rear of a news-stand. It showed a white-haired woman in a long black dress with white cuffs and a white bertha standing behind and gesturing with both hands toward an eager-faced young man in army uniform and wide-brimmed campaign hat. The young man was brandishing a rifle with a bayonet fixed to its barrel. The poster read, "America, Here's My Boy." Flora turned to look at her innocent soldier, but he had got off.

On the way uptown, thinking of her affair with Billy, Flora recalled:

- a crumpled letter burnt to ashes;

- a man's mangled body, his limbs in a bloody pile on a suburban London rail line;

- sexual abandon in a hotel on the south coast of England;

- a scrap of blue cloth.

When Flora returned to Lijak Rare Books and Prints, still shaken by her vision of Billy McKenzie, she walked into a scene – Lijak made scenes often, this time with poor, plain Alice Neff, who had just been hired on. Both were in the glassed-off rear office. "Oh, Meez Neff, my God, my God!" Lijak was exclaiming. "It eez ca-tastrophe. What can I think? What can I do?" He turned to Flora. "Ah, hello, Pet. Such staff I have!"

Alice, who was very young and new to the city (she was from Buffalo), was sitting in silence, looking mortified and fearful. Her large round black glasses and page-boy haircut made her seem even more defenceless.

Lijak, in his shirtsleeves and checked vest, was pacing, smoking a cigarette, and casting ash about. To Flora, Lijak said, "Ah, Pet, the horror, I am out not five minutes, Meez Neff has let Dr Neu-brander go away! Dr Neubrander! Ach, ach, ach!"

Alice had been cataloguing a shipment of books that had just

4

arrived from the London shop when Dr Arthur S. Neubrander came in. Dr Neubrander, an amiable bachelor of inherited wealth, was a physician who lived and worked on the upper East Side. He was a passionate bibliophile, but not yet a steady customer of Lijak's.

Lijak had gone down to the shops on the ground floor to buy cigarettes, and in his absence, Dr Neubrander had come in for a chat with Lijak and not finding him and having always the air of a busy man had left. Their lifts must have passed in both directions.

"Ach, Meez Neff, in future you must tie Dr Neubrander in that chair" – Lijak waved his arm at a plush armchair, one of two he had put in the outer salesroom with a table ashtray between them for the comfort of his clients – "tie him and not let him go."

Flora said, "Oh, Wilfrid, do stop! Miss Neff, pay him no heed. He's spouting. And joking. He barks but does not bite. And Dr Neubrander will be back." To quiet her husband she said, "I see the books have arrived." She nodded toward two large shipping crates with their tops prized off that sat by Alice's desk.

"Yes, Pet, the shipment from London – wonderful books! Lovely! Look, look, look!"

From a small, neat pile of books on Alice's desk Lijak chose one. He carefully handed it to Flora, who by now had pulled off her gloves and removed her hat, a cloche she had been wearing tugged down tightly over her ears, and coat, a thick blue woolen ankle-length garment with a fox fur collar, and hung them by the door and was sitting at her desk facing Alice's. Alice by this time seemed less taken aback, though she still looked wary.

The volume was bound in dried, flaking black leather. Its pages were vellum. Alice had already prepared the tag, which read, "Gautier de Lilles. Alexandreis, seu Gesta Alexandri Magni ('The Alexandriad of Gautier of Lilles, or the Deeds of Alexander the Great'). English. Second Half of the Fourteenth Century." Alice had also recorded the price (£200/$991), the incipit (how the book starts) and the explicit (how it ends), and, as noted in the colophon, who had copied it (one Thomas de Wrentham) and when (Anno Domini 1391). Where Thomas de Wrentham had done his copying could not be learnt.

Flora said absently, "Yes, lovely," and returned the volume to Lijak. She was thinking of Billy.

"Marvelous treasures, each one!" Lijak exclaimed, gesturing at the trunk and the pile of books on Alice's desk. "We have doubled our New York stock. Some of these are sold already." He fired one last shot at Alice: "Dr Neubrander would have been enthralled!" Then he said to Flora, "Any luck down there?"

"Down there? Oh. No, not much, really." Flora smiled blankly. "The Madame was unhelpful. She seemed flustered and confused and had nothing to say about the plants."

"The Madame" was Madame Miryam Roy, an herbalist and purveyor of medicinal plants who had been recommended to Flora by the botanical specialist at the Public Library, a Mr Sims. Madame Roy maintained a small, cluttered, fragrance-filled establishment in Greenwich Village, toward the end of Commerce Street, near a tobacco warehouse.

That afternoon Flora had been consulting with Madame. She had brought Madame ten Photostats taken of plant illustrations contained in a manuscript that Lijak had discovered in Europe. Flora had hoped Madame could help identify the plants.

The manuscript, a parchment codex one and one-half inches thick, six inches wide, and nine inches long, could not be dated but was surely ancient. It was written in an unknown, unreadable script that resembled the Latin, Greek, and Cyrillic alphabets, but was none of these. The manuscript also contained numerous extremely odd illustrations – precise drawings of plants that existed nowhere in the world, puzzling diagrams of the Zodiacal months and their days, and most strangely, depictions of small, naked women, some standing in round tubs, some reclining in channels that resembled the inner recesses of the female body. Many of the women grasped cords tethering stars that hovered above their heads, some others held stars in their hands. Groups of women, stripped to the skin, seemed to cavort and gambol with one another in pools of green water.

The manuscript – plants, stars, women – was like no other in the world, and no scholar who had perused its folios could explain its nature or purpose. It was simply an archaic mystery, inscrutable and alluring.

Lijak had discovered the manuscript in 1912 in an Italian monastery called San Giuseppe, fifteen miles south of Rome in the Alban Hills. Immediately he arrived in their London flat from the Continent, before even fully unpacking, he showed his find to Flora.

"Here, Pet," he said, his voice breathy with excitement, "is strange manuscript. The strangest I have seen. Look here." He pulled the volume from its oilcloth wrapping and laid it on his desk. "The cover – no signature, no title, just plain. Now look." He carefully opened the volume to the first page: a drawing of fourteen green leaves arranged randomly and overwritten in a peculiar script.

"The writing, Pet. Look at it. There is nothing like this writing seen before. It is unknown. Completely."

"What on earth, Wilfrid? How bizarre!"

"Bizarre? Oh, Pet, yes, bizarre! All these pages are of this writing. Nothing is familiar writing, Pet. All unknown. Now - now, now, now, now, look at these pages!" Turning through the codex, folio after folio, he showed Flora the manuscript's fantastic illustrations.

"My God, Wilfrid, what is it?"

"I don't know. I have seen nothing like it before. Or heard. No one has. This is unique."

Flora stroked the manuscript's creased vellum cover, which, front and back, was of a dull grey colour, tinged faintly with pink. The cover and quires were bound together by a leather thong that wound through three holes and tied in a knot at the middle hole. The codex gave off a faint odour, like the smell of a room that had been closed and airless for too long.

"It was with other books, piles of old junk mostly. The monks were keen to get rid of all that material, so I paid them seventy pounds for the lot. Very cheap. In addition to the cash, they wanted help with additions to their theology works. So, I arranged for material to be brought from Rome. Writings of Church Fathers, Lives of Saints, missals, other things in return for this." He smiled softly. "It made them happy."

The manuscript now rested on a wooden display stand draped in green felt in the very centre of Lijak's New York sales office. Below the volume lay a white card on which Flora had penned Lijak's description:

A Great Cypher Codex of Roger Bacon of the XIIIth Century
Once Belonging to the Emperor Rudolph II of Bohemia
Brought to that Country in 1595
And Presented to
The Emperor by John Dee of England,
Emissary of Queen Elizabeth I

Lijak based his account on a letter in Latin that he had found attached to the manuscript. Written on paper and dated 1667, the letter was from the rector of Charles University in Prague, Marcus Marci, to a renowned Jesuit scholar in Rome, to whom Marci had apparently sent the volume. Marci said in his letter that the volume had once belonged to the Emperor Rudolph II and suggested that it might have been written by Roger Bacon, the English monk-scholar of the 13th Century. Marci's suggestion had been only that, but it set off the excitable Lijak.

Lijak, whose bibliophilic scholarship was profound, knew that John Dee, the 16th century English astrologer and occultist, had acquired some of Bacon's writings for his personal library. Lijak knew also that Dee had visited the court of Rudolph II in Prague in the 1590s. For Lijak, the conjecture was irresistible that the manuscript had been written by Roger Bacon in cipher, that Dee had brought it to Prague, and there had sold it to Rudolph. The conjecture immediately became a certainty in Lijak's mind, and ever after he referred to the artefact as the "Bacon Cipher," as did Flora.

From the first, Flora had been drawn to the strange manuscript. In London, and now New York, she had worked to lay bare the Manuscript's secrets, trying to divine its underlying language and to attach sounds to the characters on its pages. Recently she had been concentrating on the plant illustrations, consulting botanical guide after botanical guide at the Public Library. She hoped that if she could identify the plants depicted in the Manuscript, their names would be a key, for her or for others more adept in the arts of decipherment, to the script and thence the language.

Flora had telephoned Madame Roy taking care to mention the Public Library's botanist and explained her problem. "I'm a plant enthusiast myself," she said, "I dearly love flowers, especially in the wild, but I'm having so much trouble with these, as did Mr Sims. He thought perhaps you..."

Madame Roy, born in Budapest, was dark, plump, and middle-aged. She had a growth of fine black hair on her upper lip. When Flora encountered Madame Roy in her Commerce Street establishment the Madame was wearing a colourful satin dress, in which greens and reds predominated, and a silvery satin turban. It was warm in the room and Flora found the atmosphere close.

Sitting at her specimens table, which served as desk, Flora opposite, Madame Roy lifted the first Photostat from Flora's portfolio, and studied it carefully in silence, holding it in the light of a large electric lamp she kept on her table. She set the first aside and examined the next, and the next, increasingly affected by the images, which she seemed to find disturbing. Her clever black eyes shot to Flora's once, inquisitively, then returned to the images. When she had seen all of them, she whispered, "No. No, no, no. There are not such plants. They have no names. They do not exist. I think it is old witchcraft. That is all. Witchcraft. I cannot help." She shoved the portfolio and Photostat to the far edge of her specimens table, toward Flora, and lit a cigarette. When she exhaled, she made a f-f-f-f sound and sat motionless, her lips compressed, letting her cigarette burn. Her eyes did not meet Flora's and would not.

Flora tried asking questions about the individual drawings. "Yes, witchcraft, Madame Roy, perhaps, but I think I have identified two of these plants, this one, the one with the three long stems and the three bunches of spearhead leaves" – Flora maneuvered a Photostat back toward Madame Roy – "is it *Datura* do you think? Madame Roy, could this be *Datura*? – I think it likely." Madame Roy remained silent.

Flora offered another Photostat. "Or this one, Madame Roy. Could it be Lords-and-Ladies? *Arum maculatum*?" The second illustration depicted a rising poker-shaped spadix (light purple in the original folio) enveloped in a hood (coloured a vibrant green in the original). In the right margin of the Photostat a roughly drawn nude woman, shown frontally, stood gazing upon the spadix, reaching toward (or perhaps gesturing toward) the part, not quite touching it with her right hand.

The manifest sexuality of this second illustration eluded Flora's conscious mind at the time, but later, much later, reflecting on her visit to Madame Roy, she understood the evocative power of the Manuscript. And how it had driven her mad.

To Flora's query Madame Roy gave no answer.

Flora sat for a moment puzzling what to do, then, concluding there was nothing *to* do and that her trip downtown had been wasted time, quickly reassembled her portfolio and said goodbye, to no response. She left Madame Roy without leaving a fee – Madame Roy did not object – and, hurrying in the bitter cold and whipping wind to catch an uptown bus, encountered the ghost of Billy McKenzie.

The office clock whirred and struck the half hour: five-thirty. Lijak Rare Books and Prints would soon be closing for the day. Flora and Lijak would walk to their hotel, the Waldorf-Astoria, where Lijak had begun living in 1914 and where, late in 1917, Flora had joined him; Alice would take a Broadway bus north to the Upper West Side, where she occupied a bed-sitting room.

Flora had gone to the window and had stood, hands on the frigid sill, not listening to her husband or Alice. Recollections of that long-past affair with Billy were flooding in upon her now — recollections of its passion and lust, of its brevity, and of how the affair had ended. Of course, that.

The snow had stopped. It was dark now, and the city's lights had come on. Below in 42nd Street, automobiles and buses glided noiselessly to and fro past Bryant Park, where electric lamps illuminated expanses of untracked white. As Flora gazed down, the view misted over and swam in her eyes.

OZZIE

He wrote:

TO: azad.hosseini@gu.edu
FROM: mark.morehead27@gmail.com
SUBJ: Flora Lijak

Dear Professor Hosseini:

I am a researcher interested in the Lijak Manuscript. I understand
(thanks to Google) you are an expert on the work of Flora Lijak
the radical and feminist author. I am a student this semester at GU
(poli sci). I am not in any of your classes but I was hoping to be
able to talk with you about the Manuscript and Flora Lijak. I am
in particular interested in what she might have said in her letters,
diaries etc. about it, anything that could throw some light on the
Manuscript itself. I would very much appreciate some guidance
from someone knowledgeable in literature on how I could research
this. May I meet with you at your office and discuss Flora Lijak?
Thank you very much.

Mark Morehead

She replied:

TO: mark.morehead27@gmail.com
FROM: azad.hosseini@gu.edu
SUBJ: Flora Lijak

Hi Mark,

I really don't know much about Flora Lijak. A while back I edited
a book on women writers of the 19th century (it's called Gender

and Anarchy), and one of the contributors did a piece that mentioned Lijak in passing. That's probably why Google thinks I'm a Lijak scholar. I doubt there *are* any Lijak scholars – she's pretty obscure. Also, Lijak manuscript? Don't know what that is. Something she wrote and didn't publish? I'd be happy to talk with you, however. My office hours are Tues and Thurs 10-12, New North 346.

AH

Azadeh Hosseini – her friends call her "Ozzie" – clicked Send and quickly forgot the exchange. That was one week back. Now she's at her unruly desk (books, papers, journals, pencils, blue and red BICs, coffee cup, flat-screen, keyboard, mouse, small green felt frog with big eyes and depraved grin (a gift from her younger brother David) in New North 346. She is grading a stack of twenty or so blue books, the harvest of a pop quiz she gave the day before in Major Brits, a mid–level English course. (She is Assistant Professor of English Literature, Georgetown University.) Tomorrow, the 17th of February, is her birthday. She was born thirty-seven years ago in Tehran.

At just ten o'clock Ozzie hears a soft knock-knock at her office door, which is open a slit.

"Yes?"

A youngish, unfamiliar male enters. He's wearing a quilted green parka, Levis, and hiking boots. Snow – it's a wintry, blustery morning outside – has dusted his shoulders and hair. "Professor Hosseini?"

"Yes?"

"Hi. I'm Mark Morehead. Unnh... I sent you an e–mail? About Flora Lijak?"

"Flora...? Oh, yes! Right! Right, right, right. So, hi, come on in, uh… Mark. Have a seat." Ozzie gestures toward a lone round-backed chair, upholstered in a fuzzy red fabric that sits by her desk.

Mark is bearded with that three-day-old look she doesn't much like. He's nice featured, though. Intelligent looking. (His wire–frame glasses help.) He's no undergrad – Ozzie puts him in his thirties. He has a slightly shy, nervous manner. He takes a seat in the round–backed chair.

"Mark, I've got some students coming in this morning, but I'm happy to talk till they get here."

Ozzie has two students due in this morning. They are to give oral reports on books they have chosen from a list Ozzie has post-ed on Canvas, the U's academic software. Kevin Mulvaney is the first at 10:15.

Kevin has light red hair and pink skin. He suffers from aller-gies. He sports a small soul patch. When he makes it to class he is bleary-eyed and looks hung over. Invariably. He won't have read his book, whatever it is.

Gwen Monda is scheduled for 11:30. Gwen has doe-like brown eyes. She participates well in class and in the required Can-vas postings – Ozzie has her students comment on the class read-ing and, politely, on their fellow students' comments. Gwen can be aggressive, but she is very bright. She will know her stuff.

"Sorry, I should've called."

Ozzie smiles in agreement but lets it go. "So, Mark, you're a student?"

"For this academic year. I've got a kind of sabbatical from work."

"Oh, good for you! Where do you work?"

"NSA – National Security Agency."

"Oh." She laughs. "Wow. A spy. I've never met a spy before."

"Are you sure?" he asks, loosening a little, smiling. "How do you know?"

"We-ell, actually that's a good question, isn't it? If they're any good at their jobs I suppose you don't know. Point taken. George-town's full of them, of course, at least former spies. They teach courses. But I don't know any – I think. So, what do you do at NSA, Mark? Or am I not allowed to ask?"

"You're allowed to ask. I'm not allowed to tell you." That smile again. A nice smile.

14

"Stops a lot of conversations, doesn't it? Are you a codebreaker?"

"I can say I work at NSA and that I'm an engineer and that I do research. I can also say I work at Fort Meade, but that's really about it."

"Fort Meade. That's in Maryland somewhere?"

"Right. We call it the Black Box. It's up near Laurel."

"And you work in the Black Box."

"Yes."

A pause. Conversation stopped. Ozzie remarks on this, and they both laugh.

They chat a little about Mark's courses – Poli Sci at Georgetown, Electrical Engineering at George Washington. He tells her he likes them.

Ozzie says, "So, Flora Lijak – you're interested in her. Why's that again?"

"The Lijak Manuscript – the LMs."

Which is, Mark says, the most mysterious manuscript in the world. He tells her it's been carbon dated to the early fifteenth century, but no one can say where it was produced. He tells her of the manuscript's unique and so-far undeciphered alphabet, of its spidery illustrations of imagined plants and their root systems, its diagrams of stars and the Zodiac, its depictions of women frolicking together naked in pools of water. He tells her how the manuscript was brought to light in London in 1912 by one Wilfrid Lijak, a rare book dealer and the husband of Flora Lijak. How its script has defied the efforts of scholars and expert codebreakers over the ensuing decades who have tried to read it. How it rests now in the Weisert Library of Rare Books at Columbia University, donated to that institution in 1967 as a tax dodge by the New York book dealer Hans-Peter Schmidt, who had bought it from Flora's companion and heir Alice Neff, but who was never able to sell it for what he thought it was worth.

"The Weisert?" Ozzie smiles. "I went to school there, Columbia. Undergrad." Ozzie has a brief recollection of red brick buildings and green patinaed roofs and autumn leaves. "The Weisert was one of those places nobody ever went – it was hidden away in the basement of Butler Library back then."

"Still is. I've been there. About a year ago I made the pilgrimage to see the Lijak. Awesome to see it up close, right there in front of me. You can view the Manuscript on the Web – the Weisert's put up terrific high-res shots on their site, all the folios – but I wanted to see it for myself, like, you know, the real thing, and I got their permission to visit. Stunning if you're a Lijak nut."

"Umm. Okay, this bizarre manuscript – you say nobody can read it – so, what do you want to do with it?"

"Read it." He laughs, making a face. "Fat chance. But if I can't do that, I'm thinking maybe push the boundaries a little of what we can say about it. I'd settle for that. The Lijak's such an enigma, such a mystery that any work on it that goes anywhere is an achievement. I've been messing with it for years. I write about it for the Lijak list-serves – there are a bunch – and I correspond with like-minded headcases."

"Where does Flora come in?"

"She's kind of peripheral, but I was thinking, like there's a possibility that if we looked at her... whatever she left, her novels, letters, whatever, especially letters, maybe we could turn up something interesting and new about the Manuscript – history, contents, whatever. I mean, people have done this already, gone through the Flora Lijak material, whatever was available, but not recently and not too systematically. So, I thought I'd try to take a fresh look at her. She worked on the Manuscript herself, by the way, and she was very serious about that. I've seen some of her work-notes. They're in the Library of Congress. They've got a Flora Lijak Collection."

"You're kidding! Wow. Live and learn."

"I've gone through it. It's mostly her music, not very interesting, but it's got other stuff, too, including notes she took on the Lijak. You can tell from them that she was trying to identify the Manuscript's plants. I think she was trying to match the names of the plants with the text in Lijakese and figure out the values of the characters – classic decryption technique. But I've reached kind of a dead end with her so I thought I'd consult with someone who knows about her."

"Well, as I e-mailed you, I'm no Lijak expert. But let me just check *Gender and Anarchy*. I think it was Kay Brockes who did the piece that mentioned her. Kay's at UC San Diego. Does women's stuff. Hold on, I keep a copy here in the office, let me see if I can fish it out."

Ozzie swivels her heavy wooden chair around to search through the books of varying size and condition that she's crammed into the long, high shelving behind her desk. The books are not or-dered, either by subject or by author; some lie horizontally on the volumes that stand upright. She brushes her fingers lightly and lovingly over their spines. "Oh, c'mon, c'mon, where are you? Just a sec, Mark..."

She finds her quarry: "Right, here we go, *Gender and Anarchy* and..." Ozzie leafs to the index... "and yes, right, it's Kay and she does mention Lijak – one of Kay's things is rescuing lost wom-en writers – and on pages... one-ninety-two, one-ninety-three... she says..." Ozzie reads aloud to Mark:

Flora Lijak (1864-1960) began her career as writer in 1897 with a popular novel, *Ribeiro*, set in revolutionary Italy of the 1830s. Li-jak's protagonist Ribeiro is an over-refined, almost effeminate young man by day who by night goes about incognito doing daring deeds. The implied androgyny here is of note as is the projection of the female author, merging herself with her protagonist. In *Ribeiro*, as in other of her works, Lijak invented a male persona for herself. The practice, a kind of literary cross-dressing, was adopted by numerous women novelists of the day. Publishers were only too happy to print their work, and quite conventional people read it, unaware of its sexual significance.

"Kay says Lijak wrote three other novels, but *Ribeiro* – I'm paraphrasing now – that was her best. Got translated into Russian in 1907. According to Kay... the Soviets made a big deal of the book. Reprinted it and reprinted it. Over two-and-a-half million copies sold. Wow. Considered her a major writer, absolutely revered her, put her up there with Hemmingway and Jack London in their pantheon of approved foreign authors... Taught *Ribeiro* in all their schools... Made a movie of it twice... Second one had a score by Shostakovich. Amazing. But... she never had another success. After *Ribeiro* something went out of her. Kay says:

> Her subsequent novels were critical and financial failures. In 1908 Lijak stopped writing altogether and moved to the U.S. with her husband, the Polish émigré Wilfrid Lijak, where she took up teaching music and composing. She taught for many years in the music department at Sacred Heart College in Manhattan. Lijak died in obscurity in New York in 1960, cared for by her long-time companion Alice Neff.

Kevin Mulvaney has edged into view outside Ozzie's office. He is slouching against the wall across from her door, which Mark has left open. Kevin is carrying an umber colored day pack, probably with the book he hasn't read in it. He looks guilty.

Ozzie gives Kevin a glance and a small, fluttery wave to let him know she sees him.

"Mark, my first student's arrived. Here's what I can do. I've got a Women's Lit study package that I give out to my classes. I'll send a PDF of it to you. It's a kind of guide to the field. It can point you in certain directions – encyclopedias, journals you may not know, bibliographical resources, Web links – that kind of stuff. But honestly, I don't think it'll help you much. As I say, Lijak's pretty obscure, so there may not be much on her." Ozzie folds her arms, smiling.

The signal. Mark gets up and stands awkwardly – nervous

again – and thanks her.

He exits; Kevin enters.

Ozzie's eyes follow Mark, though.

Evening. Ozzie is home, a small apartment she rents on Wisconsin Avenue. She lives just south of the Cathedral, close enough to campus to walk, yet far enough, half an hour or so, to give her some exercise. She worries about her weight. She's noticed a bulkiness in her thighs lately, a little push-out at the sides she doesn't like. Altogether she's an attractive woman, though, with her deep black hair and brilliant eyes (inherited from her Persian father) and her tall, rangy legginess (her American mother's).

In the kitchen she takes some already-baked chicken from the fridge, chops it up, throws it in with some leftover pasta, and microwaves the mix. She pulls a package of salad greens (Spring Mix, so-called) and bottle of salad dressing out of the fridge, puts the greens in a soup bowl, and pours on the dressing (not too much – more weight control), and carries everything out to the table in her dining area. She's already poured herself a glass of wine, a cheap Shiraz from Australia that she picked up at Pearson's on her way home and that tastes good. Across the room the TV is tuned to the NewsHour. Amna Nawaz is talking to some jowly pol about South Carolina. Ozzie mutes it.

Her day:

Kevin Mulvaney had chosen a study of John Keats. As expected, Kevin's discussion of the book was wobbly. He could not explicate major poems that the author had taken great trouble to analyze. Kevin will get a C. Which is death.

Gwen Monda had read a fat bio-historiographical work on Chaucer, which she managed to get control of by judiciously outlining it and learning the outline. An A for Gwen.

The Gwens are why Ozzie teaches. They make up for the

Kevins. There are way too many Kevins, bright kids who don't do the work, who waste their parents' money and everybody's time, and who are so, so disappointing.

For her Gwens Ozzie works hard. Her copies of the books she lectures on are dog-eared and full of notes on style and diction, on metaphors, similes, themes. She does her own plot summaries and structural diagrams. She has even sketched out maps of the wanderings of Jane Eyre and Tess Durbeyfield. All this she puts up on Canvas, and it becomes electronic, clickable for her kids to download.

They appreciate her work, the Gwens do anyway, and give her top reviews, also on Canvas: "She's knowledgeable, clear, engaging, and genuinely cares for her students... Probably the best professor I've had at GU... Awesome..." (With some outliers: "Very hard grader... Assigns too much work... Makes you memorize poetry... Avoid...")

Ozzie has been at GU four years and has come to think of the university, like her small apartment on Wisconsin Avenue, as home.

Yet she feels a vacancy in her life. On her way home this afternoon, on 37th Street north of Reservoir Road, a woman and a girl loped past her on the snowy sidewalk. They were almost-look-alikes – a mother and daughter. Both were wearing gray sweatshirts and dark blue running tights. The mother, hatless in the cold but wearing a gray ear-band, looked about Ozzie's age, somewhere in her late thirties. She was trim, though her hips were those of a mature woman. The daughter was what... fourteen or so? She was slender and narrow-hipped, and, like her mother, hatless but wearing an ear-band. As they jogged ahead, distancing themselves from Ozzie, they bantered easily with each other, laughed, once even playfully bumped hips. At R Street they turned east.

I'll never know that, Ozzie thought. I didn't as a daughter, I won't as a mother.

Ozzie and Tom had thought about having children. They'd

talked it over. Two, they thought. A daughter and a son, perhaps. That would be nice. But they would put it off until they got their careers going.

They were living in Somerville, a suburb of Boston, when Tom died. Ozzie was teaching at Boston University, her first real job; Tom was a junior lawyer with a Boston law firm. They'd been "introduced" by mutual friends, and things worked out as the friends had hoped. It has been five years since Tom's death, and still Ozzie cannot not think of him daily.

Memory: her queen-size bed under the window and the window open in the late spring. Through the window a breeze carries in the scent of lilacs. Tom came over in the evening and for the first time, stayed. When they wake, each to the other's sleepy smile, it is late. His whiskers are scratchy on her face; she finds this funny. From somewhere outside a dove coos in the morning. They have not made love before; now they have, and that made all the difference.

Toothbrush?

Didn't bring one, he said.

Next time, she said. Plan better. Or: don't plan, don't, don't, don't, don't plan. Ever. No, silly idea. Of course plan.

He laughed his way of laughing: a so endearing, so lovely pufflet of breath through his nose.

Breakfast?

Here?

How about one of those places up on Broadway? Weekends that's all they serve, breakfasts all day long for the Tufts kids who've pulled all-nighters.

She didn't know that. She had not gone up there much.

They went to a place Tom knew on Broadway, Sound Bites, where they had orange juice, bacon, pancakes, butter, syrup, and coffee, surrounded by students quietly peering at their laptops and clicking at their keyboards, or, leaning back, drinking black coffee, yacking with friends. Ozzie and Tom were in a row of booths for two. Tom, in love, said, I like the way you push your hair back with both hands when you're nervous. And: I like the way you work your face just before you're about to say something.

Ozzie could only gaze at him.

They spent the day. Doing laundry could never be so right. Later, they sat in the little park below Morrison and watched the young marrieds, some pushing strollers, others hovering over children on training bikes, the children pedaling in directions none too well defined, small helmets on their small heads.

From there they walked out to Alewife, then back to her place and the rest of the weekend. Both had work; both neglected it. That was how it started, really started.

In midsummer two years later, they married. Tom had proposed on the bike path on the south bank of the Charles just at the pedestrian crossover from BU. It was a Saturday morning on a spring day, spring Boston style – a chill was in the air, though the sun was bright. Runners passed them on the bike-path as did cyclists, in-line skaters, speed-walkers, and one fool on wheeled skis, shoving himself along on thin poles that clicked on the asphalt; out on the choppy river you could see racing sculls, red and yellow kayaks, powerboats. Just as Tom was saying, "I love you," a runner-mommy – short-cut brown hair, and the hint of a double chin – in gray sweats and pushing a runner's baby buggy jogged by, and though she couldn't have heard, she turned and smiled at them.

An omen.

Ozzie didn't take Tom's family name, Curtis. Hosseini-Curtis might have worked, but she remained Azadeh Hosseini. Always a laugh, she told Tom, feminists asserting their independence by keeping their fathers' names, but I'm doing it.

On a drizzly May morning nine months after their wedding Tom was killed. He was driving alone out to the garden plot they'd rented on a farm just east of Walden Pond; Ozzie had stayed home to work. The garden was an extravagance – the gasoline alone made it uneconomical, not to mention un-Green – but they liked the day out on a weekend, liked the work, liked watching their tomatoes and cucumbers and squash grow, and they liked the farm's resident clucking, quacking fowl, its two milk cows, and the dungy, animal smell of the place.

Midafternoon that day an officer with the State Police came to the door. Ozzie happened to be home. He said that he was very sorry, that Tom had been involved in a traffic accident on Bedford Road, that Tom hadn't survived. He repeated that he was very sorry. He gave Ozzie the name of the hospital they had taken Tom to. He said she didn't have to come identify the body, that they had enough information, his driver's license, the other contents of his wallet, for that. He gave her his card and said she could call him if she needed. He was a kind man. His last name was Paquin. She remembers it to this day.

Bedford Road, south of the Turnpike, is two-laned and hilly. At a point where the road crested, perhaps a mile from the farm, the other driver in his heavy Volvo had tried to pass a pickup truck. The State Police said he was probably doing eighty. Tom in their white, low-slung Acura was perhaps doing forty-five or fifty. They hit head-on.

"The airbag in the Acura steering wheel did not deploy," the police report said. Tom suffered a concussion and a massive loss of blood. He was dead before they levered him out of the car.

They say that in some deaths you don't black out, that when your blood pressure falls to zero and your brain is starved of oxygen, colors pale, and you actually white out, which perhaps explains those near-death experiences of people who survive some terrible trauma during which they think they've seen the shining gates of heaven or the face of God Himself and have come back to tell everyone how beautiful it all is in the sweet by-and-by. Ozzie has always wondered what Tom's last vision was – was it black or was it white?

The driver of the Volvo did survive (his airbag "deployed"), though badly injured. He was charged with negligent homicide. Since he had not been drunk or on drugs, since he had no prior offences, and since he was suitably remorseful, he received a suspended sentence of one year.

Ozzie, stunned with grief, moved in a bubble of pain. Immediately after the accident friends helped with food and showed other kindnesses. Grace came and stayed a week. Her father Sadeq called repeatedly from California. David visited, though he did not stay. A colleague took over her classes – there was only a week to go in the semester. The chairperson and others in the department were superb, save one, an alcoholic teacher of writing in his late middle age, who hit on her obliquely in his creepy way. She'd permitted him to hug her in the hall outside the departmental office – why? – and unclinching but remaining close, he said, "Time of great loneliness, I know, I know." The tone of his voice, the look in his eye said, "Keep me in mind."

Numbing. Just numbing.

After the funeral in Ohio, when they – her family and friends, Tom's people – had all gone home and she had returned to Somerville and their empty apartment and its silence, a silence so hard to hear, she fell on her – their – bed and wept, crying, "My baby, my baby, why oh why oh why oh why?" She expected no answer and got none.

For months the tears came easily. Once, sitting at the table in the kitchen where she and Tom had always breakfasted together, she looked at his empty chair and went crazy, screaming, sobbing, banging her fists on the little table. She staggered from the kitchen to the dining room to the entrance to the living room, where she leaned on the doorjamb, moaning and moaning.

She had never felt such pain. She had not known there was such pain to feel. She wanted to die.

The memory of Tom no longer wounds. It induces a mood. By now she recognizes the mood and knows memory as an enemy.

Ozzie taught one more year at the U but decided to leave Boston – there was too much of Tom there. Rumors that one of Georgetown's Fem Lit professors would retire turned out to be true. Georgetown advertised the post, Ozzie applied. She had the strengths they wanted: she had published several long articles in good journals and had delivered interesting, edgy papers at conferences. She had edited a well-reviewed book, her *Gender and Anarchy*, on changing sexuality in late nineteenth century America and Britain as reflected in the lives and work of women writers of the time. Topics – she had persuaded eight scholars, all women, to contribute articles – ranged from birth control to Boston Marriages, feminist utopianism, and free love in the revolt against Victorian sexual mores. She was known and was considered a comer in the field.

At the MLA meeting, held that year in January at UC Santa Barbara, Wallace Ransom – "Wally"– a pear-shaped man in his late fifties, who had just been appointed Chair of the English Department at GU, and two GU senior faculty members interviewed her in a campus hotel room with a stupefying view of ocean breaking on dark brown rock, wave after wave. She got the job easily.

Since moving to Washington, she's had two "experimental lovers" – her term, she likes calling them that. One was a friend of friends, as Tom had been. He was bright, kind, and not bad looking. It lasted a while but didn't work out: he bored her. She supposed he bored her because he was not Tom.

The other was an old boyfriend from high school, Will, living then in Philadelphia. It was February. He sent her a valentine with a note. He had left his wife. He had moved into an apartment. He had heard about Tom. He wanted to see her. Could he visit?

She called and got his voice mail. She had had a small speech in mind, but then, flustered, didn't say it, blurting out instead something about thanking Miss Jones (their senior-year English teacher). Will couldn't possibly understand that. What she had meant was that Miss Jones was a great encourager of bashful, sensitive adolescents and brought out the best in them, and that that's what she felt like now, a bashful teenager. She became more flustered and finally just said, "I'd love to talk. Give me a call when you can," and hung up.

He returned her call. Could he come down some weekend?

Yes.

This weekend?

Yes.

He came down. He was not so different. He had the same fine hair, thinner now. His fuzzy beard was unfamiliar, but his smile was the same and he was as funny as ever. He didn't talk much about his wife or why he had left her.

She fell in love, deeply.

Then he went back to Philadelphia and back to his wife.

To explain why he went back, Will wrote a letter – paper, not e-mail, because, Ozzie suspects, it was safer that way – giving all his self-serving excuses, at the end of which he suggested "keeping in touch" by using his office phone so his wife wouldn't know. Ozzie threw the letter away, insulted and angry, thinking, Oh, oh, oh, you prick.

When she thinks of Tom she sees snatches of their past, for the most part a restricted collection of quick scenes that occur randomly, but again and again – Tom taking a call on his cell, Tom chopping onions in their kitchen, Tom reading a brief, boarding a kayak, launching a frisbee – to no good end.

Sometimes if she has soft music playing, she sees herself dancing with Tom. They hold each other in a poised, elegant ballroom embrace. (In real life they never danced much, only at other people's weddings, and then inexpertly.) The vision of the two of them in each other's arms, a solitary duo gliding gracefully over some polished floor, is appallingly sad.

The hurt is worst in the evenings when she is home from class, no necessary reading to do, no papers to correct, and, as now, dining alone.

On the NewsHour Nawaz is speaking directly to the camera. A young black woman comes on with the illuminated West Wing of the White House as background. She's apparently listening to Nawaz. She replies, speaking to the camera. Ozzie, who's moved now to her living area couch, leaves the two of them mute, talking away to each other in silence. They make her think of the kids at Gallaudet University, a school for the deaf and hard-of-hearing over in Northeast. Ozzie sees them around town, regular college kids to look at them – they've got the dress and the moves – but they are utterly silent, communicating with each other by sign language and by gestures of their eyes and lips. As at any other decent school, they read sophisticated stuff and talk it over, but they talk it over with their hands and faces. Ozzie wonders how they do that.

I am alone, she thinks. Should I go back on the pill? I haven't considered that for a while. Should I see da Silva about it?

Francesca da Silva is Ozzie's dark-as-nutmeg, Brazilian-born OB-GYN. Da Silva is married but has no kids. Ozzie thinks maybe when you know enough about birthing it's too scary to think of doing it yourself. Or maybe da Silva just wants to do her job and thinks kids'll get in the way. Some people shouldn't be parents. Again, she wonders, should I go back on the pill?

Do I want that? A lover or two?

No.

A husband?

Don't even think of it.

She'll see da Silva in three months or something – three? four? she's not sure – spring, anyway, for a pelvic. So, go back on the pill? Maybe. She'll figure it out then.

Ozzie thinks of that guy she saw in the morning, Mark Whosiwhatsis, who, nervous and so serious, didn't know what to do with his elbows. She wonders if he had a wedding band. She hadn't noticed.

Ozzie's cell rings. It's Grace calling from Hartford.

"Hi, Mom."

"Hi, Oz. Happy birthday."

"Hey, thanks."

Talking with Grace has gotten easier over the years. Ozzie starts with the usual: "How's it going up there?"

"Oh, fine. Not much to report, really. Warren came over last weekend." She means her Significant Other – her term, she hates calling him her "boyfriend" – Warren Laessig, a doctor with Hartford Pulmonary Associates. Warren is lean and athletic, a widower, a nice man. They do sleepovers on the weekends. "He's been trying to teach me cross-country skiing if you can believe that."

"God, Mom – wow!"

"At my age! I kept tipping over and falling on my can. Warren's so patient." Grace is just on the fringe of seventy. She is tall and slender. She pulls her dark gray hair – no phony coloring for her – together at the nape of her neck and the result is most handsome.

"Where do you ski?"

"So far just in the park." Grace laughs. Elizabeth Park is a green space two blocks south of her large house in West Hartford. In the summer, Elizabeth Park is grass, flowers, shrubs, and trees, in the winter, a series of flat, snowy planes, about Grace's speed for skiing.

"Did you get my card?"

"I did, Mom. Thanks. Very nice." The card arrived yesterday. On its cover was a black and white sketch of a peacock feather. Inside, the inscription read, "With All Love for your Birthday." Grace herself had written, "Love to you, Ozzie. Mom." The card was subtle and understated, like Grace, who is correct and punctilious by nature and who did all the conventionally right things as parent, but who after law school became distant and as Ozzie grew up seemed always to be receding. Grace has never remarried.

When Grace and Baba returned from Iran and divorced, Grace changed. She started law school when Ozzie was eight, finished in three years, and went to work immediately in Hartford at a woman-owned firm doing family law, where she has stayed. All the Welles' – Grace, Ozzie, David, Grace's mother Marian, known as Moo Moo, and father, James, known as Papá – lived in the big house. Papá died an alcoholic's death a quarter of a century ago. Moo Moo, who raised Ozzie as much as Grace did, is in a nursing home outside Hartford, suffering from vascular dementia. David is in New York. Ozzie thinks of Grace living alone in that huge hotel of a house. What does that do to her?

Grace asks, "Have you heard from Sadeq?" She's almost forgiven Baba his sins, though there's still a catch in her voice when she says his name.

"He sent a card. A nice card."

"Mmm."

The opposite of Grace's, Baba's card was a large frilly affair with a varicolored explosion of buds and blossoms on its cover along with the inscription, "For a Wonderful Daughter." The card had a fuchsia-colored border sprinkled with fine silver glitter (Baba's Persian taste for *froufrou*.) Inside were more flowers and the inscription, "A Bouquet of Good Wishes for Her Birthday." At the bottom Baba had written, "Love," and under that, "Baba."

"Love" was written in English, but "Baba" was in a child's Persian script, the kind Ozzie can still half-read. Coming in from the right – Persian script reads right to left – looking like the beginning of a little smile is the character "b," and under the half-smile a single dot; then, connected to the smile's left up-curl, a tall, vertical line, an alif, the two together spelling "ba." This pattern repeated once gives: "Baba," meaning "Daddy."

Sadeq Hosseini. Hardworking. Intelligent. Eye for the ladies. Sucker for a friend's get-rich schemes. Ageing now, and barely employable, Baba is living in a one-bedroom in Van Nuys in the Valley north of L.A. He collects Social Security but still has to work in a local bakery owned by immigrant compatriots. Clever in Iran, here he's had an unerring instinct for the bad deal. When he and Grace split, he moved to California and early on managed to buy and flip a couple of apartments and build up his bank account. Over the years, though, overconfident maybe, he put money into a variety of businesses he didn't understand – gas stations, mattress outlets, carpeting stores – none of which did well. The most recent was a chain of laundromats in West L.A., an enterprise that made a little money, but only a little – not enough, anyway, and not what Baba had expected. Thanks to the way the deal was structured – the debt and cash flow–- Baba ended up owing the former owners.

The last time they talked – a month back, he called – he said he was learning the bakery business. "It's not hard work, but I'm on my feet all day, and that's a problem." Ozzie had been at a Victorian Lit conference at UCLA in November and had visited him. His face had grown lined in a way she hadn't noticed before, hopelessness finally breaking in over the old entrepreneurial optimism. Baba's state worried her.

Ozzie's earliest memories of Baba are not from Persia, a land almost dream-like to her in its hazed distance, but from America. One is of Baba and the beach at Santa Monica, where he lived with his American girl friend, a cuddlesome blonde named Valerie, not the first and one of a long string. Baba is holding Ozzie's left hand, and they are walking barefoot on the hard sand down by the waterline. David, who is two years younger than Ozzie, is with them (as part of the divorce settlement the two children would visit Baba once a summer for two weeks), but Ozzie can recall only the dim presence of a small other.

She and Baba detour once up onto the softer dry sand and step over washed-up swaths of yellow-green kelp with their ribbony blades and so squeezable bell-like floats. Associated with the sand and kelp somehow are broad, brown wooden planks – the Santa Monica pier – and the sight of the vast blue water which she learns at some point, maybe that very day, is called the Pacific. It is her first sight of ocean. Baba has a merry smile and twinkling eyes and is all happiness as he lifts her to see the water, the whitecaps, the pelicans. She learned later Baba's fortunes were in one of their periodic declines even then. He was, and is, a great dissembler. She loves the man.

Ozzie and Grace chit-chat, the subtext being Grace's worry over Ozzie and her life. You can be happy, Grace has told Ozzie, but you have to want to. Grace has stopped saying this, not because Grace doesn't care, Ozzie thinks, but because it does no good.

In that confused, inchoate period after Grace and Baba had come back from Iran, with Grace not yet in law school and Baba absconded to California, Grace would put Ozzie and David to bed and sing them lovingly to sleep. One of the songs she'd sing was "Turnaround": "Where are you going, my little one, little one...?" Grace knew all the words, as does Ozzie even now: The tiny child maturing, grown, out the door.

With babes of her own.

Ozzie has wondered if she wants babes of her own. She doesn't know.

In the silence she can hear Grace wanting to ask more but refraining.

"Well, I just wanted to call, Oz. Do have a happy birthday."

"Thanks, Mom."

Ozzie notices a text has come in from David:

Happy birthday, sis! Buzz sends her love. 37? We've got 37ers in the neighborhood. They dodder around and bump into things. No no no no. Seriously 37's not so so bad. Love to you. D

David doesn't phone, doesn't punch on when you phone. Texting's pretty much it with David. "Buzz" is short for Meredith, David's girlfriend. Ozzie responds quickly:

Thanks, turkey. Say hello to buzz.

David, Grace's favorite, Ozzie's rival, is handsome, like Baba. He has Baba's spare build and something of Baba's deceptive smile. David is self-employed at some not easily definable niche job in Web videos – made-for-client short pieces and podcasts. He seems to be making money. His girlfriend is an "aggregator" –

she configures restricted Web sites to pull in the content of other Web sites, order it, display it, distribute it, archive it. Her clients run to banks and investment companies. Like David, she's slender and athletic. They run and work out together. They live in a loft on Mott Street in SoHo – Greenwich Village, south of Houston Street – renting at below-market rates from friends who are away long-term, maybe a year more. When their friends get back David and Buzz will migrate somewhere else. They don't seem to be in a big hurry to get married, have kids, or do anything substantial with their lives. Ozzie thinks of them as Web Folk, temporary and transient, as impermanent as the contents of their flash-drives.

Ignoring the TV, which is still mute, still showing the NewsHour, Ozzie, not hungry, pecks at her chicken pasta. The apartment is quiet, only the fridge making noise, snuffling like a horse when the condenser shuts off.

She thinks of her morning visitor again. Mark.

On a whim, she goes to her desktop to do a search on "Flora Lijak."

And enters another world.

CHAPTER I

"A Large, Loud American"

25 May 1895

149, The Grove
Hammersmith

Dearest Evie:

Last night's Evening went <u>splendidly</u>. We decorated the hall
with pictures of great Russians – Tolstoy, Tourguenieff,
Chaikovsky etc. Volkhovsky – you met him Nov. last at tea
at the Garnett's, do you recall, a short slight nervous man
with a ferocious beard? – who planned the proceedings didn't
want fancy dress but forgot to say so in the invitations & so
of course everyone came dressed up to the nines. I wore my
black gown & green cape.

The Stepniaks, the Rossettis, the Garnetts (Connie & Edw.
as well as his sister Olive), Fisher Unwin, all the other Free
Russia people, Mrs Sparling, Perriss, Mr Stevens came.
Kropotkin came in very late, beaming & nodding to all.
Volkhovsky had been looking very pulled down & fretful the
day before but he was ecstatic with the turn-out & the way
the evening went.

And what an evening! Max Ritschl played violin & I did
Chaikovsky's Dumka, a very difficult work. Esther Palliser
sang Russian songs. Stepniak gave a talk but simply told

everyone to read Russian literature. Byles & Picton made tiresome speeches. Mrs MacDonald's samovar spilt into Olivia Rossetti's shoe.

Fannie Stepniak had a large, loud American named William McKenzie in tow & introduced him to me. Mr McKenzie is living in Mile End & is writing up stories of workers & their families many of them Jews from Russia for the American press. He seems very young. He is an Anarchist & has some connexion with Kropotkin. He is quite the 'Yankee', in both the bad & the good sense. He was interested to hear that I am writing my novel.

W. is in the throes of a 'crying cold' & did not attend & is still feeling highly indisposed this morning. Shall we see you Sat. aft. at the Stepniaks?

Loving Sis

Flora's "Evening" was put on by the Society of Friends of Russian Freedom, a group of anti-Tsarist Russians living in London and their English sympathizers. Flora had been a founding member and worked for it tirelessly. The Society's overt purpose was to publicize outrages committed by the Russian government against the Russian people and so bring pressure to bear on the government to reform. To this end the Society published a monthly newspaper, *Free Russia*, which Flora helped edit and for which she translated countless articles from the Russian press. The Society also put on galas such as this one, held on a bracing, starlit May evening at Barnard's Inn Hall, Holborn, to celebrate its work and make itself more widely known to influential members of the British public. The Society's British members - intellectuals, university professors, eleven members of Parliament, publishers, progressive religious figures, even the Countess of Carlisle, Rosalind Howard - gave it a stamp of moderation and reputability.

But the Society had a clandestine side too, one not wholly

known to its English membership: it helped Russian political prisoners escape prison or exile, sent funds to revolutionary groups in Russia, including terrorist groups, and smuggled books and pamphlets in both directions across the Russian frontier. Flora engaged in this dangerous work, travelling to the Continent, carrying funds and accompanied by trunks full of forbidden publications. To pay for these activities the Society established the Russian Free Press Fund and solicited contributions to the Fund from well-wishers of all nationalities.

Tsarist spies in Britain, of which there were many – Feliks Volkhovsky claimed there were more in London than in any other city in Europe – reported to St Petersburg on the Society's activities; Russian agents in London tried when possible to obstruct the Society and its work.

British authorities also took an interest in the Society, despite its respectable membership. The Special Branch of police, which had originally been created to put down Irish political agitation, had expanded its responsibility to include all foreign revolutionary and Anarchist groups, particularly after the Greenwich Bomb Outrage of the year before, when a young French Anarchist named Martial Bourdin had eviscerated himself whilst carrying explosives up the hill toward the Greenwich Observatory. The Special Branch kept a careful watch on the Society.

Flora finished her letter shortly after breakfast and sent the hired girl, Sarah, a quick, sprightly young thing, to post it in a pillar box just up The Grove in Goldhawk Road. In those days of no telephones, one communicated either by telegraph or through London's superbly organized postal system, which in some areas, including Hammersmith, scheduled twelve collections a day, starting as early as 8:15 a.m. Sarah, who liked to dash places, dropped the letter in the slot well before 9:15 a.m., the time of the second pick-up of the morning. Evelyn Bowles, Flora's beloved sister, who was renting a small flat in Highgate four miles to the northeast of Flora, would receive the letter in the late afternoon.

Flora's performance of Tchaikovsky's *Dumka* the night before had been stunning. Volkhovsky introduced her: "The wonderful pianist Mrs Lijak has consented to play this evening Dumka of Pyotr Ilyich Tchaikovsky. The Dumka of Tchaikovsky is very Russian composition, a song of the countryside and of our birch forests, very sad, very beautiful..." The audience applauded politely as Flora, all in black, walked briskly to the piano, a polished maple baby grand which workmen had positioned that afternoon at the very end of the hall in front of the hall's great fireplace and which was surrounded, Russian style, with buckets of red, white, and yellow flowers.

Flora sat and waited for the applause to end and for the sounds of the audience – the throat-clearings, the coughs, the shiftings of chairs – to die down. When the hall was close to silent, she straightened her back, paused, and, fingers arched high, started the first soft strumming notes of the piece, a folk-like Russian tune in a minor key. She played the first section solemnly and slowly, lost in the composition, her eyes closed, her body swaying with the tempo. In the livelier central section, she struck the keys vigorously, even jauntily, rocking her shoulders, and in one dramatic sequence, so different to the rest, smiled as she kept her left hand in her lap and ran her right to the highest register of the instrument, playing a small, trilling tune, then resumed the quick forward movement. The last section was slow (that folk tune again) and with it the piece quietly came almost to its end, trailing off into a melancholy silence, a silence that was shattered by the surprising final three crashing chords in a dark and sad C minor.

The audience sat silent for a moment, then rose en masse to applaud, some waving their programmes and yelling, "Brava, brava!"

Flora bowed and bowed, glowing with the success, and returned to her seat among her fellow participants in the evening's event, all of whom were standing and applauding her as well. The applause died down; everyone took their seats.

The participants – there were eight – sat facing the audience in a row of spindly gilt ball-room chairs. To Flora's left, at the very end of the row, sat Feliks Volkhovsky, one of the two Russian founders of the Society. To her immediate right sat Sergei Stepniak, the other.

Stepniak, an energetic giant of a man – rooms seemed unable to contain him – was the foremost anti-Tsarist publicist of his age. He was a prolific writer and a passionate speaker. His family origins were a topic he avoided, but he apparently had been born in the Ukraine to Russian parents. His real name was Sergei Mikhailovich Kravchinsky. In England he adopted the name "Stepniak," which means "man of the steppes," as a kind of nom de plume and nom de guerre. He lived with his wife Fanny Lichkus in Bedford Park, a comfortable, newly built community, fashionable among London's artistic and literary set.

Feliks Vadimovich Volkhovsky was Ukrainian. In the 1870s, whilst a law student at Moscow University, he had travelled among the Russian and Ukrainian peasantry preaching political and social reform. He had been arrested and imprisoned numerous times, often after peasants had complained to the police about his activities. During one extended period of solitary confinement, he went almost deaf. In 1878 he was tried for revolutionary agitation and exiled with his family first to Tobolsk, then to Tomsk in Siberia. There his wife Yevgenia, depressed by the deaths of two of their three daughters and by the loneliness of exile and fearing that they would never be allowed to return home, shot herself dead. In 1889 Volkhovsky managed to escape, fleeing first to Japan, then Canada, then England. He lived in Bedford Park, too, not far from the Stepniaks, with his surviving daughter, Vera, a dark-eyed twelve-year-old and already a beauty.

After Flora's performance, William Pollard Byles, MP from Shipley and member of the Society's Board, rose and spoke, delivering a smug, bragging speech about British political institutions

– so like him, Flora thought, and so tiresome.

As Byles spoke Flora's mind wandered to the bustle of preparation for the soirée earlier in the day: sunlight pouring through the
high windows; rose-cheeked Olive Garnett adorning the whited
walls and oak timbering with swags of Russian drapery, so Oriental
in aspect; Volkhovsky hanging pictures of great Russians in a line
on one wall, banging with a hammer, cocking his head, fussing,
complaining of his lumbago; the Rossetti girls, Olivia and Helen,
busily setting out cake plates, teacups, spoons, forks, tea utensils,
napkins, floral arrangements – and Mrs MacDonald's samovar – on
tables in the small room off the main hall.

Flora, to test the pitch of the piano that afternoon and see
how it rang in the hall, which was high-ceilinged, played a bit of
Beethoven, a bit of Bach, then, wide-handed and solemnly, the
first chords of the *Dumka*. The piano was fine, though the hall
sounded cavernous. She hoped when it was full of guests its sound
would be warmer. So it turned out to be.

When Byles stopped talking, he sat down to tepid applause. Then
the American Esther Palliser rose and to Flora's accompaniment
sang two folk songs in her lovely soprano. The second, "Evening
Bells," brought the programme to a close. Then the guests, vol-
uble, gesticulating Russians and staid, reticent English, rose from
their seats and milled about the room in a buzz of talk, mingling
in small groups, drinking tea, and eating cake.

Stepniak, flushed and happy with the size of the audience and
the reception its members had given the programme, rushed up
to Flora and embraced her, telling her in Russian she had played
beautifully. Then he stood back still holding her and said, "Bulochka, what a beautiful gown! Black with your lovely hair – so
striking! Will you be photographed in it? You should, you really
should!"

"Bulochka" was the Russians' pet name for Flora. Everyone
used it. It meant "muffin" in Russian, and was a play on her maid-

en name, Bowles. Stepniak had thought it up. Someone – was it Anna Olefskaya? – said Stepniak called her that because her face in fact looked like a muffin, but that was cruel and not true. Flora's face was beautiful in an austere way, her forehead high and intelligent, her nose straight, her lips even. She had nimble, wide set brown eyes that played over the face of anyone she was talking with. And she did have thick, captivating hair, which she had tied up and back that evening.

Stepniak broke away to speak to Constance Garnett as his wife Fanny, a short, vivacious woman, came over leading by the hand a tall, young-looking man she had detached from the group surrounding Pyotr Kropotkin. Fanny said in English, "Dear Flora, let me introduce Mr McKenzie, Mr William McKenzie. He is excellent American journalist. He is living in East End and is writing about the conditions of the workers. Mr McKenzie, this is Mrs Flora Lijak. She is writer and journalist. Like you. She is member of the board of *Free Russia*, and she has written many things for it. Also, she translates from the Russian, which she speaks very well." Fanny, her attention now elsewhere, wandered silently away, leaving the two of them.

McKenzie smiled engagingly and said, "Hello." Flora said, "How do you do?" They shook hands. This, their first physical contact, was short, yet each noticed the other's touch and later each would remember the moment. Her hand, he thought, was soft and warm, surprisingly, since she had banged away so at the piano. His she found large and engulfing, and rough and callused as well, a hand that had known work.

McKenzie was tall and large-chested. His face was broad, open, eager, an American face, and his brash, inquisitive eyes looked squarely into hers. The effect was of a vast innocence. In those eyes, though, Flora also detected melancholy and wondered what lay behind that. His left cheek was scarred.

McKenzie said, "You play piano very well, Mrs Lijak. You must have studied for some time."

"Oh, thank you very much. Yes, I studied in Berlin in the

'80s. It was a great experience. I studied under Spitta."

"Spitta?"

"Philipp Spitta. Bach scholar and a masterful piano teacher. I owe him a great deal. He died last year. A great sadness for me. He was too young."

A decade ago, when she was twenty, a small inheritance allowed Flora to study piano at the Berlin Higher Academy of Music with masters like Spitta. Before, though she loved the instrument, she could afford to take lessons only intermittently.

In Berlin, Flora became a Bohemian. She walked about the city in an ankle-length black dress, the hem of which she held up with safety pins. She had adopted her black clothing when she turned sixteen, after reading the biography of Giuseppe Mazzini, the Italian revolutionist. She told her Mama and sisters then that she had gone into mourning for the state of the world. (She was never able to convey to them her real reasons for wearing black.) She habitually dressed in mourning until her marriage to Lijak.

McKenzie said, "And you speak Russian?"

"Yes. I learnt it first here – in London, I mean – from Sergei Stepniak. My mother invited him one day and we got acquainted then. Also, I spent two years in Russia. This was after Berlin. I was in St Petersburg a year, then I lived on an estate with a family, relatives of Sergei's. I travelled a lot as well. One gets to know the language."

"Well, I don't know a word of it. Seems pretty complicated."

"It is."

"What have you translated?"

"Oh, I do all the Russian contents of *Free Russia*. There's lots of that, so it keeps me jumping. Other things, too. I'm just now bringing out a book called *Tales of Russia*. Short stories by Russian authors. Walter Scott's publishing it here, in America it's with Scribner's, so I'm very happy about it. And two years ago, I did a collection of stories by V.M. Kosinsky, a wonderful Russian writer, not well known outside Russia, or inside for that matter, but he should be, he deserves a wider audience - there's an intense psychology in all his work. Fisher Unwin published it. He's over there. Fisher Unwin, I mean" - she jerked her head in a small laugh – "not Kosinsky, Kosinsky's dead. Consumption. And now I'm writing a novel."

"A novel! Good for you! What's it about?"

"Italy. And the struggle for unity and freedom there in the 1830s."

"Ah, that's a very fine theme. It's the kind of theme I'd like to write a novel about, maybe I will someday – revolutionary!"

McKenzie spoke loudly, like the Russians. It seemed to Flora that he did so by nature, that he put no thought into it. She supposed it was because he was American and that his loud manner was simply there, like the Niagara Falls. And she noted with amusement his drawling accent. When Americans speak, she thought, how they mush everything and take out the high notes.

"Well, if you want to be a revolutionary writer, Mr McKenzie, why don't you write something revolutionary about your Chicago or New York? What brings you here?"

"I wanted to see things, see some of the world. I found a couple of newspapers in the States to pay my way while I have my fun."

"Fun? Is the East End fun?"

"You bet it is - in its way."

"And you actually live there?"

"I do. I wanted to from the start. When I got here I took a cab to Cheapside and just walked east. I met a bobby who gave me the address of a minister who lives over there, Father Buxton, good man, works with the poor. So, I went and found him and rented a room down the way from his place. Needham Lane, just off Commercial Road. Not too bad a neighbourhood, decent enough landlady. I took it because I needed a room to keep my belongings safe in and where I could go to write up my notes. Then I went and rented another place, my real East End place. A lot cheaper, and I can tell you, it's a wretched place and most certainly not safe. Thieves, con-men, burglars, fences, all of 'em a lively bunch. Make for good copy. My papers keep wiring for more."

"I see. And how is it you are here this evening?"

"Oh, I've gotten to know some Russians in my neighbourhood, and they're interested in what's going on back in Old Russia. They're all Jews and they all want to bring down the Tsar. Well, Mr Kropotkin came over a while back and gave a lecture in Father Buxton's church – in Bethnal Green, close to me – and I went and got to talking with him afterward and one thing led to another."

Fanny Stepniak was back. "Flora, may I steal Mr McKenzie from you? I have a gentleman, you know him, Mr Serov, who wants to meet him."

Ivan Maximovich Serov was standing alone a short distance away. Serov, a gaunt, shaggy young Nihilist who had fled Russia for reasons unknown to Flora, was dressed as ever in the one suit he apparently owned, a mud-coloured frock coat smelling of benzine and a mismatched pair of duck trousers. He nodded and smiled to Flora.

"Oh, please, please, please, Fanny." To McKenzie she said, "Well, some time you must tell me more about your Russian workers, Mr McKenzie, I should like that."

"With pleasure, Mrs Lijak."

As McKenzie left, Flora turned, not to converse with anyone, but to think. What struck her most about McKenzie was not his height or his loud voice. No, what struck her most were his eyes. They reminded her of those of a youth in a painting she had seen years before in Paris. Sojourning in that city in 1885 on her way to Berlin to study music, Flora visited the Louvre. Among the works she saw there was a portrait of a young man by the Florentine painter Franciabigio. The young man stood resting his left arm on what looked like a balustrade and gazed directly at the viewer. He had long, dark hair and wore a black cloak and a wide-brimmed black cap. The left side of his face was partially lost in shadow. Above him stretched a blue sky traced with wispy white Italian clouds. In the youth's eyes Flora sensed an elusive, mysterious melancholy, an air of untellable sadness that wrung her heart. The portrait of that youth would haunt Flora to the end of her days. William McKenzie's eyes, she thought, resembled the young man's.

Balancing a teacup and a small plate of cake, Richard Lane Hodgson of the *Pall Mall Gazette* approached Flora. Lane Hodgson was young, stout, and fair-faced. A schoolboy friend of one of the Garnetts, Lane Hodgson retained a schoolboy's habit of mockery. He was no friend of the Society, and everyone knew it. Flora wondered why on earth Volkhovsky had invited him. To convert him, she supposed. She thought there was little chance of that. She nodded obliquely in greeting, and asked, "Are you enjoying the evening, Mr Hodgson?"

"Other than the music, particularly your playing, Mrs Lijak, which was as always a delight, I must say... no, no, I'm not."

"I'm so sorry. Why is that?"

"Ah, your London 'Rooshians' – so much posturing, so much talk. All these boring speeches that always say the same thing. Brave words far from the fray. Stepniak, Volkhovsky, Kropotkin – they are quite safe here in England and they live very nice lives. But if there is to be a Socialist revolution in Russia, I can assure you it will not begin in Bedford Park. Your Mr Stepniak in particular is a noisy windbag."

"That's most unkind. And unjust."

"Well, he is. 'Man of the Steppes' indeed! One thinks of wild Cossacks and sabres and such. So impressive to the impressable English. He is a humbug."

"You underestimate the man, Mr Hodgson."

"You say." Lane Hodgson sipped at his tea.

———

On a hot day in early August 1878, Adjutant General N.V. Mezentsev, Chief of the Special Gendarmes Corps, the Tsarist secret police, a sadist and torturer, was taking his daily walk in St Petersburg's Mikhailovsky Gardens. He was accompanied by two aides. That day, as usual, Mezentsev began his walk at the main gate of the Castle, a two-storied, coral-coloured building that served as headquarters of the Corps. He turned left into the park, intending to walk for half an hour or so on the park's undulating paths. Because the day was hot, he had loosened the collar of his blue police tunic and kept to the shade under the park's spreading elm trees. From time to time he spoke with his aides, but was mostly silent, and the only sound the party made was the crunch of their well-polished, heavy boots on the beige gravel of the paths.

Sergei Mikhailovich Kravchinsky, the man later known as Stepniak, was strolling in the park that morning as well, carrying a rolled newspaper under his left arm. Kravchinsky approached Mezentsev and his aides from the opposite direction. When they drew close, Kravchinsky started as if surprised to see Mezentsev, then, smiling, said, "Your excellency, it's good to see you this morning. We met at the opera last spring" – and still smiling broadly, his eyes friendly and confident, he drew closer to Mezentsev. The General took him for a well-wisher of some sort, possibly a man wanting something, but strange to meet here. "Boris Godounov," Kravchinsky said. "Madame Borisovicha introduced us." When Kravchinsky had got to within one metre of Mezentzev, he seized the Italian stiletto concealed in his newspaper and sprang at the General. Before the General or his aides could think or act Kravchinsky had plunged the stiletto, which had a needle-sharp point that widened quickly to a thick blade, between the General's upper ribs on his left side, piercing the rib cage and stabbing directly into the General's heart.

At just that instant, Ivan Grepin, Kravchinsky's fellow conspirator, following the General and his aides on the fast pacer Varvara, a beautiful chestnut mare, galloped forward, grasped Kravchinsky under his left arm, helped him onto Varvara, and carried him down Nevsky Prospekt past astonished spectators – "Who are these men? Why are they two on a horse? Why are they galloping so?" – to Italian Street, where Kravchinsky was given another horse, held for him there by Boris Yurchenko, a third conspirator. The three, Kravchinsky, Grepin, and Yurchenko, fled in different directions and not one was caught by the police. Mezentzev died on the spot.

So went the story Flora had pieced together from various accounts of the incident and believed. She had not heard any of it from Stepniak himself, who was reluctant to talk of the matter.

Flora said, "Sergei Stepniak is no humbug. If you're saying he is in order to irritate me, Mr Hodgson, you are not succeeding. You are only making a fool of yourself, and not for the first time. Which is merely sad."

"Ha ha. Where is Mr Lijak?"

"Home with a cold."

"Lucky man."

Shaking her head dismissively, Flora strode to the far side of the hall and began speaking with the shaggy Ivan Serov. McKenzie had left Serov to speak with other guests.

As the evening wound down and guests began departing, McKenzie said his good-byes. He shook hands with Kropotkin, Volkhovsky, and Sergei and Fanny Stepniak, and made a point to say good-bye as well to Flora, promising to tell her more about his workers in the East End. She assured him again that she would enjoy hearing about them. As he was leaving the hall, something – he wasn't sure what – caused him to turn round and look for her, to look once again on her beautiful face and russet hair.

Too late, he missed her glance.

OZZIE

Sitting serenely in her armchair, she brings her right hand to her mouth and blows a kiss. She draws her head back and nods, folding her hands in her lap. She smiles. Her eyes crinkle. She nods again to someone off camera.

Here Ozzie freezes the frame.

Flora Lijak's face, fixed now and motionless on Ozzie's flat screen, is worn away by time. Her eyelids and cheeks are heavy, her mouth drawn. Her gray hair, braided in back, is looped carelessly up and over, her skin parchmenty, translucent-seeming, woundable. She'll die in a year.

Ozzie has just viewed to its end a black-and-white video featuring an aged Flora Lijak. The video, reproduced from a newsreel filmed by British Pathé in New York in 1959 and available on YouTube, records a visit paid to Flora on her ninety-fifth birthday by a delegation of Russians from the Bolshoi Ballet, who were performing in the city at the time. The newsreel's images of Flora, gritty, grainy, fleeting, are the last known of her.

Ozzie has spent her evening tracking Flora on the Web, drawn ever deeper into her mystery. She's found only fragments of Flora's life, but they are enough for her to sense how strange that life must have been. In addition to this stunning video, Ozzie has turned up:

Flora's short obituary: "Author of *Ribeiro* Dead... No immediate survivors... Taught choral and orchestral music..." *The Times*, July 29, 1960.

Wilfrid Lijak's: "Authority on Medieval Manuscripts...Exiled to Siberia as a Student... Discovered 'Lost' Bacon Work..." *The Times*, March 19, 1930.

The Library of Congress's Finding Aid for its Flora B. Lijak Collection. (Tantalizingly, the Finding Aid mentions a Diary Flora kept.)

Lijak's sales catalogue of 1914 ("Rare Books and Prints. Incunabula. Woodcuts. Maps. Early Printed Books.")

Five issues of *Free Russia*, a publication of something called the Society of Friends of Russian Freedom. All are from 1894. They feature "Mrs F.B. Lijak" on their mastheads as a member of their Editorial Committee.

A short article ("By Our London Correspondent") in the *San Francisco American* describing a "gala" put on by the Society of Friends of Russian Freedom in 1895. The article notes "the pianistic artistry of Mrs. Lijak."

Five or six photographs of Flora – the same photographs – show up at various sites around the Web. The earliest, and for Ozzie the most appealing, is a tintype put up by an Irish historical society showing Flora at age twelve. In it she's posing with her four sisters and her mother Mary Bowles. Flora and Evelyn, the two youngest of the girls, are kneeling in profile on either side of Mary, who is seated facing the camera, hands pillowed in her long, thick skirt. Flora's other sisters – Alice, Edith, and Helen – are standing to the rear, hands at their sides. The portrait contains the usual Victorian clutter – a bowl of wax fruit on a high, slender table placed to the right of Flora, two potted palms flanking the standing girls, and, hung on the wall behind the group, festoons of tapestry.

Though Mary Bowles appears solemn (her wide, homely face emphasizes the effect), the girls look happy enough. Flora is quizzical and coy and has a hint of mischief in her face. And skepticism

– she doesn't quite trust the camera. Her hair is combed high in back and is bound with a wide, dark ribbon. Thick ringlets spill down her neck and over the front of her right shoulder. She is all innocence.

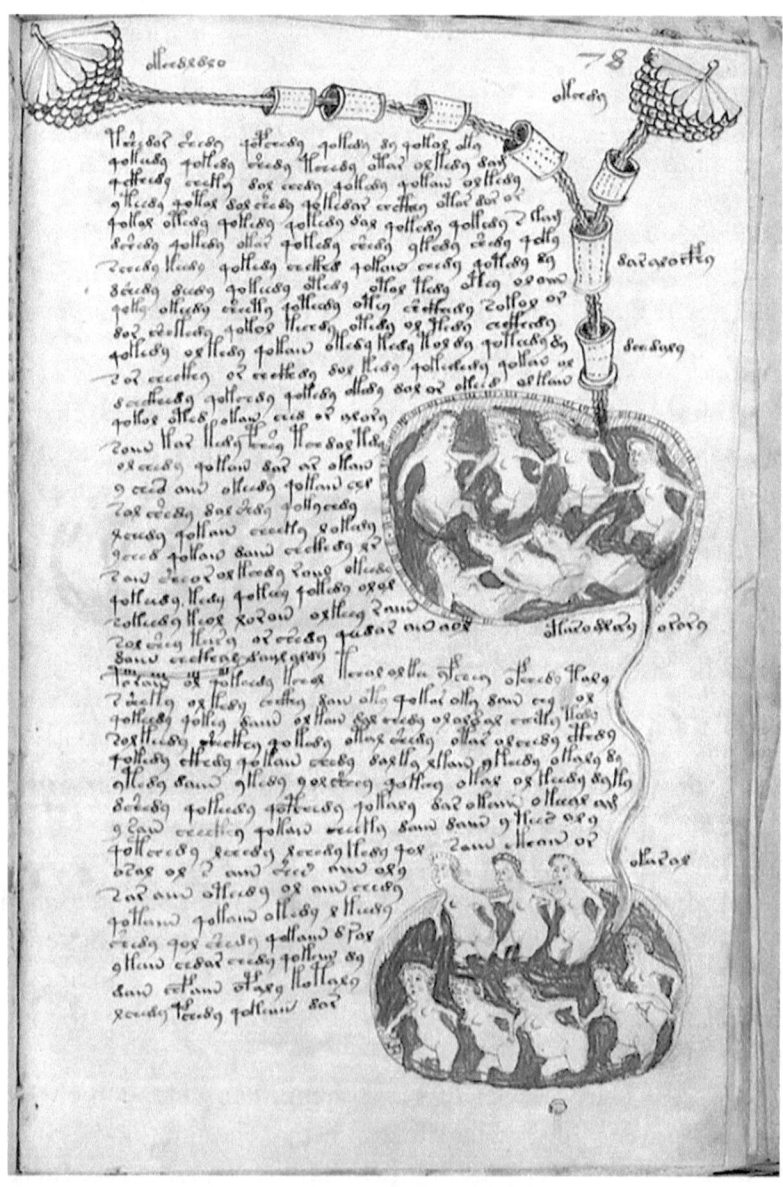

The others show Flora at various stages of her life, from young woman to the ancient person in the video. In all of them, her face is open, intelligent, kind.

At the Weisert Library's site Ozzie paged through the Library's high-res images of the Lijak Manuscript, pausing on this folio or that, fast-forwarding through most. Mark Morehead called it the most mysterious manuscript in the world, and, yes, she admits, it is one odd number with its depictions of plants that never were, of suns and moons and stars in bizarre arrays, its little naked women. These last stand singly, knee-deep in fluid-filled tubs, or frolic in groups in shallow pools. They cluster in circles of thirty or thirty-one around signs of the Zodiac. They are all buck-naked, their vaginal clefts like little commas, their nipples mere dots on their tiny, round, gravity-defying breasts; they have bulging, preg-nant-looking abdomens and short little legs bent at the knees; their faces, crudely sketched, gape into distances and at sights un-knowable. They are beyond weird.

The Weisert has put up five photographs of Flora's husband, Wilfrid. Four of them are conventional likenesses – a man in a business suit not quite looking at the camera. But one – the earli-est, like the tintype of Flora – Ozzie found striking, arresting even. It's a sepia-toned portrait in three-quarter view taken in London in 1892. In it Lijak is a handsome young man possessing a thick brush of hair and goatee. He's wearing steely pince-nez specta-cles, from the right lens of which a double cord drops to a button on the breast of his dark suit. His face is taut: he's been exiled to Siberia and has gotten out, somehow, no one knows how, but somehow, and did so not long before this photograph was taken. Though he is in the safety of England, his eyes are wary still and fearful, the eyes of someone who has suffered. This is the young man Flora will meet and marry.

Ozzie replays the video of Flora and the Russians. It opens with a shot of a Manhattan street and a halted taxi, from which emerge

the Russian visitors – a beautiful ballerina, a handsome male dancer, and a pretty young woman, their interpreter. The women wear
pillbox hats, clingy dresses, and white gloves, the man a well-cut
suit.

The day is splendid. The Russians pause on the sidewalk to
gaze up the front of a massive brick apartment building, the London Terrace Towers, where Flora is living with Alice Neff. Behind
them, at some distance, runs an elevated rail track. This, Ozzie
recognizes, has been transformed into today's High Line park.

The scene changes to the interior of an apartment and a shot
of its entrance door. The door opens, and the beautiful ballerina
enters, smiling, bearing a large bouquet of flowers. The young
interpreter and the male dancer follow her in. The camera pans
after the three as they approach a very old woman dressed in black
seated in an armchair at the end of the room: Flora.

The ballerina leans to present Flora the bouquet. Flora, extending both arms to receive it, beams warmly on her three guests,
but doesn't rise from her chair. A walking cane hanging beside her
from the crosspiece of a floor lamp suggests that rising might be
painful.

The camera pulls back to reveal another person in the room,
a woman in her late middle age, who's standing and speaking to
the Russian guests: Alice Neff. Alice is friendly and gracious in
gesture, the Russians attentive.

Now a close-up of the Russians and Flora seated together: the
ballerina hands Flora an envelope from which Flora extracts what
must be a birthday card. When Flora reads it, she is delighted and
bursts into another smile.

Here abruptly – and puzzlingly – the video cuts from Flora
and the Russians to a portrait hanging on the wall behind Flora.
The portrait is of a young man. He is wearing a flat, dark hat. His
hair, which is deep black, flows to his shoulders. His face, turned
to the viewer, is obscured partly in shadow. The portrait looks
Italian, from the mid-Renaissance perhaps. The image, which is
blurry, lasts only a few seconds. Probably from that summer in

Florence, Ozzie thinks, when Flora wrote *Ribeiro*.

The scene shifts back to Flora and the Russians. As the latter watch, Flora writes something in the title page of a book. She is probably signing a copy of *Ribeiro* in Russian translation. Then, smiling, she presents it to the ballerina.

The Russians rise. The two women buss Flora on her cheek, and the handsome male dancer, bowing deeply, kisses her hand. After which comes the final close-up of Flora blowing her kiss to someone off camera. The video goes to trailer, unreadable markings flash past, the end.

Clearing her screen to Desktop, Ozzie closes her eyes and leans back in her chair. In the silence her thoughts drift from the aged woman whose image she's just seen to the coy little girl in the tintype. Between the two lie eighty-three years, more than a lifetime for most. That little girl grew to adulthood, became a revolutionist, met and married Wilfrid Lijak, smuggled forbidden literature into and out of the Russian Empire, and wrote a best-selling novel.

Then, at some point and for whatever reason, she lost her imaginative power. Though she produced three more novels she was never able to repeat the success of *Ribeiro* and in time ceased writing. She ceased her political activity as well and, as far as Ozzie can learn from the Web, dropped from sight, a Lost Woman Writer, another one.

Hoping to find something of Flora in her work, Ozzie downloads an ePUB version of *Ribeiro*. It's a Google Books scan of the first American edition with its olive-brown cover, its title impressed into that cover in art nouveau gilt lettering. She begins to read.

She is astonished.

CHAPTER II

"Be Silent."

Flora Bowles Lijak was born in County Cork, Ireland on 11 May 1864, to William Bowles and his wife Mary Catoe Bowles. She was the fifth of five daughters.

Six months later, William Bowles died. It happened like this. Bowles, professor of Mathematical Philosophy at Queens College, Cork, had a lecture to give and walked the two miles from his home to the College in a heavy rain. After delivering his lecture in sopping clothing, he returned home, and that evening came down with a severe cold and a high fever. Mary Bowles, who believed remedies of illnesses should resemble their causes, put her husband to bed and for two days she and her older daughters poured buckets of cold water over him. Bowles did not demur, but endured Mary's treatment. Within the week he expired.

For Flora her father was not even a memory; he was someone others talked of. All her life she wondered what it would have been like to have had a father, particularly one as brilliant as hers.

Mary Bowles in her youth had had a wild beauty. She had thick russet hair, which she let grow long, and a fine-featured, open face. These she retained even after bearing her five children. She was so well known for her looks that Arthur Fitzhugh, the Irish Pre-Raphaelite, sought her out in Cork to sketch her in pastel. He sketched William as well and left for posterity the only likeness of the mathematician. Fitzhugh sold the portraits for a pittance to Bowles, and they hung side by side on a wall in the Bowles' living-room in Cork. The very small Flora sometimes watched the portrait of her father hoping he might say something to her and trying to imagine him laughing and playing with her. Age gave her more sense, and she stopped the practice. Fitzhugh's portraits of the Bowles' are stored now at the National Gallery in Dublin.

After William's death, Mary moved her family to London, where she took work as a librarian at Queen's College in Harley Street, an institution for girls and women (not related to Queen's College in Cork). Mary also began tutoring pupils in mathematics. The household of six women lived in a small cottage in Hampstead in a kind of cheerful poverty.

At the age of twelve Flora suffered two ordeals, one immediately following the other. The first was a horrific skin disease. While dressing one morning Flora noticed a blemish on the outer side of her left thigh about three inches above her knee. The blemish was pink in colour, the size of a halfpenny, and resembled an ordinary scab. Within an hour, however, the blemish had swollen to an ugly, encrusted carapace that was as wide as her palm and that had the texture of pigskin. Further, the rash had turned fiery red and had become hot and painful to the touch. Over the next few hours the rash spread, covering her thighs and belly, and a clear fluid began seeping from fissures in the rash. Chills and fever seized her. She could not keep food down.

In her vast old age Flora will remember that illness and her mother's anguish at her plight. Of the physician who came to treat her, however, she will recall only a wide, florid face and a reddish chin-strap beard. Because her illness and treatment were part of the family lore, which she was told later, Flora will know that he diagnosed erysipelas and recommended warm poultices and a good diet. The warm poultices appealed to Mary Bowles's faith in homeopathy, and she dutifully carried out the doctor's orders. Flora recovered.

Flora's other ordeal lasted much longer, her lifetime.

Because the Bowles' were so very poor, Flora, at age twelve, was sent off alone to Manchester to live with the family of William Bowles's older brother Charles, who managed a colliery in a barren outskirt of that city. (At the same time, her beloved sister Evelyn was boarded out to relatives in Ireland.)

Before Flora and Evelyn knew they were to be separated from their mother and other sisters, Mary, despite the expense, had a portrait photograph taken of herself and the five girls. The photographer, a Fleet Street artist, posed Mary seated with the two youngest girls, Flora and Evelyn, kneeling, one on each side of her, and the older girls standing behind. Mary gave small tintypes of the portrait to Flora and Evelyn, hoping the girls would find them comforting when far from home. When Flora arrived in Manchester, however, she hid away her portrait and avoided looking at it, for, far from comforting her, it made her sad.

At Euston Station, in pallid morning light, amidst crowds, hissing steam, the shouting of porters, and the clanging of bells, a desolate Flora said good-bye to her Mama, who knelt to embrace and kiss her. Mary Bowles said, as she had said before, "Your Uncle Charles is a good man and Aunt Elizabeth is a good woman. They are both kind to give you a home when I must work and save money. It is for the best, and sometimes hardships which are unavoidable make us stronger. We shall write you, your sisters and I. And soon" – here Mary's wide face became intense – "I can't say when, but soon – we shall all be back together again. Oh, dear Flora, they'll take good care of you! And you must be a good girl and be grateful and be helpful to them."

Flora nodded, in the way that children do when they know they must agree with an adult.

Flora's journey to Manchester took seven hours (she was put on the slow train in second class) though it seemed much longer. She arrived in the late afternoon, not hungry, fortunately - Mary had packed her a lunch-basket of bread and cheese, a sausage, and a sweet biscuit – but quite frightened, though wishing not to show her fear.

A kindly porter fetched her trunk from its place on the luggage rack, to which place he had hoisted it in London, and helped the little girl disembark into the dense, pushing crowd.

"I reckon you'll be met here, young miss," he said.

"Yes, sir, my uncle is to bring me to his home."

"I see."

The porter busied himself with other passengers, but tarried on the platform, keeping an eye on the little girl, who waited alone, grave and silent, holding her small basket that now was empty of food. Beside her was her trunk, almost as large as she.

Presently a tall, thin-faced man wearing a black suit and black top hat loomed over her and greeted her from his height with a solemn yet brief nod.

The tall, thin-faced man said, "Are you Flora Bowles?"

She replied, "Yes, sir."

The tall, thin-faced man then said, "I am your Uncle Charles, child. Do come," and took her hand.

Catching the kindly porter's eye, Charles tipped his head at Flora's trunk, then escorted Flora briskly through a gate to the street (followed by porter and trunk) into a wilderness of conveyances – broughams, cabriolets, hansoms - and the odour of horse dung and horse sweat. Charles selected a hansom, rewarded the porter with a coin, and, with Flora's trunk deposited in the vehicle, drove off.

Mrs Bowles, a lean, sad-eyed woman visibly older than her husband, met them in the bricked yard behind the Bowles' black iron picket fence. She said, "Welcome, child," but her look and embrace, for she did stoop down to clasp the child in her arms, were far from truly welcoming.

The newly arrived Flora was first exhibited to the Bowles' children (a boy, Jack, the eldest, and two girls, Edna and Ethel) in the Bowles' comfortable parlour after her arrival and "clean-up." Jack's lip curled as his eye wandered over her. The girls, in identical frocks, were subdued. After she had got to know them, Flora found the girls quiet, like their mother, and obedient; Jack she found cold, taciturn, and unfriendly.

Flora settled in and began her new life. She was given a tiny upper room intended once for a servant, which was appropriate, for servant she was to be, helping the general who came in days, a plumpish, disagreeable woman named Rachel Moss, with the domestic work.

Charles (he considered this a great kindness) arranged for Flora to take lessons. For these she would walk to a near-by house occupied by an elderly woman named Miss Branch. Miss Branch taught sewing, drawing, arithmetic, piano, and French. Other girls attended Miss Branch's lessons. One, a dark-tressed child named Juliet, was clever and kind, and Flora liked her, and they made friends. Juliet loved piano as did Flora. When Miss Branch played a lively tune on her piano, Juliet and Flora would grasp each other's hands and dance and laugh. Juliet was Flora's only good memory of Manchester.

Though she could not have articulated the feeling, Flora sensed early on that much in the Manchester Bowles' household went unsaid. She discovered that Charles, far from being a good man, was cruel. He beat his children, particularly Jack, over the slightest wrongdoing, smiling when he did so. He beat their old dog Spotty as well, for... for who knew what? – in any case, smilingly, as the beast cowered. Charles never beat Flora, though she too transgressed (she once was caught taking apples from a neighbour's tree). An accusing glare, a burst of angry talk, savage mockery when she practised her piano lessons – these were his weapons against her. She was his deceased brother's child, not his own, and that is perhaps what restrained him, though he had no fondness for George Bowles or his family. When, on Flora's first day in Manchester she showed Uncle Charles her tin-type portrait of her Mama and sisters, he drew his mouth into a thin, hard line and muttered, "All girls," shaking his head at the thought. "My foolish, improvident brother had no means. And now you are a burden." After only a few weeks in Manchester Flora came to loathe her uncle.

She then became difficult, sometimes neglecting her domestic tasks or performing them indifferently. She tried to befriend her ill-treated cousins, even though they, particularly Jack, disdained her as the poor relative and the girl who never suffered beatings when they must, and at first rejected her attempts at befriending them.

Jack's feelings toward Flora were the first to change. One day after he had been whipped smartly by his father for some small misdeed he went to sit in the shady, high-walled back area. He had loosened his shirt and was studying a red gash on his left shoulder, cut there by his father's belt. Flora approached him quietly and put her hand on his arm.

"I'm sorry, Jack," she said. "He mustn't beat you so."

Jack looked up. "Ah, you. Well, he will. It's his way. It can't be helped. Me, I'm just waiting to leave. Once I'm old enough, I'll say good-bye to him forever. I'll get out into the world and make my way in it. I intend to work and do well."

"You will, Jack, I know it. You'll give him what for. So shall I one day."

"'Give him what for'?" Jack laughed, this time good-naturedly, forgetting the stinging across his shoulder. He studied her a moment, then said, smiling at her, "You're a good 'un, Flora." It was her acceptance.

After that, not only Jack, but the girls too came round and began to behave in a friendlier way toward Flora. On some nights, when Uncle Charles and Aunt Elizabeth had gone to bed, Flora would tip-toe down to the girls' room and there the three, in delicious secrecy, would talk. The talk was often of Charles's hard heart and his delight in others' pain, which the girls' maturing minds had begun to notice. None yet knew the word "sadism." The young Flora paid little heed to a certain film of reticence that came over her cousins' faces when the girls spoke of their father, neither looking at the other.

One night as Flora lay asleep above stairs Uncle Charles quietly entered her room. He approached her bed and, kneeling, drew back her checkered coverlet. This woke her. She said sleepily, "Hello, Uncle Charles. What is it?" Uncle Charles did not answer but began to touch and caress her small legs. His hand drifted (outside her night-dress) to her small tummy. His actions puzzled her; she could not conceive what he was about. She pretended sleep. He left.

Some nights later he returned. This time, after caressing her, he lifted her garment and stroked, trembling, her nether parts. When Flora cried out, his left hand capped her mouth, suffocatingly.

"Be silent," he whispered. He stood for a moment as she lay trembling, then backed from the room.

In the morning Uncle Charles's harsh black eyes were unapologetic. He even affected a slight smile. He did not threaten to punish her if she spoke of the matter. Punishment was understood – his was the house of punishment. The rest of that day Flora was uncommunicative with Rachel Moss and the Bowles children and ate little. That night and the following nights she slept only fitfully, frightened that her uncle might return.

At Miss Branch's, Juliet noticed something was wrong with her friend. She put her hand in Flora's and asked, "Are you feeling ill?"

Flora said, "No."

To cheer her friend Juliet said, "Shall we play 'The Frogs and the Crickets'? Do let's!"

"The Frogs and the Crickets" was a piano exercise Miss Branch had taught them in which one girl would play a tune in the lower register and the other answer her in the upper. The two girls had loved the game.

Flora turned away.

As days ensued Flora became herself again. But one night Uncle Charles returned to her room. Once more Flora pretended sleep, hoping, foolish little girl, that she could by this means escape his caress, dream him away, herself fly to a Land of Nod and there find safety. But she could do none of these. All her life Flora will remember, but not remember, how on that night her small limbs had been forced apart and her shoulders pressed to the mattress by a large hand.

And the rest.

Charles returned to her room other nights, leaving her days desolate. Flora could not remember how often he did so. She remembered his whispering, "This is love, child. Love. I am loving you."

Till the end of her life Flora would recall the odour: it was that of fish.

One day Flora announced to Aunt Elizabeth that she would drown herself in the horse-pond. When Aunt Elizabeth asked why, Flora would not say. Flora thought that her declaration led to talk between Aunt Elizabeth and Uncle Charles because after she made her threat Uncle Charles never reappeared in her room. What her aunt might have said to Uncle Charles Flora could never know. Much later in her life she would wonder, Had Aunt Elizabeth any inkling of the nature of her husband's crimes? Had she other occasions to talk with him about other children? About the girls?

Charles sent Flora back to London with a letter to Mary Bowles complaining of Flora's "wilful and rebellious nature" and of her bad influence on his own children. He wrote that he "could no longer tolerate her disruptive presence" in his house and that she must leave. He hoped and prayed that her character would improve. By that time, however, Flora was another creature.

When Mary asked her why Uncle Charles should send her home and write such a letter, Flora would never reply.

Soon after her return Flora experienced a series of convulsions that came on with no warning. The first occurred as she was rising to leave the breakfast table, having eaten in silence. Half out of her chair she threw herself to the floor and, eyes closed, rolled back and forth the length of the room, screaming not words but mere sound in parched-throated anger, all the while kicking wildly and thrashing her arms. Her seizure over, Flora lay panting on the floor, exhausted, as her distraught mother and sisters surrounded her, imploring her to speak.

Mary Bowles cried, "Oh, Flora, dear, what is the matter? What can it be?" Mary feared her daughter had gone mad.

Ignoring them and their attempts to comfort her, Flora rose unsteadily and went to the room she shared with Evelyn and Alice to commune with herself, which she did for some hours, resisting company. In the days that followed, she had two further seizures and exhibited the same behaviour: a period of silence, then convulsions and unintelligible screaming.

Mary Bowles tried to understand and assuage Flora's distress, but Flora would tell her only that the Bowles household in Manchester was an abode of misery. She could not think of let alone mention her Uncle Charles's acts.

Mary, smothered in guilt for sending Flora away to such a home, rebuked herself mercilessly. She called in a physician, who diagnosed "hysteria juvenalis" and recommended warm baths of sulphate of magnesia. The baths brought an end to Flora's seizures, and her troubles seemed to abate.

Flora's mother and sisters schooled her and treated her lovingly, and she brightened. Best of all, when funds for lessons were available, she studied piano. Increasingly skilled, she learnt difficult pieces and took much pleasure in performing them. Great music, she was finding, moved her deeply; music became her passion and gave her much happiness.

During the summer of her sixteenth year Flora visited Ireland to stay with relatives (the same who had boarded her sister Evelyn). It was in the library of their large old house in Cork that she came across E.A. Venturi's memoir of the Italian revolutionary hero Giuseppe Mazzini. Mrs Venturi's sketches of Mazzini's life as journalist and her account of the part Mazzini played in the struggle for freedom in Italy resonated with Flora's own feelings and ample imagination, and she vowed then that she would fight for freedom and justice herself, perhaps, like Mazzini, as a writer. It was at this time that she began to wear black always and to view herself as a revolutionist.

OZZIE

It's a glorious, breezy, open-skied Sunday afternoon, early in March. Mark Morehead, Ozzie, and Mark's son Oliver, an energetic child who is not quite six, are strolling on the gravel towpath of the old C&O Canal. They're at Fletcher's Cove, a picnic and boat rental park two miles up the Potomac River from Georgetown. Passing them in both directions, on the towpath and on an asphalted bicycle path that parallels the Canal and follows it into Georgetown, are cyclists and joggers. Across the bicycle path and down a slope is the park, and beyond that, visible through a line of sycamores and willows, the gleaming Potomac.

Mark had called. He thanked Ozzie again for the PDF on Women's Studies she sent him.

I looked at your book *Gender and Anarchy*, too. The piece that mentioned Flora, it just mentioned her, like you said. Not much help.

Right.

So, I'm still at a dead end. I'll write something up for the list–serve, but I think that'll be about it.

I got curious about Flora and did some checking. Not a whole lot out there on her, not on the Web anyway. Type her in, you mostly get a bunch of hits on the Manuscript, which I guess is understandable. Certainly one odd item. Good luck on breaking it, by the way.

Tell me about it.

There's this video, Russians visiting her in like 1959? And there's a video of it?

Yeah – I've seen it.

Like Kay's article, not much use to you, I guess.

No. Fun though. To look at.

Yeah. Very. Quite a woman, wasn't she? Revolutionist, best-selling writer. I read *Ribeiro*, by the way. Her big success? It's a real page-turner, some kind of great work — at least in the intrigue genre. Seems to prefigure classics of the form. Might even be better than that. Not sure. Might get inspired to do a paper on her — you know, Lost Woman, Lost Masterpiece et cetera. Kind of like Kay. But she's maddening — so little to go on with her. I tried to work out a timeline on her, on her life? But there's so much blank space.

Yeah.

Pause.

Well anyhow, I was thinking, I'm going to be out with my son this Sunday. If it's a nice day. I'm taking him for a walk down by the Potomac. Not too far from Georgetown. Like to come along? In the afternoon? Sunday afternoon? Be fun for us.

She wavered. She wanted to say, as she had said to others, I'm not seeing guys these days, but Mark seemed nice and she could use an outing, so she said, Oh. Sure. Thanks. Yes, sure.

She regretted it instantly but felt she couldn't back out.

They met in the small parking lot across the Canal from the park, where an entrance drive comes down from Canal Road. Mark, who was there waiting with his son when Ozzie arrived, waved happily when he saw her and shouted, Hi, how are you? and then, when they'd neared one another, said, Hey Ollie, say hello to... He hesitated.

By then Ozzie had kneeled and put her hand on the little boy's arm and said, Hi, Ollie, I'm Ozzie. Nice to meet you, Ollie.

Ollie, shy, pulled himself around his father's leg giving Ozzie a quick, tentative look, then turned away.

Beautiful little boy, she thought: Perfect skin, pearly, lustrous little ears, lively eyes. Cleft in his small chin. Killer smile. She caught another glance from him and smiled back.

Mark took Ollie's hand, and the three of them crossed a bridge over the Canal to the towpath and started walking in the direction of Georgetown.

Mark and Ozzie establish: That Mark and Anne – that's her name, Mark's wife – have this one child, Ollie. That the divorce is proceeding. That Anne doesn't want the divorce, but that Mark does, that it's necessary, and that he'll get custody of his son. Mark seems pretty sure of that. Ozzie wonders why.

They establish, too, that Ozzie has been married, but that her husband has died. That Ozzie and her husband, Tom, had had no kids. That Ozzie's father is Persian and her mother American. That Ozzie was born in Tehran but brought up in Connecticut.

Ozzie finds she likes Mark. He's attentive, his face is kind. He's shy, like his son. He's bright, not intellectual but bright, which is okay, Tom was like that. People like that run the world. And Mark is tall. She likes that as well, though Tom was not.

She asks herself, Why am I doing this? And for the first time since Tom's death, as she walks with Mark in the bright sun and the fresh day, she admits to herself – or perhaps realizes – that she's lonely.

Mark has a nice voice. He's soft-spoken. His accent has just a touch of the upper Midwest. As Mark talks, Ollie is zigzagging ahead of them, dashing in short little steps, his tiny running shoes flashing red on their outside soles. When he comes to a clump of water-plants at the edge of the Canal he squats to investigate, then leaves them to scamper toward a party of geese. When he nears the birds, he slows, approaching them warily (they're as tall as he is). They do move from him, but grudgingly, not ceding him much space.

Mark's watching. "He could lose an eye. Hey, Ollie? Ollie – come on over, let's turn around and walk back this way. Might see some deer."

Ollie seems happy enough to leave the geese and dashes back to Mark.

"Hey, Ollie," Mark calls out to his son, who again is straying off, "know what this is?" Mark points toward the water. "It's the 'Canal' I told you about. They used to have big boats on it. And see this path we're walking on? Runs along the Canal? Mules would pull the boats. Along this path."

Ollie doesn't quite get this. He looks back at Mark, weighing what Mark said. Then he looks across the Canal and his face brightens. He points to two large snapping turtles sunning on a log and, still pointing, turns to Mark and Ozzie and laughs.

Mark says, "Wow! Okay! What are those?"

"Turtles!"

"Right! Turtles! Awesome!" To Ozzie he says, "He knows about turtles. Not sure about mules. Or where the Canal goes or why. Thing is, I talk to him as if he does know and he learns. If he wants to know what a mule is, he'll ask, 'What's a mule?' He's always asking, 'What's this?', 'What's that? Why, why, why?' Lot of 'whys' with Ollie at this stage."

Mark and Ozzie have come to a set of concrete stairs to their left that lead down to the bike path and from there down to the park. Mark gestures with his head. "There are benches down there. One of them looks unoccupied. Want to go down? We could sit and watch the Ollie Show."

"Sure."

"Hey, buddy," he yells at Ollie, who's examining a turned-over canoe, one in a line of aluminum canoes and dark red wooden rowboats drawn up on the edge of the Canal awaiting renters. "Hold it, come on back – let's go down here. Come on, dude, let's go down. We're going to go down and look at the river."

Ollie happily rushes up to Mark, who takes his hand again, and the three of them descend to the bike path, cross it quickly – it's heavily traveled by speeding cyclists this beautiful day – and descend more stairs to the park.

On the way down to the empty bench they pass a man and

woman who have taken over a picnic table and are cleaning fish on it, which they must have caught on the river. They're holding their catch in a picnic cooler. Both are wearing jeans, sweatshirts, sleeveless jackets, floppy canvas hats, and identical yellow rubber gloves. His white hair, which is thin and fine, is pulled back into a ponytail; her gray hair spills wildly from under her hat. She's wearing rimless glasses.

Mark, still holding Ollie's hand, stops to talk with the man. "Hi. Excuse me, I don't want to bother you, but I wanted to ask, what kind of fish is that?"

"White perch," the man replies testily, not looking up. He grabs a fish from the cooler, stabs into its belly with a long, serrated knife, and pulls out a handful of stringy guts. These he throws into a red plastic bucket. His lady – wife? girlfriend? – who is using a boning knife to filet the fish the man has gutted, says nothing, and doesn't look up either.

Mark nods and pulls Ollie away. "Hey, thanks." Mark glances at Ozzie, the glance meaning these people are really weird.

Ozzie finds his glance, the soundless communication, a kind of intimacy. She likes this.

They sit on the park bench and let Ollie explore the terrain down toward the river, among its budding willows and sycamores and the tree trunks washed up by last year's flood.

"Don't go too far, buddy – okay?"

Ollie doesn't acknowledge hearing this, but heads for the cove, a small inlet, where rowboats and canoes are moored to a dock reached by a narrow footbridge. Ollie ventures to the bridge but does not cross it.

The Potomac is narrow here, no more than a hundred yards across. On the Virginia side a granite bluff rises high over the river, at the very top of which cars on the George Washington Parkway are gliding into and out of the city, emerging into view from one stand of pines, disappearing into another, silently, endlessly. On the water a lone fisherman in a rowboat is patiently awaiting a strike. Around him, at long, unpredictable intervals, a flash of silver and white — white perch? — will break the surface, then disappear, leaving expanding rings of water.

Ozzie says, "Those two back there — ageing hippies. Nothing sadder according to my mother. My Mom's a reformed hippie. Very serious lawyer now, very prim. Back in her day she wore striped bell-bottoms and smoked pot and hash — hard to believe it to see her now, but she really did. So'd my dad. They've since grown up. At least my mom has. Not sure about my dad. They met in school. She was Smith, he was UMass. They got married and went to Iran. In the '70s. After the revolution they stayed on. Which is when I was born. And my little brother David. In Iran.

"Dad was in banking. He was an exec with the Bank of Tehran. He thought he could make a go of it after the revolution and all the Islamic craziness. But he couldn't. Mom left first. With me and my brother. Then dad left."

Ozzie does not say that Baba and Baba's family lost most of their money in the revolution, that Baba was accused of embezzling funds from the bank, that when he left and came back to America, a fugitive lucky to get out, he was miserable. She does not say that he moved to New York, leaving Grace with Ozzie and David in Hartford, ostensibly and maybe truly, to find a job in finance, failed at that, but used the opportunity to philander, at which sport he excelled. That Grace learned of it easily and, profoundly wounded, divorced him.

Nor does Ozzie say that after her divorce Grace became hard, that she pushed herself at law school and at her firm, that Grace's mother Moo Moo raised Ozzie as much as Grace did, nor that Grace worried — she said this now and then — that Ozzie might inherit what she called "Sadeq's cluelessness gene," that is, be irresponsible with her life, throw it away like Baba. When an adolescent Ozzie retreated into books, Grace took it as a bad sign.

———

Baba and Grace had their final angry days and their parting at The Pond, a country estate in the watery, eastern part of Connecticut. The Pond belonged to Grace's Uncle Bill, a retired engineer, and consisted of a rambling one-story stone house and three wooden outbuildings, all set on a hill looking west over a pond – hence the name – and low, boggy land. Thirty years back the Hartford Welles, always welcome, would repair to The Pond regularly for its hint of country life and fresh air.

There, on an autumnal weekend, Baba and Grace walked together in a meadow, talking seriously, not hand-in-hand, watched from a distance by an unseen Ozzie. Baba and Grace had had no loud arguments, nor did they tell Ozzie they were separating until after the fact. Much later, Ozzie realized that Grace and Baba were walking in that meadow about the time they split and that they were probably talking about the divorce. If so, it had to be 1987, that jumbled year when Baba left for good.

Grace, talking not long back of her marriage to Sadeq and their time together in Iran with his family, told Ozzie, "Hard to believe it all actually happened, it's so far away." Her eyes moistened when she said this, and she looked away from Ozzie. "It's like it was all a dream."

Ozzie thinks maybe that's what Grace has done with her marriage and that exotic, long-ago life of hers – turned it into a dream. Maybe that's what happens when you get old enough, the past becomes a dream.

Ozzie says to Mark, "My husband was killed in a traffic accident. Five years ago, outside Boston. Other guy's fault." This is Ozzie's standard story, short and bitter, which she habitually tells in a neutral tone. She does not say how death gave her a new role in life: widow. When she says, "I'm a widow" to people who don't know her, she finds they react mutedly, not knowing what to do with it. They usually don't inquire further. They'll say something like, "Oh, sorry for your loss" or simply nod sympathetically. Whatever

COLIN MACKINNON

they do, the subject gets changed.

Mark reacts differently. His face goes serious. He says, "I'm so sorry. Must have been terrible."

Ozzie senses Mark means what he says. Maybe because he's divorcing, she thinks. Death, divorce – one or the other, that's how marriages end. When he mentions Anne, Ozzie has noticed, a curtain comes over his face. She thinks it's to cover pain. She understands that.

In one of her phone conversations with Grace – it wasn't that long ago – they'd talked for a time, then Grace, probably when she thought Ozzie wouldn't bristle, asked, "Is life passing you by, Oz? You can't grieve forever." To keep things civil, Ozzie made some response that took the conversation elsewhere, but thought, Oh yes you can. It may be self-indulgent, but oh yes you can. Grieve forever.

Baba knows this. Grieving forever makes sense to Persians. Baba has a story about a madwoman in Tehran who'd loll around one of the traffic circles they have there. "Everybody knew her. She was very old. White hair. She always wore a long red dress. Her face and her arms were brown from the sun and skinny. She always had a smile on her face. Talked to herself. Crazy woman. Nobody bothered her. Nobody seemed to know where she stayed or how she lived or who took care of her. People told a story about her. They said she'd lost a love when she was young – he died somehow, nobody knew how – and she grieved for him from that day on, never talking sense to anyone. She was there when I left. Still at it, still sitting in that traffic circle, smiling." He snorted. "She must be dead now. Joined her lover."

As Baba told the story he seemed to half-believe it, but then he said, mixing Persian into his English as he liked to do with Ozzie, "*Chairt o pairt* [nonsense]. She was just *divooneh* [crazy]."

Baba's story was his way of commenting on Ozzie's habit of grief – indirect, Persian, letting you draw your own conclusions. Choose grief if you must, he was saying, but don't forget, the woman was mad.

Ozzie recalls Baba's story from time to time. Maybe I am a mad woman, she thinks, sitting forever in a traffic circle, life passing me by.

Mark asks Ozzie about her name.

"It's pronounced Ah Zah DAY, stress on the DAY. It means 'noble.'" She snorts a laugh. "Misnomer, unfortunately, just my father's wishful thinking. Most people call me Ozzie."

She tells Mark of Grace, of her brother David and his girl-friend Buzz.

Mark says that his father died a few years back. That he served three years in the Air Force out of college. That he has two sisters, one, a nurse in Rochester, not married, the other, a Special Ed teacher in Orlando, married. That his mother lives near the one in Orlando. That he has two nieces and a nephew. The American Family.

Mark's cell rings. He pulls it from his shirt pocket and after a short hesitation excuses himself and takes the call. Listening, he glances at Ozzie, glances away, saying little in the conversation, just some "yeses" and "rights" and finally "Okay, see you then. Fine." The conversation ends. No explanation.

Spy, she thinks. He's on sabbatical, but they're calling him anyway. Probably part of the deal.

With his phone out now, Mark shows Ozzie shots of Ollie: Ollie dressed for Halloween last year in a black and white penguin suit with a large, droopy orange felt bill; Ollie at the beach, boney little body in striped swim drawers, fat face; Ollie perched on a snowboard with other children in a park, everybody laughing. More shots follow – all featuring Ollie – maybe a dozen, Mark so proud, explaining where they were taken and when.

Mark produces one final shot: Ollie with his mother on a gray-planked deck somewhere.

Anne. She's sitting forward in a wicker chair, surrounded by lush plants, and has her arms around Ollie from behind, who's standing between her legs, both facing the camera, both smiling. Anne's a good-looking brunette. She's trim and tanned. She's wearing off-white slacks, a simple, earth-toned top, a necklace of dark stones.

Ozzie wonders what she's like, Anne, why they're divorcing. Sex? Money? Is she touchy when the moon's full? Is he? And Ollie – why only the one child? Is that the problem?

Ozzie senses – from something in Mark's face, something in his voice when he speaks of it – that the divorce is breaking his heart.

Ozzie pulls her own cell out and shows family photos to Mark. He regards each curiously, as Ozzie swipes them past, explaining who they are, where the shots were taken. He smiles, nodding, as if acknowledging Grace's elegance, Baba's still-noticeable good looks, and David's.

Ollie's back from exploring the cove. He hangs on Mark's knee, stealing more glances at Ozzie, warming to her.

Mark says, "Hey, buddy, hey - want to count backwards? Show Ozzie, okay? Start with one hundred. By fives."

Ollie inhales deeply and pulls himself erect. "One hundred," he says. "Ninety-five. Ninety..." He counts down smoothly, slowing only once – going from forty to thirty-five – recovers, gets them all right, down to a triumphant, loud "Zero!"

"Cool! Let's do the letter game, okay? Want to do the letter game?"

Ollie nods.

"You choose."

"Ummmmm... 'N.'"

"'N'... Okay, uh... Nose."

"Nice."

"Next."

"NetFlix."

"Near."

"Noise."

"Okay! Let's change the letter – want to change the letter?"
Ollie bobs a "yes".

"Okay, I'll choose. Uh... 'B'."

"Boy."

"Bicycle."

"Big."

"Bite."

"Bug."

Not six and he recognizes letters, Ozzie thinks. Mark's show-ing him off. He is adorable. Do I want that? Do I want a child? Tom and I did. Once. But now? Even a charmer like this one?

"He's a good reader," Mark says, as Ollie wanders off again to explore. "He likes books, figuring out what they say."

"So, he's a codebreaker. Must be the genes."

Mark smiles. "Yeah. His teachers like him. Anne – to her cred-it, Anne limits his time on his Wii. She sets aside media-free time."

"Beautiful little boy."

"He is. Though he can have huge meltdowns. They come out of nowhere – he squalls and kicks, cries his eyes out. Hard to believe it when you see him like this, but he can be that way."

Ozzie regards Mark. He loves this child, even with his melt-downs. And the boy obviously loves him. They're close, they're physical, there's lots of hugging. Not distant, the way Grace was. How attractive that is.

"He's shy," Mark says, "but he likes you."

Ozzie nods, pleased. And, she thinks, you like me too. What do I make of that? You're a married man. Would you be like Will, my experimental lover, Will, who was simply adrift, taking other people down with him, Will, who finally went back to his wife?

Mark has become quiet. Both he and Ozzie are comfortable with that. In their silence they watch the river and the lone fisherman.

Ozzie thinks: Making love again. That's what this is about, isn't it? What would that be like? With this one? With anyone? She remembers Tom's body, its silkiness, its warmth, how it fit so well to hers.

She thinks, This is just a friendly walk in the park. I can still cancel. But I'm seeing da Silva next week. So, should I go back on the pill? Not for this one. Necessarily. But still, should I go back on the pill?

Ollie, on the other side of Mark, is leaning on him and beginning to look sleepy.

Mark says, "Hey, we better go. This guy's tired. He's going to go home and crash. Aren't you, buddy? Aren't you?" Mark grabs Ollie and tussles him around saying "Aren't you? Aren't you?" as the little boy struggles and giggles. To Ozzie he says, "Hey, I had a good time."

"Me too." She means it.

"Can I call you again? Maybe take another walk or something? Or go out? See a movie?"

"Sure."

Is he being polite? she wonders. Am I? Or what?

He smiles, taking Ollie's hand. "Great."

In the parking lot there is much ado buckling Ollie into his booster seat in the rear of Mark's car, a shiny yellow Mustang convertible. After snapping the little seatbelt but before shutting the door Mark says, "Okay, buddy, say, 'Bye-bye, Ozzie.'"

The little boy, no longer shy with her, waves and smiles his killer smile. "Bye-bye, Ozzie."

Mark gets in, starts the car, and waving goodbye himself pulls his Mustang up the drive to Canal Road, where it vanishes.

If he'd wanted to go out again, he'd have had a suggestion, Ozzie tells herself. He won't call, he was being polite. Maybe he will, though. His smile looked real. What do I want?

CHAPTER III

"You Could Just Call Me Bill, You Know."

"Two, four; three, seven; six, one; three, five; four, one," Flora read under her breath, making tiny, almost imperceptible marks with a finely pointed hard-lead pencil in a book, a collection of short stories entitled *Keynotes*, by George Egerton, the *nom de plume* of the English feminist author Mary Chavalita Dunne.

Flora made her first mark in the margin of the page she had selected, two lines down from the top; she made her second mark over the fourth word in that line: two down, four over — "two, four." She repeated the process on the next page, "Three, seven," making a small mark by the third line from the top and another over the seventh word in that line. She continued with the pages after that, "Six, one; three, five; four, one," marking each in the same manner.

It was Wednesday afternoon, 28 May 1895, four days after the Anglo-Russian soirée. Flora was upstairs in the house in Hammersmith she shared with Lijak, in a bright front bedroom that she and her husband had turned into a kind of office, where they occupied opposite ends of a long deal table. Lijak had left for the Reading Room of the British Museum to study medieval art and ancient techniques for producing ink and pigment. Flora was alone.

Using a technique known as the Nihilist Cipher, based on a grid containing the Cyrillic alphabet and in common use among Russian revolutionists, Flora was slowly and carefully concealing in Egerton's stories a message for a comrade in St Petersburg. The message described when and how a shipment of prohibited books and pamphlets was to arrive in that city.

When she was done Flora would bundle *Keynotes* with several other English works, these unmarked, and, using a pseudonym, post them to a recipient in St Petersburg thought unlikely to be under strict surveillance by the police. This person would pass the books on to Flora's real correspondent.

The servant girl Sarah tapped twice on the work-room door, which was slightly ajar. "A gentleman to see you, Ma'am," she said. "A Mr McKenzie."

"Mr...? Oh, yes. The American."

The morning after the soirée McKenzie had sent a note addressed to Flora at the *Free Russia* office (he had got the address from Kropotkin):

American Press Association
34 Throgmorton Street, E.C.

May 25, 1895

Dear Mrs. Lijak,

May I call on you and Mr. Lijak sometime and see you at your work? If so, when might that be convenient?

Wm. McKenzie

She received his note a day later and replied:

26 May, 1895

149, The Grove
Hammersmith

Dear McKenzie,

Weekday mornings Mr Lijak and I are generally to be found in the Free Russia offices 3, Iffley Road, Hammersmith.

Afternoons we are at our residence, as above. You are most welcome at either place.

Flora Lijak

Sarah entered the workroom and presented Flora with McKenzie's card:

William B. McKenzie
San Francisco American
331 South Port Street
San Francisco, California

"Yes, yes, yes. Right. Tell Mr McKenzie I shall be down presently. Bring him tea. And bread and butter. And the blackberry jam."

"Yes, Ma'am."

Flora finished her work, rushing slightly and not bothering to verify its accuracy – she would do that later – because of her waiting guest. She closed her *Egerton* and put it and the Russian text she had enciphered in it in a sewing basket at her end of the cluttered table and descended to the parlour.

"Ah, Mr McKenzie, good afternoon!"

McKenzie rose quickly and agilely from the sofa. "Good afternoon, Mrs Lijak." They shook hands. For the second time (the first was at the soirée) they touched one another. This time, however, each detected an import in that touch that went beyond casual gesture.

"I happened to be in the West End this morning," McKenzie said, "and I thought I'd come further out and see your operation. I hope it's not inconvenient."

"No, no, no, not at all. We are accustomed to receiving guests at odd hours. As are some of our guests – odd. But you can see there isn't much of a... an 'operation' here, just my husband and me, and really mostly me these days. Wilfrid's out."

When she said this Flora caught a look in McKenzie's eye

suggesting that he was not entirely displeased that Wilfrid was absent. She went on, "I'm working here. I can be quite monkish about my work, by the way, but don't worry at all, I was in need of a break. Have you had tea? Did you find the blackberry jam satisfactory?"

He smiled. "'Satisfactory?' Most 'satisfactory.'"

Her smile met his. A thought of the beautiful day struck her. "You know, it's such a lovely afternoon it's sinful to be indoors – shall we take a walk? There's a park not far from here. We could go there and have a stroll. Would you like that?"

"Why, yes indeed!"

"I have a student coming later – I give piano lessons – and I must return for that, but we do have time for a walk and a talk." Putting on her black jacket and her new straw hat with its lovely cornflower-blue band, she called to Sarah, who was clattering dishes in the tiny scullery behind the kitchen, "Sarah"– the clatter stopped – "Mr McKenzie and I are going to the park if anyone should inquire."

"Yes, Ma'am." The clatter resumed.

"Let's go first to our *Free Russia* offices – they're not much, but you should see them. They're on our way."

She led McKenzie briskly round a corner and over to the Iffley Road and to the modest grey brick house with bay window that Sergei Stepniak had leased on behalf of the Society.

"Look there," Flora said and gestured with her head at a middle-aged man in black bowler-hat and dark suit standing quietly at a lamppost up the street. "One of our friends."

McKenzie tensed.

"They are always about, sometimes here, sometimes in front of our house. We see this one frequently. We call him 'The Limpet'." Flora laughed. "No fear, he's harmless. And stupid. In Paris when Wilfrid and I are followed we will often nod and bow to our escorts and they will sometimes nod and bow back to us. Our English spies" – Flora gestured again toward the man in the bowler-hat – "I am sorry to say, are ruder. When one addresses them, they pretend not to notice. Well, let's go in."

Flora unlatched the door. (Because it was after one p.m. the bookshop was locked and closed for public business.) McKenzie, after glancing furtively up the street at The Limpet (who eyed him back), followed Flora inside. There, Leonid Shmuilovich Shishko and Nikolai Vasilyevich Chaikovsky, two Russian propagandists-in-exile, both middle-aged and bushy-bearded, were at work editing and correcting proofs in Russian of a new pamphlet by Stepniak on tactics for the revolution entitled, "What Must We Do? The Beginning of the End." ("We see no other path save violence," Stepniak wrote in his summation. "We look to bombs and dynamite.")

Flora, speaking English with Chaikovsky and Russian with Shishko (who didn't understand English and as long as he lived never learnt it), introduced McKenzie as an American journalist. Smiling, each shook McKenzie's hand and went back to work.

Flora showed McKenzie the front room shop: the counter, the till, the display shelves filled with books and pamphlets (in English and Russian), and in a glass showcase back issues of *Free Russia*.

"*Free Russia* comes out every month. Here's a copy. The latest. It's yours. Take it home and have a read if you haven't seen it. It's most informative."

Saying good-bye to Shishko and Chaikovsky, Flora led McKenzie to Ravenscourt Park, where they seated themselves on a bench in the sun. In the splendid weather black-stockinged nurses were out, some playing with the toddlers in their charge, others pushing prams along the paths, as many as three abreast, chattering and laughing amongst themselves. Elderly persons walked dogs or, wrapped in blankets, lay dozing in bath chairs.

At the park's northern end copses had been cleverly combined with grassy lawns to suggest English countryside; at its southern end lay a triangular pond, round which shrubbery and more trees formed a number of connected shady recesses.

"This park was done by Repton," Flora said. "Humphry Repton. Landscape architect. Beginning of the century. Designed it as part of a vast estate that has since been broken up. The core of the park remains, however, which is where we are now."

"Good. Glad to hear that – that it's been broken up. It's a park for the people now. For everybody."

"Ha. I see your Anarchism extends to parks."

"Estates."

"Well, I could not be an Anarchist. One has to be too good. Pyotr Kropotkin and my friend Charlotte Wilson are perhaps the only two persons I know who are good enough to be Anarchists." Charlotte Wilson, the wife of a stockbroker, had founded with Kropotkin the Anarchist paper *Freedom*, which she edited. Mrs Wilson refused to live on her husband's earnings and took to raising chickens whilst dwelling in a cottage, Wildwood Farm, on the northern edge of Hampstead Heath.

Flora said, "You might be surprised to know that Kropotkin is actually a prince – did you know that?"

"A prince? No."

"Well, he is. Not that that's unusual – the Russians have throngs of princes – *knyazy* they call them – and he's one. I don't understand the system, it goes far back. He may, however, be the only Anarchist Russian prince. He is mystical and monumental as only Russians can be. And he's the kindest, gentlest man in the world. And terribly sad away from his country. Kropotkin and I went once to the Regent's Zoo. We came upon an aged Russian wolf lying in his cage. He did not move at all; in fact, he scarcely breathed. Kropotkin said, 'He is a Russian in exile. He is alone and among foreigners who do not understand him. He is a prisoner. He pines for his homeland.' Kropotkin carried on talking like this until the wolf eyed us sadly – he had thick white eyebrows – and began to make melancholy noises. In Kropotkin, I believe, he sensed a fellow countryman. Well, Kropotkin, as I say, and Charlotte may be good enough to be Anarchists, but the rest of us, I fear, do not measure up, and that is the fatal flaw of Anarchist theory."

McKenzie looked her straight on. "The Capitalists are stealing from us. They always have, they always will. It's our right to fight back in whatever way we can. I am part of that struggle. And we will win it. It may take time, but we will win it and put an end to… things as they are. We are many, they are few. And we will move History." McKenzie's face had hardened.

Later, when she was trying to make sense of things, Flora would recall the vehemence of his look.

"Umm. So, tell me about yourself, Mr McKenzie. Where in America are you from?"

"'Mr McKenzie' – you could just call me Bill, you know. I'd like that."

"Fine. Bill it is, then. Bill, I'm Flora."

At this McKenzie extended his hand in a joking way. "Nice to meet you, Flora," he said and laughed. Again, they touched. McKenzie's joking way of seeking her hand concealed something not a joke. Flora sensed this; the moment passed.

"I'm from San Francisco. Or Oakland, really, which is across the Bay. I was born and brought up there. My father was a miner and a farmer. My mother taught piano. She was a music teacher like you."

"Ah, good!"

McKenzie nodded. "And she took in boarders to make ends meet. She's gone. So's my father."

Those three laconic statements concealed immense hurt. McKenzie believed that he was illegitimate. That the man, Laughlan – "Lockie" – McKenzie, who was said to be his father, was not. He knew that the boarders his mother Nell McKenzie took in were sometimes more than boarders. He believed that one of them, some itinerant shoe salesman, perhaps, or a prairie dentist new to the city, had had the honour of being his father. Poor Lockie's last venture after failure as farmer was to manage then buy a general store in Oakland, a city which was then booming. He staked what savings he had on the store and, much against his principles, took out a small loan. After booms, however, come panics, and Lockie was ruined in one. He lost his store and ended as a night watchman on the docks in Oakland. He died by drowning himself in the Bay for reasons unknown but surmisable.

Lockie, a kind, decent, hard-working man, who on Sundays after church loved to take the small McKenzie oystering in the hard-packed grey sand of the Oakland shore, failed in life through no fault of his own. He had been ground down like many another good man by the Capitalist system, which impoverished him and drove his wife to take up with transients and himself to end his troubles in the Bay. The memory of Lockie and the thought of all the horrors and humiliations that had led him to suicide sometimes brought McKenzie to a rage he could never articulate. He carried it on his person like a bomb.

"I've got a half-brother, Frank. Couple years older. He lives in Oregon."

Frank had been a good boy. Frank had studied hard (as had McKenzie), learnt his mathematics through trigonometry, and took up telegraphy. Frank had become a stationmaster on the railway in Oregon and had a wife and two sons in some small town up there. Frank's prospects with the railway seemed good, and he was at peace with the world as McKenzie could never be. McKenzie and Frank had not seen one another in years and never wrote.

"The Bay's my real hometown," McKenzie said. "Got my first job there. Out of Oakland – shrimping. For a bunch of Chinese. Then I worked up and down the Coast, mostly hauling timber down from Oregon and Washington State, but also fishing. Terrible work, fishing. When there's catch below you break your back all day and into the night. You're out a week maybe, then you come back and collect your wages, which are never much. To get work you show up at the docks when you hear they're hiring and join the crowd – and it can be a crowd when times are bad, let me tell you – you join the crowd of all the other men looking for work. The guy doing the hiring, we call him the 'crimp'. The crimp stands at the gate to the wharf and looks the crowd over. If he nods at you that means you got work. But if he doesn't like the cut of your jib – if you're weak-looking or you look like a trouble-maker – you don't. And for hiring you he takes a percentage out of your pay. The bosses give it to him directly – you, Jack Tar, you never see it."

It was on a cruise out of Half Moon Bay on the California coast – the name enchanted Flora, she had never heard it before – that McKenzie had had an accident – a full net, a snapped cable – that almost cost him his eye and left a triangular scar on his cheek.

"And the bosses wouldn't have given a damn. It would have been 'Tough luck, old guy. Go home and study your Bible.'" McKenzie considered his scar a badge of honour.

McKenzie finished high school in Oakland though he had to work to earn money and did a year at university in Berkeley. Early on he became an organizer with the Coastal Seamen's Union and wrote flaming editorials for the union paper. After that, and minimizing his radical past, he got himself hired onto a San Francisco paper, which he left after a few months for a paper in New York to become their man in San Francisco. When his New York paper fired its man in London for being in drink once too often, McKenzie pushed to replace him and was accepted. In London he picked up work with another San Francisco paper (The American, not the one he had quit) and wrote for them anonymously, an arrangement the New York paper quickly learnt of and at first objected to, then ignored.

He laughed when he told Flora the story. "They figured it'd keep me from asking for more money." He laughed again. "Which wasn't true. I mail in my longer articles. Takes them ten days, the articles, to reach New York, sometimes two weeks to San Francisco. Otherwise, I wire stories in. Got to watch the word count, of course. Editors get mad if you go over budget."

"What's your day like?"

"Oh, well. In the mornings I'll buy a bun or some kippers for breakfast, then I head for the American Press offices. Late. No point in getting there early, nothing's happened yet. I read the papers there, talk with the boys, try to find out what's going on, which isn't easy all the time. When I hear a likely story, I'll report it. I follow the rich Americans – my papers always want to know what they're up to. The U.S. Consulate's not too far from the A.P. There's a guy there I'm pals with. Once in a while he'll give me a tip. I've gotten some good stuff from him. I don't mix too well with the embassy types, but I give it a try. Maybe I'll go to a Turkish bath, get my hair cut. Evenings if nothing's happening I'll eat in a pub.

"I find bully stuff just in my neighbourhood. Working people, their lives. Stories of men who sleep in parks, get pushed around by the police. Women slaving all day making matchboxes or pulling fur from rabbit-skins and earning pennies at it and then getting beaten when their drunken, useless husbands come home. I take it all down, then write up what I've seen and heard. Every day without fail. I'll turn it all into a book someday – I will!"

He cocked his head. "So – speaking of stories, Flora, I've told you mine – what's yours? These Russians – how is it you're so thick with them?"

"Well, as you know, my husband's Russian. That is, he's a Russian subject. He's actually Polish by race. He's a chemist and has a degree in that science from Moscow University. In Russia he was a revolutionist and was exiled to Siberia but escaped. Before he and I met I had been in Russia. I had got to know Sergei Stepniak here in London. My mother had made his acquaintance. Through Sergei I became interested in Russian matters and I went to Russia to live and to learn the language. To support myself I taught piano and English. I made dear friends there, especially among Sergei's family, people who were struggling for freedom and to whom dreadful things had occurred – exile, imprisonment, torture, execution. I returned home five years ago and I sought out their friends and supporters here and have tried ever since to help. Beyond my work with the Russians, I'm writing my novel."

"Ah, yes, the novel – and how's that going?"

"It progresses. Fits and starts. I'm working it up, but it wants development. And depth of detail. I shall travel in Italy this summer looking for" – she smiled – "'stuff' to include, which will be a great help."

As their conversation ambled about in this pleasant way, Flora found herself silently asking, Why has this man come and why are we sitting together here in Ravenscourt Park on this fine afternoon? She knew part of the answer. From the looks McKenzie had given her the night of the soirée and from his enamoured gaze now as they sat chatting on their sunny bench in the park, his sentiments toward her were obvious. But what of hers toward him? She thought, I was glad to see this man and I am most happy now to be in his company. How can this be? I am a married woman. I love my husband. This is folly in more ways than I can enumerate. Why, then, do I not send McKenzie – Bill – packing? Why allow a charade? Why give him the least encouragement, which in the end will hurt him?

When Flora tried to answer these questions she could conclude only, Because I am drawn to him. At this she felt a great confusion.

No such confusion troubled McKenzie. Flora Bowles Lijak stirred him more than any woman he had ever known, and he had known not a few.

It had become late. Flora exclaimed, "Goodness, my pupil will be arriving soon! I must be returning." She looked at McKenzie and felt regret that they must part, then felt guilt at feeling regret. She had almost put her hand on his arm but caught herself.

On their way back, they spoke little, each thinking of the other. When they turned into The Grove the sight of her house suddenly reminded Flora of her cipher. Bother! she thought. It must go out this afternoon! It may contain inaccuracies, and I shall have to correct them if it does, immediately, and I've a pupil coming. Bother! Her thoughts then returned to McKenzie. This strange man at my side – what do I feel for him? Why do I so enjoy being with him? If only the human heart, even one's own, were as easy to read as a cipher!

At 149, The Grove they said goodbye and shook hands, touching once again, each noticing the touch of the other. At a cross street, McKenzie turned back to look for Flora, as he had done at the soirée, but she had gone inside. So, hands in his pockets, his copy of *Free Russia* rolled under his left arm, he walked down The Grove to Beadon Road and the Metropolitan District Station, where he caught a train and began his journey back to Mile End, dead in love.

"One, *two*, three, one, *two*, three," Flora sang. "The second beat is forte, do treat it as such, Kate. Yes, yes, that's right, very good, you're getting it. Good, good, good."

Kate Murray, Flora's student, a quiet, pigtailed girl of thirteen who was devoted to Flora, was playing her set homework (not very well and she had practised so!) at Flora's mahogany upright in the sitting-room. (Sarah had cleared the tea and bread and jam from the room and was at this moment on her way to the Hammersmith Post Office with a parcel of books destined for St Petersburg.) Above the piano hung a photogravure of Haussmann's 1746 portrait of J.S. Bach, a gift from Lijak to Flora. Haussmann's sharp-eyed but kindly-faced Bach seemed to wish well to all in the room, including Kate Murray, who was not a natural pianist but who deserved praise for her efforts.

"Now the triples... are... coming... The triples... are equal in length to the pairs, so, la-la la-la-la la-la la-la-la, and all the notes of the triples are absolutely equal in length, each to the other. Don't pound the first note, Kate, that stretches it out, no, no, no, don't pound, dear. Try it again, please, Kate. Start at bar 14. Never fear, you'll soon get a knack for triples, they're not so hard, really. So again, from bar 14. La-la..."

Kate got through her triples better this time, so Flora let her play uninterrupted. Flora was scarcely thinking of Kate in any case. Flora was wondering what had come crashing in on her.

OZZIE

He has beautiful eyes, Ozzie thinks. That's the thing.

He called again. She said yes, again.

Maybe because of his eyes, she is thinking. She didn't remember them when he called, not exactly. Now she's studying them. They are: bluish green, not quite hazel, flecked with silver. Lashes long, brown, tending toward blond.

Beautiful.

Mark suggested dinner when he called, and now he and Ozzie are in Zaytinya, an upscale mezze restaurant at 9th and G. They're in the balcony at the rear, alone. It's early evening, customers are few.

Mark and Ozzie chat – of his day, of hers. They find they like some of the same music – pop groups, all with female lead singers as it happens. The Lijak Manuscript comes up ("Haven't solved it yet. Maybe next week.") as do Ollie and his whales project for pre-school: Ollie has had to draw a whale and learn three facts about the species. He has learned six.

As they talk, Mark is leaning forward, arms on the thick, white tablecloth, not knowing he's being examined. At his left elbow sits a vase of shimmering lavender glass that contains flowers Ozzie can't identify. They have small, orchid-like blossoms and yellow petals, bordered with rusty red and speckled with the same rusty red.

They're as beautiful, almost, as this man's eyes, Ozzie thinks.

The first small plates arrive, *hummus* for Mark, *bantijan* – spiced baked eggplant – for Ozzie. Persian has a word for eggplant that sounds like *bantijan* but isn't quite. Ozzie can't remember it.

As they start to eat, Mark says, "Unnh, I want to say something."

His eyes are on hers. His voice has an edge.

"About Anne and me."

Right, Ozzie thinks. This is the point of tonight. Anne.

She nods.

He starts matter-of-factly: "Anne's a vice president with a fancy lobbying firm on K Street. M. Grayson Associates. They're not that old, but they've grown fast. They've got a bunch of lawyers and some ex-congressmen. They're big in the industry. Grayson was on the Hill for a long time. His senator, Donovan – remember Donovan? – Donovan died on him. Now he's cashing in like they all do up there. Anne joined them a couple of years back. She'd been with a PR firm, on 20th Street just around the corner from Grayson. She thought they were going places and she was right. And she likes her job and she's good at it. Problem is, she drinks."

Oh. Oh, oh, oh. So that's it, Ozzie thinks. This poor guy.

"Occupational hazard in her industry. They do a lot of liquid lunches. They entertain clients at home with liquid evenings. And all that became a way of life for her. For us. Anyhow she's... an alcoholic. And that's what killed the marriage. I just don't love her anymore. Terrible thing – falling out of love."

His eyes move from hers, to the beautiful flowers, back to hers.

"Anne's in denial about it, the alcohol. Or maybe it's avoidance. I don't know. She knows she's got a problem, but she won't even think about going into a program or anything. The 'problem' runs in her family. Her father was a drunk. Small town lawyer in Kentucky. That's where she's from. One time he got hammered – she was like fourteen years old – he got hammered and chased her around the house with a knife. She had to run out into the street to get away from him. He never got hauled in for it." Mark sets his mouth, shakes his head. "Small towns."

Anne, Ozzie thinks, that confident, attractive, stylish woman in the photo on Mark's cell, Anne once was a child who had to flee a knife-wielding father. She is now an alcoholic, a wife who is being divorced, and a mother who will lose her child.

People live on their lawns, Grace the lawyer likes to say, meaning, under their façades all families have secrets, lots of them, some very dark. You can't know.

"I'm so sorry, Mark, really. These things are just godawful. For everybody. My grandfather was an alcoholic. I know what you mean."

Papá was a quiet man, who loved Ozzie— he called her "Li'l Snort" – and never lost his temper with her. Papá was tall and rotund and had a fleshy, wattled throat. When Ozzie thinks of him, she sees an elderly man sitting in a lawn chair on the back porch of their house in West Hartford. It's summertime. He's wearing Bermuda shorts, street socks, and street shoes. The shorts expose his skinny, spindly calves. He has a cone-shaped glass in hand containing a gimlet, lime-tinted and straight up, his favored hot-weather drink. Forced out of Hartford Life because of his drinking – Grace's take – Papá yellowed away and died of cirrhosis at the age of seventy-four.

Ozzie asks, "This thing, this... Anne's problem – has this been going on for a while?"

"Years. She wasn't that big a drinker when we got married. It crept up on her. And me."

A short silence.

"Took me forever to get moving... on the divorce. I just couldn't do it. When she's sober she's bright and funny. And we'd had some really good times together. She's a good person. And she's the mother of my son. I didn't want to say good-bye to that life. And also, like, you think you're enlightened, right? – you think alcoholism's a disease and you've taken that vow about sickness and health. So... you think you should stick by her... that if you leave her it'd be like running out on a pal who's sick and in trouble. But it just went on and on and on, the problem, and as I say, I don't love her anymore. And of course in all this I had to think of Ollie. I have to get my son away from her. When I realized that, I realized that it really was over, that life, and that I had to move, had to end it."

"How's Ollie taking it – the separation?"

"Jury's out. I really don't know. He didn't like it when I moved out, it confused him. But I see him all I can. We go to parks and hang out, he does sleepovers easily – doesn't mind leaving the house." Mark smiles at the thought. "I don't think he's mad at me for deserting him, or Anne, I'm pretty sure of that. But I do worry. With his meltdowns he may be acting something out, I don't know. So, I've got to move on the divorce and make it as easy as possible on him. And hope for the best."

"I'm so sorry, Mark. Divorces can be terrible, for all concerned."

It was Grace who broke the news to Ozzie that she and Baba were divorcing. Ozzie had gone to bed in her small room – the room all her own – in the Welles' house in West Hartford. The light in the room was dim enough so that the luminous stars pasted on the ceiling over her bed had come out. The stars were a pale yellow-green, the color of a luna moth, against the sky blue of the ceiling. They are on the ceiling of that room to this day.

Baba had put the stars there when they – Grace, Ozzie, and David – were living with the Welles', and Baba was in New York, allegedly looking for work. Baba had come back for a weekend visit, and the four of them were out wandering through some roped-off street fair not far from the house – rock bands, arts and crafts, food stalls – when Baba went to buy everyone ice cream in cones and somewhere among the tents and stalls had found his glow-in-the-dark stars.

When Baba put them up that evening he said, "See all the stars in the heaven? And see the biggest one in the exact middle? That's the star named Azi and she looks over you as you sleep. She smiles because she sees you and because she loves you."

Then, perhaps a month later, when a sleepy Ozzie is lying under her stars, especially the one named Azi, Grace comes into her room and sits on the bed beside her. Putting her hand on Ozzie's arm, Grace says quietly, "Ozzie, honey, uh... Your father's gone away. He's not in New York anymore, he's gone to California."

Ozzie does not know what California is.

"When is he coming back?"

"Honey, he's not coming back."

Ozzie doesn't understand this.

Grace says, "We're going to live apart. You'll live here with me and Moo Moo and Papá and David, and your father is going to stay in California to live and work. You'll see him. I promise. He loves you and he wants to see you. He does."

"Not coming back?"

"No, Ozzie."

Incomprehension is followed by disbelief.

"Why?"

"Because we think it's better for everybody, including you — I mean this, Ozzie, including you — that your father and I live separately." Grace, sighing, dreading what she knows must come and whose repertoire of affectionate gestures was limited, gives Ozzie's arm a series of gentle pats. Ozzie begins to wail, to weep violently and, it seems, endlessly, while Grace, sitting by the bed, rests her hand softly on Ozzie's shoulder and — this, too, Ozzie remembers because it is so singular, so unlike her mother — a warm tear of Grace's own falls onto Ozzie's face.

Grace must go on that night to tell David, who at four will not quite grasp the news. David will react to Baba's absence when he notices it. He will do so by going wary and elusive, the little child father to the man: David's always been good at slipping away, evading. It's his style.

After Grace left Ozzie in her bedroom, Ozzie, a clear-sighted child, made a connection: she recalled being with Baba and Grace at The Pond perhaps only a few weeks before. The three of them were standing in the graveled apron in front of the garage some distance from the main house. Baba suddenly knelt and pulled Ozzie to him in his large arms, holding her, rocking her gently, and, inexplicably, began to cry. His tears, because they were tears and because they were inexplicable, frightened Ozzie. He kissed her face and hair and, his voice strained, said, "I have to go, Azi Joon. Bye-bye, bye-bye, I love you."

Then he was up, swiveling away in that abrupt manner Persians can have, and not looking back, headed for his rented car. As the car moved up the long, pot-holed drive that leads off the property, Ozzie, now puzzled more than frightened, waved her small hand toward it but saw no return wave.

Lying in her bedroom under Baba's yellow-green stars, Ozzie realized that Baba's embrace at The Pond was his farewell to her and began weeping again, this time silently.

Later Ozzie learned from Grace that Baba simply could not tell her himself that he was departing forever and had to leave that task to Grace and that he had said a separate, quiet farewell to David, who was napping at the time in the stone house. Ozzie forgave him. His tears were enough.

"So anyhow," Mark says, "that's how it is with Anne. Wanted to let you know."

Ozzie nods. He's told me all this, she thinks. So soon. He's serious about me. He's also lovely and kind and decent.

The talk shifts from Anne, and Mark lightens. Ozzie tells him she has read two more of Flora's novels and that they are really pretty good. "Maybe not as good as *Ribeiro*, but good. A lot of sexual violence in them, by the way – like in *Ribeiro*. There's an attempted rape in one of them, in another a cruel uncle gets a charge out of whipping his son. There's a homoerotic side to the whipping – when she describes the uncle and the pleasure he gets out of beating his son she talks about 'love that dare not speak its name.' Pretty explicit stuff for her day. There's something behind those scenes – in her life, Flora's life, I mean. Got to be. You wonder what."

Mark talks of the Lijak Study Group at Fort Meade, five guys and a young woman, who meet irregularly to brainstorm on the Manuscript. "We've been in existence for decades. Literally. No closer to a solution than we were in 1945, when the group got started."

"'We dance round in a ring and suppose,'" Ozzie says, "'But The Secret sits in the middle and knows.'"

Mark's look is questioning.

"Frost. 'The Secret Sits.' Just the one short couplet. I've always liked it. Seems to fit your manuscript. And the 'headcases' who try to break it."

"I'll tell the Study Group about it. Maybe we'll make it our motto. We don't have a motto." Looking away, he chuckles at the thought in a way Ozzie finds pleasing.

They decide it's time to leave and split the check, each tossing a credit card into the waitress's fake-leather card folder. As they are getting up, Ozzie's hair brushes Mark's face. Both notice this, neither reacts.

Just outside the door they hug briefly.

Mark says, "I'd love to see you again. Would that be okay?"

"Sure. That'd be nice."

It would, she thinks. Yes. Quite nice.

At home Ozzie Googles "Mark Morehead" and finds little. He's not on social media and he doesn't tweet. Intelius knows him: he has an address in College Park, Maryland, a Maryland landline number, an age (thirty-seven), and relatives (Anne Morehead, Oliver Morehead, and, implausibly, Agnes Moorehead). When Ozzie Google Earths the address she finds a pleasant-looking brick split-level with a large, well-tended yard. In the driveway sits a black SUV. Other houses like it lie to the right and left. He's real.

A text pings in from Mark's cell:

> Great to see you tonight. Here's a group I mentioned. Can't get them out of my head. Thought you'd like them.
>
> https://www.youtube.com/results?search_query=o'donnell+waves

The link is to a YouTube video of a singer named Cait O'Donnell and her band. The video, produced by the band itself, is not some fuzzy, jerky, hand-held, badly lit, pirated thing. It's slickly shot with good sound, at least for YouTube.

She's pretty, Cait, with her long red hair. She's standing at a mic, swaying in blue backlight, a spot on her face, her eyes half closed. She's wearing a sparkling, snug-fitting, blue-and-silver sequined top, dark-gray, mannish trousers, and clunky-heeled boots, and has jammed a man's dark gray fedora onto the back of her head. She's rocking with the beat, dancing. Behind her, eyes on her, the guitarist is playing lean, flinty riffs of an almost-tune, and behind him, on risers, the bassist and drummer are lost in their own spheres.

Cait starts a song about making love on a beach:

We loved and then we loved some more,
Chased the moonlight on the shore,
Waves out there and waves in me,
Oh, I'll take it, baby, take it…

Cait has a lilting Irish accent and a gorgeous, throaty voice. She pulls the mic from its stand and caresses it, holding it close to her lips – wickedly, it's a penis, right?

Tell me that you love me true,
Tell me, baby, tell me, do,
Waves out there and waves in me,
Oh, I'll take it, baby, take it…

Cait wants her lover badly and she repeats:

Waves out there and waves in me,
Oh, I'll take it, baby, take it...

Waves. I've felt them, Ozzie thinks. With Tom, with Will.
Waves.

The beat, the throbbing, pounding beat, and Cait's stationary,
thigh-grinding dance – rock music, Ozzie thinks, it's all fucking.
Mark's seducing me with this video, Mark with his beautiful eyes.

CHAPTER IV

Here She Took Her Leap.

After his walk with Flora in Ravenscourt Park, McKenzie rode the Underground back to the East End, pondering what to do. McKenzie had known women and had loved some of them, as he thought and in his way, but he had never loved anyone as he loved this one.

When he arrived at his room – the one in Needham Lane, the better of the two he rented – he splashed water on his face from a basin, sat at his table, and composed a blandly-worded but far from innocent note:

May 28, 1895

American Press Association
34 Throgmorton Street, E.C.

Dear Mrs. Lijak,

It was so kind of you to receive me today. I feel we have very much in common. I do hope we may meet again. Yours,

Wm. McKenzie

This letter would be enough, he thought, just, to signal a lover's plea. She would understand perfectly.

He walked up to the Commercial Road and dropped his note into the red pillar box there, wondering what Flora would think and do when she received it.

You live by taking chances, he thought. You risk your fortunes on the play of a single card. This is my card.

To pass the time that evening he read the papers, smoked, went for a walk (oblivious to the familiar, softly uttered enticements, some of them coarse, emanating from darkened doorways), and finally had a series of pints and a solitary supper in a large public house, The Angel, grateful for its noise and its gift of anonymity. Later in his room he dreamt of Flora lying in his arms, of her lips responding to his.

After Kate Murray had finished her piano lesson and left, Flora spent her evening with Lijak, reading, writing letters, and conversing as if nothing out of the ordinary had occurred that day. She did not mention her visitor and their walk in Ravenscourt Park. That night she lay awake in the bedroom that she and Lijak had shared for three years. The faintest of light entering from the street fell on the objects in the room – the dark oak wardrobe rising beyond the foot of her bed, the single straight-backed chair, the oak dresser (a mate to the wardrobe) and oil lamp, the cheval glass, the folding Chinese screen – all these familiar to her, yet all now oddly alien. The only sound was that of her husband in his bed breathing through his mouth in innocent, trusting sleep. Once he turned onto his right side and faced her. She dared not look on him.

She thought, I am an independent woman earning my way in the world through my music lessons and my translations from the Russian. I am taking notes for my novel. I am planning my trip to Italy. My life until this afternoon had seemed reasonable.

Yet I want to see McKenzie again, listen to his tales of places I can scarcely conceive, and – I know and I admit this to my shame – to gaze into his handsome face. What folly.

After breakfast, Lijak set out for the British Museum Reading Room. As was her practice, Flora went upstairs to work on her novel. Flora did all her work – her translations, her writing for *Free Russia*, now the first drafts of her novel – at her lap desk, which sat on her end of the worktable she shared with her husband. The lap desk, a gift from Lijak, was an elegant, hinged affair that opened into a slanted surface covered in dark brown leather. Along its edges and top the leather was decorated with gold leaf in a symmetrical vegetal pattern that hinted of Morocco or Algeria. Its sides and lower edge offered receptacles, lined with purple velvet, for pencils, pens, ink bottles, note paper, envelopes, erasers, pins, postage stamps - whatever a writer might need. Lijak had recently bought the expensive piece in Paris because, he told Flora, he loved her and because it reminded him of her and of her work, at which he very much wanted her to succeed.

This morning, she spread an empty sheet of lined paper before her and stared at it. What to write?

Her novel, entitled *Ribeiro* after the name of its hero, was set in the Italy of the 1830s, a period of violent struggle by Italian patriots to drive out the Austrians, who occupied the north, and unify the peninsula under one independent and democratic Italian government. She had read Garibaldi's *Memoirs* (the Werner translation, 1889) and had been stirred by its accounts of battles won and lost, of treacheries, executions, and failures, then, after decades of fight, the rebirth of Italy, free and united.

Ribeiro's face, she knew and had known for years, would be dark and melancholy, like that of the youth in the Franciabigio portrait she had seen a decade before in the Louvre. The haunting eyes of that youth she had never forgotten. This morning, though, as Flora tried to imagine and body forth her hero on that empty sheet of paper, her thoughts kept drifting to the real person whose dark and brooding face so reminded her of the Franciabigio youth: William McKenzie. She tried to dispel these thoughts but could not, and because she was sitting at the extravagant gift from her loving and supporting husband, felt guilt all the more.

————

Mid-morning, Sarah brought the post up with tea. Amongst the letters was McKenzie's note, the purport of which Flora understood immediately.

It is madness, she thought. Shall I respond to this? If I do, what shall I say?

After hesitation, she decided she would answer him, but she would do so in a neutral tone (mentioning Lijak), a tone she thought and hoped, truly hoped, would be discouraging. She took out notepaper and wrote:

29 May, 95

149, The Grove
Hammersmith

Dear McKenzie,

I, too, enjoyed our talk. I am sure Wilfrid would like to make your acquaintance as well. The Stepniaks hold at-homes every Saturday afternoon

But here she stopped and, as if controlled by supernatural agency, laid down her pen. Here she took her leap and altered forever the course of her life. She tore up her note and wrote another:

29 May, 95

149, The Grove
Hammersmith

Dear Bill,

I, too, very much enjoyed our talk. May we have many more.

Flora

What she had written contained not a hint of dishonesty or scheming or betrayal. Her language was conventional and inno-cent-seeming, yet, like that of McKenzie's note, freighted with the unspoken.

Her hands tremulous, Flora inserted her note into an envelope, addressed and stamped it, and called Sarah to post it; McKenzie's note she put amongst her other correspondence, all of it open to her husband's scrutiny if he wished to see it, which he would not. To place it there in easy access was to declare – oh, so falsely! – its innocence, and hers.

To break her anxiety as Sarah was leaving, Flora asked playfully, "And will you be saying 'hello' to Teddy on the way?"

Sarah, a winsome girl, naturally graceful and possessing an easy laugh, had a "looking romance" with the greengrocer's boy, Teddy Elsworth. Old Elsworth's shop was in Goldhawk Road; Sarah contrived whenever possible to pass it whilst on an errand. Teddy, who made deliveries, was known to appear in The Grove from time to time, walking up and down, undoubtedly hoping to catch sight of Sarah – Lijak had seen him more than once and had laughingly remarked on it to Flora.

Sarah flushed. "We're going dancing Saturday night, Ma'am!"

"Dancing! Oh, splendid! Can you dance, Sarah? I cannot." Flora, though a skilled pianist, had never learnt to express herself in bodily movement.

"Oh, Ma'am, I do! 1 so love dancing!"

Eyes averted, Sarah confided that she and Teddy had "taken walks together in the park." She meant Ravenscourt Park. At this, Flora's guilt welled up again for it was in Ravenscourt Park just the day before where she and McKenzie had sat and talked, McKenzie's looks betraying his emotions, she herself increasingly confused and bewildered. Worse, it had been in Ravenscourt Park that she and Lijak had strolled in their time of courtship, and it had been there, within one of its shady retreats, that she had finally accepted Lijak's offer of marriage.

When Sarah banged the door shut as she left with the note, Flora knew that she – Flora – had taken some irreversible step down a path that led she knew not where.

The next day, a grey morning that promised rain, McKenzie received Flora's note at the American Press Association. He tore the envelope open, read its contents, and felt rapture. Juvenilely and stupidly, like the adolescent Teddy Elsworth hoping to see Sarah, McKenzie pocketed Flora's note and took the Underground to Hammersmith, having no plan other than to look from a distance at her house, knowing, or thinking, or hoping that she was inside, then leave.

Before he had got to 149, The Grove, McKenzie saw the police spy, not The Limpet, another man, this one wearing a bowler-hat with a dent in the crown and a long blue coat. He was leaning against an iron picket fence reading *The Standard*. As McKenzie passed, the man lowered his paper and gave him a look that lingered. The man had pale blue eyes.

They don't bother to hide, McKenzie thought. That's part of their fun.

Without breaking his pace, McKenzie walked nonchalantly north, eyeing number 149. At Goldhawk Road he turned right and took a different way back to the Underground, hoping he had not been seen from the house and regarded a complete half-wit.

Flora and McKenzie encountered one another a few days later. Sergei Stepniak was giving an evening lecture on Russian literature at Essex Hall, a Unitarian meeting place just off the Strand, and Flora and Lijak decided to attend.

When they arrived, the minister, Moncure Conway, a dignified, middle-aged man adorned with a salt-and-pepper beard, was introducing Stepniak. As Conway spoke – he was a Virginian and had a soft, pleasing Southern accent – the Lijaks slipped into a bench toward the rear of the hall, which was crowded. After they had got seated Flora scanned the audience to see if McKenzie were there. It seemed all the English and Russians of the *Free Russia* set had come – Spence Watson, Fisher Unwin, Byles, Picton, Olive Garnett and her sister-in-law Constance, Fanny Stepniak, of course, Feliks Volkhovsky and his pretty daughter Vera, Kropotkin and his wife Sophie, Ivan Serov – that strange young man – as well as a gratifyingly large number of others less involved in Russian affairs, among whom Flora recognised Richard Lane Hodgson of the *Pall Mall Gazette* and Bernard Shaw.

Then she saw McKenzie. He was seated beside Pyotr Kropotkin, only four benches down. Her heart clenched. She was hoping McKenzie might be present, and present he was. He had surely got her note by now.

McKenzie in fact had come to the lecture, which he had heard about from Kropotkin, in hopes that Flora would be attending. Before she arrived, he had numerous times looked round the hall for her only to be disappointed. Once more, arm on the bench-back, he turned to search the hall, and their eyes met. His said, Yes, I have received your note. He smiled and turned back round.

We shall meet after the lecture, Flora thought. What shall I say? What will he?

Conway finished; Stepniak rose to speak. His subject was "Tourguenieff and Nihilism." Striding back and forth on the platform, his deep, full voice rising and falling dramatically, Stepniak talked of the Russian Nihilists, a word, he informed his audience, that Tourguenieff had popularised. Nihilists were young persons who took nothing on faith, who questioned everything, particularly Russia's backward political and social arrangements. What they did believe in was science. There were thousands of them all over Russia. Stepniak referred to the character Bazaroff in Tourguenieff's novel *Fathers and Sons*, Bazaroff the young physician – a practical scientist – who dies after contracting a disease from a patient. Stepniak described his death scene: "Bazaroff is in coma. It is time of last rites. The priest is anointing him with oil. One of Bazaroff's eyes opens and he sees the priest and the smoking censer, candles, icon, and when he sees these he seems to shudder – shudder! – at the horror of it all. Thus passes a man of science surrounded by superstition. *Fathers and Sons*, you will be glad to hear, has just been translated into beautiful English by Mrs Garnett, who is with us this evening." Here Stepniak extended his hand toward Constance Garnett and nodded. Mrs Garnett smiled all about and nodded back to Stepniak for the recognition. "And you may now read this masterwork of Russian literature in English!"

Stepniak spoke without notes, brilliantly, for an hour, his thick accent adding to the effect of mastery and expertise. When he finished and had taken all the questions he wished to take, Flora followed her husband to join the swarm of congratulants surrounding him on the platform. McKenzie, she knew, feeling trepidation, would be among them.

Indeed, after separating himself from the Kropotkins McKenzie approached Flora and Lijak. He bowed to Flora and said, "Good evening, Mrs Lijak," flashing a friendly, expectant smile at her husband.

Flora said, "Hello, Mr McKenzie. Wilfrid, this is William McKenzie. Mr McKenzie was at the soirée. Fanny Stepniak introduced us there. Mr McKenzie is also a friend of Kropotkin's. Mr McKenzie, my husband Wilfrid."

"So glad," Lijak said distantly, surveying the hall and crowd as he took McKenzie's hand. Lijak had no use for Kropotkin, whom he considered an unworldly fool, nor for Kropotkin's Anarchism, which he thought preposterous. If this man was an associate of Kropotkin's, Lijak was thinking, why then...

Flora said, "Mr McKenzie is American. He's from San Francisco. He's a newspaper man."

"Oh?" A spark of interest lit Lijak's eyes briefly, then went out as if doused. "Will you excuse me, my dear?" he asked Flora in Russian, then in English, smiling at McKenzie, he said, "It is good to meet you, Mr McKenzie, but I must speak with some persons before they have gone." He went to join Constance Garnett and Olive, who were conversing.

McKenzie and Flora were left alone amidst the crowd.

Flora began: "I thought Sergei's lecture very fine."

McKenzie said, "It's so very good to see you."

Measuring his gaze steadily, returning it, her eyes glowing,

Flora said, "Yes. And to see you."

There was a silence. Instead of telling her that he loved her, which is what he wanted to do, McKenzie said, awkwardly, "Well, I can't say I know anything about Russian literature. I'm going to read some of this Tourguenieff – he sounds good all right."

Flora picked up from this. "Oh, you must. Connie's a fast friend of ours" – Flora gestured toward Constance Garnett, who was speaking with Lijak. "She translates from the Russian like an angel. And as Sergei said, she's just done *Fathers and Sons*. I'll introduce you." She made no move to do so.

McKenzie and Flora chose to talk inanities and to joke – at Stepniak's untamed beard, at Bernard Shaw's get-up (a coarsely-woven German hunting suit and knee-high laced boots) – but beneath their talk and joking lay something each sensed but could not articulate: desire, and with the desire, danger, which Flora felt more keenly than McKenzie.

A voice just behind Flora said, "Good evening, Mrs Lijak."

The voice was Richard Lane Hodgson's.

Flora turned. "Oh, Mr Hodgson. You. 'And all should cry, Beware! Beware! His flashing eyes, his floating hair!' How are you, Mr Hodgson?"

Lane Hodgson, who, though only thirty-one, was balding painfully and self-consciously, smiled at Flora with some effort. To McKenzie he extended his hand. "Dick Hodgson, *Pall Mall Gazette*."

"Bill McKenzie."

Flora said, "Mr McKenzie's a writer for the American press."

"Ah. Papers? Magazines?"

McKenzie mentioned his San Francisco and New York newspapers.

Lane Hodgson crimped the side of his mouth and nodded slightly to the right obliquely, indicating that he was favourably impressed. "Where are your offices?"

"I use the American Press Association for correspondence, especially cables. But I don't have an office there. Sometimes I borrow a desk. Or a typewriter. I live in the East End. Commercial Road, Whitechapel, Bethnal Green – those are my 'offices.'"

Lane Hodgson laughed. "Working out of one's diggings. Good enough. But do you write about the goings-on over there in Bethnal Green?"

"Among other things – yes, I do."

"And are your countrymen interested in all that? Match-girls and costermongers?"

"Some must be. They buy my stuff. Maybe they've read Dickens."

McKenzie added, "I emerge from time to time to cover the rest of this city. And country."

"Umm. I knew another American newspaperman. Kennan, George Kennan. Know the fellow?"

Flora said to McKenzie, "Lectures on Russia. He's in America now."

"Don't know him."

"Didn't hang about London," Lane Hodgson said. "Travelled in Siberia. Saw some wild places."

"Oh, I've found some pretty wild places right here."

"I daresay. I've seen a few myself."

"I guess you've got a real office."

"Not two streets from here. We must have a drink some time."

"I'd like that."

At this point Lijak returned and nodded greetings all around, shaking hands with Lane Hodgson. "I fear I must take my wife away from her admirers," he said, smiling. "Flora, my dear, it's very late."

McKenzie and Flora exchanged a glance – Lijak's "her admirers" had stabbed at both of them – then McKenzie, in misery, watched Flora put her arm in Lijak's and go off with him into the night.

Next afternoon an unsigned note addressed to Flora in McKenzie's hand arrived in the post. It read in its entirety:

> You are my dear heart. I ache to see you. When may I? And where?

Horrified at McKenzie's audacity Flora burnt the note and envelope immediately in the kitchen stove – not in Sarah's presence, Sarah was dusting the upper rooms. Watching McKenzie's note catch fire and blacken, Flora whispered, I love Wilfrid Michael Lijak, my husband of three years and boon companion of five; I love Wilfrid Michael Lijak, who is good and kind and faithful and who is devoted to me.

For McKenzie she felt – she could not think the word "desire," though that was what she knew she felt – and because of her desire she felt also deep guilt, the two emotions circling in her mind like adversaries on a battlefield. In her confusion she felt one other emotion, obscure but powerful, something like dread, though that word did not capture the full force of it, not at all.

She thrust a poker into the stove and stirred the ashes of McKenzie's letter into the glowing coals till all were commingled.

OZZIE

I don't need this caffeine, Ozzie thinks. I mean, I really don't need this caffeine.

It's a gusty, sloppy-rainy late afternoon. Ozzie's in the Starbucks in the Leavey Student Center, out of the weather, on her way home. She's bought herself a grande. The soft, retro cool of the Starbucks sound is currently Billy Holiday singing a boppy, frisky "Day In, Day Out." In here, Holiday's so-recognizable voice is distant, more like background radiation than music.

Ozzie has just learned that she may be fired.

The shock came first. Now the hard-edged fear. Ozzie is up for tenure in the spring. If she doesn't get it – tenure - she'll be dismissed. To get tenure she'll have to have published a book, one she has written herself, not just edited like *Gender and Anarchy*. She has produced one, a solid work on American women poets and novelists of the mid-twentieth century called *Live or Die*. The book, which turned out to be lengthy, is a clear-eyed look at these women and how, transiting into the Second Wave, they handled sex, class, and race in their lives and their work, how those who survived – who didn't kill themselves like Sylvia Plath or Anne Sexton (hence the title, which Ozzie took from one of Sexton's poems) – evolved through the sixties and seventies, and how their work helped shape current writing by women. *Live or Die* was to be published by a prestige university press.

But *Live or Die* – that title! – has just been rejected by the academic publisher she thought had accepted it.

Ozzie carefully places her coffee container on the small, low table she's sitting at, telling herself, No spilling. No, no, no, don't spill.

She removes the container's white plastic cap with its little opening like the top of an adult's sippy cup.

The coffee needs to cool.

Yes.

Crumbs from someone else's cookie or brownie lie scattered on the table. These she disregards. She sits not thinking.

The rejection came by e-mail early in the afternoon. When Ozzie, in her office in New North, saw the sender and subject – "Re: Live or Die," she excitedly clicked open the document, then saw the first words, "Dear Professor Hosseini, we regret..." and lost her breath, could scarcely read the rest of the e-mail, her eyes first skittering over her flat-screen, then returning to "regret." She read the message in phrases, out of sequence, doubling back to gaps that hadn't quite registered: "...unfortunately doesn't fit with our current publishing plans... our backlist of such works is quite formidable" – formidable? formidable? God, they have to brag! – "... our decision is not based on the quality of the research or writing, which we are sure is high, though one reader did express certain reservations." A gut-punch that last phrase, which she found deeply angering and which left her sucking for air.

The message ended: "A more detailed account, including readers' comments, will be sent by post. Sincerely, Marc Riesner."

Riesner was supposed to be her editor. Riesner is the nicest guy in the known universe, on the phone.

Ozzie stared briefly at Riesner's message, her lungs pumping. When she had recovered enough, she forwarded the e-mail to her department head, Wallace Ransom.

TO: wallace.ran@gu.edu
FROM: azad.hosseini@gu.edu

Wally,

Just got this from Marc Riesner. I'm heartsick. Wanted to give you a heads-up.

Wally responded immediately:

TO: azad.hosseini@gu.edu
FROM: wallace.ran@gu.edu

This is crazy. Riesner's e-mail makes no sense. Drop by, we'll talk about this and how to proceed. I'm in right now if you'd like.

Wally quickly followed up by phone. "Hi, Ozzie – Wally. Uh, should have called in the first place. Uh, want to come down?"

Ozzie managed a tight, "Yep."

"Okay, see you."

Wally, you dear man, she thought, you are being discreet over the phone. Your office door must be open.

With what she hoped was a blank face, though not too blank, Ozzie walked the long hall of New North – hers is the furthest office from the Department – past the abstract painting hanging by Bill Egan's door, a big cobalt blue and fire-engine red thing that takes up the wall, floor to ceiling – it's been there forever, nobody notices it – past the office pin-boards with their pictures of children, class announcements and schedules, past the notices of upcoming events that have come and gone, of summer workshops (who needs them?), of job offers for grad students (few, impossible), past, finally, the display case of faculty books. Faculty books! Her *Gender and Anarchy* was displayed there once – now Ozzie has nothing displayed and perhaps never will again! At the Department door she made a right turn and was in.

Josette Khouri, Wally's receptionist, a dutiful, kindly, mother-of-three, with bobbed hair, looked up inquiringly.

"Hi, Josey, I'm here to see Wally." Ozzie's voice is toneless. She congratulated herself on that.

"It's okay, Josey," Wally declared from his office, "She's expected."

After he closed his door – gently – Wally turned and glowered. He brought his fists up and shook them in the face of an imaginary Marc Riesner. "Bastards!" he said, "bastards! Ozzie, I'm astounded, just astounded. But – we will deal with this." Wally touched his hand to her arm, then settled into his chair.

"Wally, it's getting late." Ozzie's eyes were tearing now; Wally's face looked distorted as in a crazy mirror. "Getting another publisher... I'm..." Stressed? Is that the word? Try distraught, try terrified.

As time for her tenure evaluation has drawn near, Ozzie has been waking in the middle of the night and remaining awake for long hours, tensed at the prospect of losing the job she loves. She woke last night, she can't think for how long, long enough, though, despite several trazodone 10 mgs. Classes went all right today, but only all right. Typical, she's told. Everybody goes through it.

"Wally, I thought my book was a shoo-in. Marc sounded so positive when we talked it over. Just a few weeks back... Did you see that, 'Reader expressed reservations'?"

"Their way of saying they're sorry."

"God."

"First off, battle stations. New submission. You've got to get one out immediately. I can think of five likely publishers."

"It took six months to get a refusal."

Wally peered at her over his glasses. "Yes. Outside readers take their time. Always happens. Academic publishing is slow and sleepy. You know that. Professors."

"Including the reader who had 'reservations.'"

"A testy reader. They come along."

"Wally, if it didn't 'fit with' their 'current plans' why did they sit on it for so long?"

"I don't know. They may have sent the thing out to a fourth reader after getting a negative. And that fourth reader took his time. Also, I've heard there've been huge personnel changes up there and a lot of confusion, fear, loathing et cetera."

"Marc survived."

"Yes. Too bad about that. Listen, *Live or Die*'s good. Quite good. We will get it published. *Du calme, du calme.*"

Wally resorts to French when someone else is desperate.

Wally's desk, as always, had administrative debris of various sorts on it, reports, schedules, letters to be read or signed, but no knick-knacks, no souvenirs, no awards. And no shots of kids because there are no kids. He does display a picture of his wife. Her name is Charmian (British). He calls her "Sidecar." You're supposed to go, "Ha ha" when you hear it. Charmian is slender and short. She has thick curly gray-and-black hair. She controls conversations. She is a foodie and cooks obnoxiously.

"Wally, what am I going to do?"

"We will deal with this."

"Wally, level with me. This is too close. It's too late, right?"

Wally's eyes shifted a nanometer.

He doesn't believe anything he's saying, Ozzie thought.

"We will deal with this. Yes, it is probably too late to get a book published before your review, at least with a legitimate house, but a book contract will do the trick. We don't need to have the printed copies literally sitting on our desks. We've done this before. There are precedents."

"Won't I need reviews? Good reviews?"

"If necessary, we can get prepublication reviews. Even readers' reports. It's been done."

Wally looked unenthusiastic when he said this — he's so not good at deception.

"Now. I know the editors at a number of publishing houses. I can get promises of fast turnarounds. I will put together a list of likelies — names and addresses and all that. I will get them to you pronto, this afternoon, maybe in an order of preference. When you get it, prepare your submission and send it out to one of them. Then get a project. Do something different. Go to Norway. Have an affair. Learn Chinese. Anything."

Ozzie mentioned Flora Lijak. Maybe research her?

Wally had never heard of Flora Lijak.

Christ, Ozzie thought.

———

Across the table from Ozzie in Starbucks a young woman in green surgical scrubs and cap, her face serious and concentrated, is writing notes into a loose-leaf binder. Around the young woman's neck hang a stethoscope and an RN ID tag.

A nurse in here on her break, Ozzie thinks, working through it.

Georgetown Hospital is just to the north of the Leavey, across a narrow access road, so a lot of the customers in here are medical – doctors, interns, orderlies, nurses like this one, who pauses now, looking up to think, taps her pen on the page she's working on, then goes back to writing.

She's dark and pretty. Ozzie notices a wide silvery band on the nurse's left index finger, but no wedding ring or engagement ring.

She's on her own, Ozzie thinks. Maybe she's got a guy, you'd think she would. She probably does. Even so, she's on her own, independent, out there earning a living. Nurses can work any-where they want, they're always needed, always have job security. Which I do not. Which I really, really do not. I've done every-thing right here at Georgetown. Now look.

If Ozzie is not tenured this year, Wally will offer her a one-year contract for the following year, time supposedly to find a job elsewhere, and then terminate her.

Four years here! Ozzie wants to cry out. All that work maybe for nothing! If they fire me, I'll be nearly forty and jobless. When you've been dumped, you're damaged goods, not wanted. And the market's beyond tight these days anyway. The jobs aren't there. I cannot be dumped, cannot. Where would I go? What would I do?

When the Welles' summered at The Pond, Ozzie's place to sleep – and her sanctum away from Grace and the others, but especially from Grace – was a plain bedroom on the second floor of an outbuilding down by the empty sheep meadow. On certain nights lying in bed she would watch the moon, a brilliant disk, pass across her room's one narrow window.

The moon's not a man, she would tell herself, the moon's a woman with a kind, smiling face, a woman alone. Like me.

Now, as Ozzie sits in this campus Starbucks, that old emotion wells up in her: I am alone.

The young nurse across from Ozzie is on her cell now. She turns out to be Iranian – she's speaking Persian, chattering in that melodious language and laughing, her face now rapt, now jokey. As she speaks, her eyes roam the room, alighting briefly on Ozzie's, then flit away. Ozzie listens, trying to pick out a word or two she understands, but can't get even a general sense of what the young woman is saying.

Gone, all that, Ozzie thinks. Those sounds – the language of my wandering father. They're just sounds. So familiar, so far away.

Like him.

Should I call him? she wonders. Call Grace? Tell them about all this, how scared I am? No, no, no, can't talk with either of them, not about this. Can't. Wanting to please your parents. And failing.

She laughs to herself: text David.

Sure.

Maybe call a friend? she wonders. Like who? Ozzie has picked up acquaintances during the years she's been in Washington, but not many, and none of them have become close. She wonders why that is. She thinks of old schoolmates, colleagues. Should she call them? Not possible. She's not been in touch, and she can't talk about this, anyway, not with anyone.

Stop weeping, she tells herself. Can't help it. I don't want this fucking coffee. The pretty nurse is gone. Maybe the rain's stopped.

CHAPTER V

"I Love You Dearly and Always Will."

11 June, '95

Florence
Pensione Gavelli
Via S Antonino 12

Dearest Wilfrid:

I arrived yesterday from Nice as I telegraphed, quite
exhausted. After a sound night's sleep – so welcome – I am
now refreshed & most comfortable here. Sr Gavelli is an
engineer with the waterworks but he owns this smallish place
& runs it (quite well) in his after hours. He is most courteous
& solicitous. The rooms are clean & quiet. The food is
French-Italian.

This morning I met briefly with our Resident Consul Sir
Dominic Colnaghi & our Vice Consul, a Mr French. Both
were highly welcoming.

Tho' only a night & a day here I have managed already
to 'see the sights' – some few of them at least. This
incomparable city is filled with such beauty it is almost
dream-like. I think of Berlin, that forbidding, closed city, and
its cold, leaden streets that I walked as a student. I then look
about this place of enchantment with its winding by-ways

which of a sudden burst onto sun-lit, open piazzas. Can one call a city a gift?

Tomorrow I present myself at the Marucelliana Library, where I hope to work. More anon, dear Wilfrid. Your loving

Flora

She had bolted. Before McKenzie's note had fully burnt in her kitchen stove, Flora knew that she must leave London and do so directly. If she stayed, she feared what she or McKenzie might do. She needed to be away, to be on her own, and without distraction write her book — especially that. Writing her book was the most important task in her life. Further, though she could not know this, her book, when published, would bring her a measure of wealth and a good deal of fame.

The afternoon she received McKenzie's note she telegraphed the Pensione Gavelli to ask if they might accommodate a change in her plans. They could; they did. The next day she rushed to Adelphi Terrace to get her letter of introduction from Fisher Unwin, who obliged on the spot. Lijak was not surprised by her eagerness to get on with her researches. He himself often packed and left impulsively for the Continent: her sudden rush seemed perfectly reasonable to him.

Over the week she bought light clothing for the Italian summer and medications recommended by her chemist husband: quinine tablets for fever ("You must be sure to take three grains a day regularly and without fail — this is particularly so if you visit Venice."), Pyretic Saline for headaches, other preparations for food poisoning and diarrhœa, and borax salt in solution to bathe her eyes should they become inflamed from work (Stepniak's suggestion, this last). Whilst occupied with these preparations and her packing she managed to call on friends (the Stepniaks, the Kropotkins, Feliks Volkhovsky and his daughter Vera) and on her Mama and sisters to say her good-byes. Within four days she was gone.

15 June, '95

Florence
Pensione Gavelli
Via S Antonino 12

Dearest Wilfrid:

I have settled in, for that is the proper expression, at the lovely Marucelliana Library (personally welcomed by Sr Achille Pavese, the head librarian, thanks to Fisher Unwin's letter of introduction) & have begun serious work. Sr Pavese has assigned a desk in the Reading Room for my exclusive use, a great kindness and honour.

Each day as I ascend the stairs to work, I pass a small statue of Minerva, her rich locks piled high under her helmet. She appears a most formidable goddess. With Minerva peering over my shoulder as it were & inspiring me, I do my work – writing up notes for my characters & scenes & furthering the narrative I began in England.

In another marvelous library here, the Gabinetto Vissieux (where I was also received most kindly, again thanks I am sure to Fisher Unwin's letter), I am reading memoirs & collections of correspondence & articles from old newspapers (especially 'La Giovine Italia' published in Marseilles by Mazzini in the '30s) that are collected & bound & kept in the Gabinetto. Read with a close eye these are a treasury of useful facts. Did you know that the local coinage of the time (scudi, testoni, paoli, a most complicated and irritating system) was minted by the Pope! of all people? My Italian improves by the bounds.

I am managing to explore the city. I walk about wearing coloured glasses against the brilliant sunlight & imagine Ribeiro dodging behind pillars & into hidden courts to elude the police. These visions are quite distinct. I see him.

The local larrikins follow one everywhere begging for centesimi. To discourage them (so I was instructed by Sr Gavelli) one holds one's hand at waist level, turns it up at the wrist, & wags one's extended index finger back & forth & says – frowningly – 'non c'e niente'. The technique works on occasion & buys one some respite from the scamps.

I have visited the English cemetery & the English churches (C of E & Presbyterian). In the churches I have met some of the English community here, mostly female, but so far have found none of them congenial. Their political & religious views do not bear repeating.

Of our officials at the Consulate Sir Dominic is affable & gracious but appears preoccupied. With what I do not know. He collects bibelots & has a social life. Mr French, I believe, does the work. He has been most helpful to me & is a great source of information.

Mr French tells me he knows ancient veterans of the struggles of the '30s & '40s & will introduce them to me. I am of course eager to speak with anyone who lived in those times. I shall need a translator but Mr French says he will help. More anon. Your loving

Flora

The young Mr French had attended to Flora from the morning she first visited the Consulate. After Sir Dominic had led her from his large office to Mr French's small one and introduced her (Mr French's office, it should be admitted at once, did have a fine view onto the shaded Via de' Tornabuoni) Mr French invited her for coffee at a nearby *pasticcería*, La Giacosa. At an outside table, Mr French listened with great interest as Flora described her "project," her novel of the Thirties. She talked of "her Russians" as well, of her work with the Society of Friends of Russian Freedom, and of her husband, an exile out of Siberia. Mr French then offered to show her some of the city.

They strolled roughly east, wandering into and out of side streets and small markets, wherever fancy took Mr French, who, like Sir Dominic, was a scholar of the city as well as of its art.

In a widening of the Via Calimaruzzo, Mr French led Flora to a darkly-patinaed bronze statue of a boar, larger than the real animal, posed resting on his left haunch and installed before a tall, arched *loggia*.

"We call him *Il Porcellino*. 'The Piglet.' Pietro Tacca. 17th century, first half. Rub *Il Porcellino*'s nose and you'll return to Florence someday however far you may have wandered."

"Well, then, I must!" The Piglet's snout above its tusks, touched so often by would-be returnees, felt shiny and smooth.

"It's a fountain, but the water's been shut off."

"I shall ask Sr Gavelli to turn it on."

"Sr Gavelli?"

"My landlord. He is also an engineer with the city waterworks. He'll be shocked."

"He probably knows all about it and in any case will not be shocked. Things go slowly here. Perhaps by the time you return – on your next visit I mean, and you will return now you've rubbed our Piglet's nose – Sr Gavelli will have restored the water."

They walked on in shade and sun and when they turned finally into the Piazza del Duomo, the grey octagon of the Battistero lay before them, and beyond it the great Cathedral with its panels of green and pink and white marble and its vast brick dome.

"Here we are," Mr French said. "Heart of the city in a way. Like the sight?"

"How could I not, Mr French? How marvelous!"

"Yes. I thought you would want to see it your first day here." After standing for a moment with Flora, Mr French drew a breath and said, "Well, I must return to Via Tornabuoni. May I order a cab for you?"

"Oh, no, no, Mr French, thank you very much, but I shall see the Cathedral, then walk a bit and explore on my own. I am armed with my little red Baedeker."

"Baedeker? Good. Then you're well-armed, but I hope that once in a while you'll allow a fellow human being to assist you." She thanked him. He paused. "You'll love Florence, you know. And Italy − all of it. 'Open my heart and you will see, Graved inside of it "Italy"'."

"Browning?"

"'De gustibus...'"

"'De gustibus...' Right − no disputing that!"

He laughed. "Quite. Well, do let me know from time to time how your 'project' progresses − I'd like that."

She promised she would. He said good-bye and walked off briskly − handsome, lithe, and English in his linen suit and wide-brimmed straw hat.

———

18 June, '95

Florence
Pensione Gavelli
Via S Antonino 12

Dearest Wilfrid:

I have been having wonderful conversazioni with a Sr Leonardo Santorelli, a friend of Mr French's. Sr Santorelli was born in 1814 (he thinks) & was a gunrunner in the upheavals of the '30s & '40s. He is of an ancient Tuscan family. For our first meeting Mr French himself kindly fetched me in a hansom to the Casa Santorelli, for that is what it is, a casa, a narrow, grey marble-fronted abode on the right bank. It has the usual vast wooden gate & courtyard. A portone leads into a small back garden of vines and herbs, where a nymph bathes in a tub (she is of grey marble like the tub, not pink flesh). Sr Santorelli dwells on the ground floor as he can no longer climb stairs.

The courtyard has a fountain, but it is simply a mossy stone trough built against one wall of the house & furnished with a tap that can be turned on & off at will (no water burbling thru the mouth of a lion or grinning satyr!).

At least one grandson lives somewhere about the building, with three children – all boys – & wife. The grandson is in banking & has interests in Austria & France. He is a stick, all formality & suspicious looks (so unlike his grandfather). The children, however, are a delight & play noisily, watched over by a crone dressed in black.

Because of the heat the youngest two are allowed to run about the courtyard quite naked like little putti in a Rafael. The eldest, a lad of eight or so named Leonardino (after his grandfather), goes about more modestly in short underdrawers. The wife has yet to make her appearance.

It turns out the elder Sr Santorelli speaks French well & so we communicate easily. He has a sharp wit still & regales me with tales of derring-do – ambushes, prison escapes, pitched battles – as well as lurid accounts of treachery & spying & hired murders. Marvelous 'stuff'. I am taking full notes, tho' Sr Santorelli sometimes speaks so quickly & with such animation, gesturing with his hands & rolling his eyes, that I am hard-pressed to get it all down. He obviously likes telling his tales, which I believe he has practised over a lifetime, he is so fluent with them. After time his energy flags (we have been meeting in the late afternoons after my work in the libraries) & I take my leave. I have visited Sr Santorelli four times now. He has begun to repeat himself & his stories vary in the repetition, but I suppose that is the result of age, not wilful prevarication. In any case I shall use the better versions! Your loving

Flora

One morning Mr French called on Flora at the Marucelliana. After begging her forgiveness for interrupting her at her work, he said, "I thought you might care to make an excursion someday. The heights surrounding the city give a charming view. We could take a cab – perhaps some afternoon – the haze lifts then."

Flora wondered, Is there no Mrs French? Have I a suitor? How odd. And how very unnecessary. She agreed to go but told herself that she would not lead him on or give him encouragement.

They made their excursion that very day, leaving from the Porta Romana and driving on a stone-paved road that wound into the northern hills. On either side lay pleasure grounds of the wealthy, marked off by elms and sycamores and fragrant bay trees and hedged by roses in glorious summer bloom.

At a terrace near the top of one hill Mr French stopped their cab and they descended by footpath to a clear space, a small piazza defined on three sides by brick wall. The open, south, side gave a view down through the limpid air onto the city and its towers and domes and bridges and, just discernable, the blue-grey Arno flowing through it all.

"Nothing like this in England," Mr French said quietly.

"Nor anywhere else, I should think."

"No." Mr French pointed at the hillside to their left. "Over there, see all the white walls and ceramic roofs and gardens? The campanile? That's Fiesole. Lovely little town. Worth a visit in itself." Mr French was all but promising to convey her there.

As they passed back through the piazza, Flora noticed a small bronze replica of Michel Angelo's "David" standing off in an ivied corner. Early in her sojourn in Florence she had viewed the huge white marble original in the Cupola Saloon of the Accadèmia di Belle Arti. Approaching the masterpiece through a long, dimly lit gallery, she sensed the force of it, a force that grew more disturbing the nearer she got. The frank male figure, muscled, bold, composed and quiet, yet menacing and ready for action, sling held in left hand, stone concealed in right – this youth would soon kill. The latent violence in this naked male and his overt sexuality made her think of McKenzie and disturbed her in a variety of ways she could not sort out. She suppressed a tremor then. The little copy in the piazza returned her to her unease and to thoughts of McKenzie and made her disinclined to conversation on the ride down the hill.

When Flora returned to the Pensione Gavelli she found an envelope addressed to her there. Printed in its upper left corner was the return address, "American Press Association, 34 Throgmorton Street, E.C., London." Flora, as she rushed to leave England, had known that McKenzie would learn where she was and would write her. She had determined to destroy without reading it any letter he might send, but in the event, could not. Heart racing, she cut open the envelope and read its contents:

June 15, 1895

My lovely Flora,

I learned from Sergei Stepniak this evening that you have gone on your Italian adventure. I send all my best wishes, but I shall miss you so. I love you dearly and always will.

Bill

Flora had seen the longing in McKenzie's eyes as she and he spoke so guardedly with one another after Sergei's lecture; more than once after that she wondered if he had seen longing in hers as well.

Far from destroying it, Flora kept this letter. She stopped seeing Mr French. There was no trip to Fiesole.

Over the rest of June and the month of July, despite the growing heat, Flora did her work. Sundays, she attended mass, each
week at a different church. She observed the priests celebrating
the Eucharist, listened to the chanting, took pleasure in the cool
darkness.

After each mass she purchased a votive candle in return for
the experience, adding hers to the flickering tables of light. As she
toured her churches, she paid particular attention to the confes-
sionals. These were usually placed discreetly off in some quiet corner. They were constructed of dark-stained wood and curtained
with thick cloth that hid persons and muffled sound. What secret
sins had these booths heard over the years? she wondered.

Once she sat in the darkness of a confessional, alone, and,
drawing closed the heavy curtain, imagined herself to be Ribeiro
acknowledging his sins to a traitorous priest on the other side
of the grille. She imagined the priest's unctuous voice purring
questions (perhaps even asking the names of her accomplices) and
leading her further and further into his trap. She heard the priest,
after learning enough to have her shot, directing her to do pen-
ance, giving her absolution, and blessing her in the name of God.

Her researches took Flora to Pisa, which Ribeiro would make his
base and where Ribeiro's English beloved, a girl named Adele,
herself a young but steely revolutionist, lived; and to Bologna to
consult records at the State Archives and to view artefacts at the
Civic Museum.

Disciplined in her work and single-minded, within weeks Flora had produced hundreds of pages of notes and the beginning
chapters of her novel. Yet day and night the entire summer she
thought of McKenzie. She hoped her longing – for that, she ac-

knowledged, was what she felt – would ease as time passed, but it never did.

OZZIE

Home from Starbucks, Ozzie changes into a dry pair of sweats —
when she'd been only a block from the stone portico and heavy
oak entrance door of her apartment building rain had suddenly
come sluicing down again, driven by a high wind that tore at her
umbrella, reversing it twice, leaving her drenched and shivering
on the sidewalk. Dry and warm now after a hot shower and sham-
poo, she sits on her sofa, petrified, thinking: this really could be it.

"*Live or Die* is good work," Wally said when she had numbly risen
to leave his office but had not yet opened the door. "It will see the
light of day. I cannot understand, cannot understand Riesner and
that crowd. But — do not let this buffalo you. Keep a grip. We will
see it through."

Buffalo? Grip? she thought. Christ.

Her laptop pings softly. It's Wally's e-mail with his suggested
academic publishing houses. He recommends starting with the
first, that of a major university in the Midwest, and says he knows
the executive editor, Ted Greene, with whom he has, he says,
"mojo."

Mojo.

She thanks Wally, then wires *Live or Die*, a new cover letter,
and her resumé to Ted Greene.

Gone. Out the door.

At this she feels a great emptiness.

Next day, Thursday, she calls Marc Riesner. He tells her what he told her in his e-mail, that he's "terribly sorry," that he feels bad about "the way this was handled," that *Live or Die* looked good to him, that if it was up to him "it would be a go," but that the board of editors ultimately decided against. And, yes, he admits, the delay was "unconscionable." Still the nicest guy in the known universe, Marc.

The remainder of her week she drifts. She meets her classes and sees her student advisees. She works out on the machines at the Field House and jogs on the indoor track there. Evenings in her apartment she watches movies and reads, listlessly. Since she gives no quizzes, pop or otherwise, she has no papers to grade. She drinks too much Shiraz. Nights she takes trazodone and alprazolam; mornings she is headachy and muzzy.

At some point David texts:

Buzz and I are going to Puerto Rico tomorrow. Hotel milano San Juan. I need a break. Hope you're okay.

She answers:

Hey, have fun. Big hugs.

Texting is good, she thinks. Very good. Betrays no affect.

No one phones, fortunately – not Grace, not Baba. She won't take calls from them in any case. She just can't. What would she say?

She thinks again and again of her book, on which she had worked so hard and for which she had had such great hope. What will become of it now? And of her? The prospect that she will not teach again, not at GU, not anywhere, is all too thinkable.

Yet how she had wanted to teach, always! One summer at The Pond, a teenager ravished by words, especially old words, she would tramp in her yellow rubber boots through the brush and fallen leaves on the woody far side of the pond where no one could see or hear her, to a rise she had once assured an amused

Grace was an Indian burial mound. There, as if standing before a class, she would declaim verse she had been memorizing from Moo Moo's old high school English textbook: "A thing of beauty is a joy forever...", "She walks in beauty, like the night... "Death, be not proud..."

She explicated the verse to imaginary students and pictured herself an adult doing so in her coming real life, which life would be one of learning and teaching. Through her touchy adolescence, through college, for which Grace paid, and through graduate school (Virginia, full scholarship), she could think of no other.

Friday morning, she sees Wally in his office, door closed. This time she does not tear up when she walks in. Wally assures her *Live or Die* will be read promptly. ("I know Ted Greene. Believe me, he's a decent guy.")

Wally doesn't say so, but he's talked to Greene. Must have. Mojo, chits... something.

Wally wants to know how she's feeling. She lies. She says she's holding up, getting better. Wally nods. She can tell he's unpersuaded and she wonders what her face shows. There are born liars, she thinks. I'm not one.

Late Friday afternoon she receives an e-mail from E.L. Greene's secretary acknowledging that her manuscript has arrived. The manuscript arrived at 3:35 p.m. Wednesday afternoon. They acknowledged receipt at 2:42 p.m. Friday afternoon.

Can this be mojo? she wonders.

Friday evening, she goes dark. She turns off her computer, laptop, and cell. She watches junk TV.

Next morning, she grocery-shops at the Singles Safeway on Wisconsin, so called because of the young and unattached who patronize it. She notes, pushing her cart through Dairy Products, that she has never been hit on in the store, surprisingly. Fine with her. In fact, thank God.

By Sunday evening her dread has softened into something closer to foreboding and has acquired a hint of sadness.

Bluesy, she thinks. Yes, that's how to describe it, that sounds about right: Bluesy.

Her apartment is intensely silent. As she sits in the old brown leather couch from Somerville, book in hand, a mood creeps in: countless evenings Tom would sit on the right end of that couch and she next to him, thigh to thigh, somebody's arm around the other's neck, each talking low. And in her desolation after Tom's death, she would sit on that same couch alone, so alone, softly crying, "Come back... Come back..."

On Ozzie's bedroom dresser rests a framed portrait photograph of Tom. He gave it to her soon after they met. He had it taken by a quality photographer and put in a quality frame and gave it to her because he loved her and wanted her to know that. In that photograph there's a hint of his boyish shyness.

When Ozzie was having her lovers, her "experiments," she would hide the photograph deep in the third drawer of that same dresser. She felt guilt of some kind, but for what she wasn't sure. For deceiving her lovers? For not letting them know she was married to a memory?

Or was it, against all logic, guilt for some betrayal of Tom? That made no sense, she told herself, the dead don't care, then immediately thought, But the living do – oh, they do. If it hadn't been for that Volvo smashing straight into Tom's future and hers, she and Tom would be in Somerville, and if she were having tenure fears at Boston U, Tom would be steadying her, as he always did, and see her through.

But there is no Tom, and Ozzie sits alone in her Washington apartment wondering: How will this end? Will I publish my book? Will I have to leave Georgetown? If that, where will I go? What will I do?

Late in the evening she decides to reconnect with the world. Mark, she sees, has left voicemails. In one he simply says hello, in that soft voice of his, that he'll try again later. He tries again later but leaves no message. Instead, he sends her an e-mail and attachment, which, together, are an endearing, heart-lifting gift.

CHAPTER VI

"The Struggle is Everywhere and Takes All Shapes."

Shortly before Flora was to leave Italy, she received a telegram from Lijak:

TO: MME LIJAK C/O GAVELLI, FLORENCE 1AUG95
FROM: LIJAK LONDON
PLEASE SEE FRIENDS GENEVA. LEAVE FLORENCE EXPECTED
DATE BUT DO VISIT. LIJAK.

Under this unrevealing message lay urgency: something had happened in Russia, Flora knew, and knew that she must go to Geneva and learn what. Doing so would add two days to her travel but it was not to be helped. She telegraphed Lijak informing him that she had changed her plans in accordance with his wishes. She also telegraphed one Salomon Ignatieff in Geneva announcing her arrival date. Ignatieff was a comrade of Lijak's from Russia, whom Flora had never met, but whose address Lijak had given her on her leaving London. "In case," he had said, presciently. On 3 August 1895 Flora boarded a train at the Stazione Centrale in Florence and left Italy for England via Switzerland.

She stopped two nights in Geneva, where she found Ignatieff living in one bare room not far from the railway station with his wife, a woman named Anna Dmitrievna, familiarly called Anutya. Ignatieff and Anutya shared a kitchen with the occupants of two other flats.

Ignatieff was a Nihilist who had committed crimes of some

indeterminate sort in Russia and had fled its police. He was living in Geneva under a pseudonym. He gave Flora a packet containing, he said, a letter and several manuscripts of revolutionist tracts that had been smuggled out of Russia by courier. Ignatieff did not know the contents of the letter (it was in a sealed envelope and besides was sure to be enciphered), but the courier, who had come and gone, said the letter contained bad news. The courier did not know what the bad news was. Flora would convey the packet to Lijak (it could not be entrusted to the post). Lijak and his comrades in the S.F.R.F., when they learnt what the letter contained, would decide what, if anything, to do. The manuscripts would be printed as pamphlets and these smuggled into Russia.

Ignatieff was a Jew from somewhere in the Crimea, where exactly he would not say. He worked as a printer with a local publisher and wrote Nihilist tracts in the German Jewish language. He was small and had pitch-black eyes and never laughed. Flora thought him the most humourless man she had ever met.

Anutya was Russian. She had wanted to leave her country ever since as a young woman she had "become political," as the phrase went. She wanted to "breathe the air" in the West and work with Nihilist comrades in comparative freedom. Her father, however, refused to give her permission to travel abroad. So, she converted to the Hebrew faith and married Ignatieff, whom she knew from the Nihilist circles in which she moved and who was willing to take her. In those days the kind of relationship Ignatieff and Anutya had entered was known as a "Mariage Blanc," a "White Marriage," contracted not for love, but for political convenience: the two, as each freely admitted, were wedded to the Cause, not to each other. Anutya's father bitterly regretted losing his daughter not only to the Nihilists, but to the Hebrews, a race he despised, and sent her a short, cold letter in which he declared that he no longer knew her. She accepted the estrangement. After they married, Ignatieff and Anutya emigrated first to Berlin, then under police pressure to Geneva.

Anutya had ashen hair and a papery complexion and was sick-ly. She was also very shy. In the room she shared with Ignatieff she slept on a chaise longue with a broken wheel. It lay against a far wall away from the window. For whatever reason, possibly because she was consumptive, she feared drafts. Under the quilting of his own bed Ignatieff kept a large revolver of American make wrapped in oilcloth. He showed it to Flora and said he intended it for use.

The night before Flora was to leave Geneva, she and the Ignatieffs strolled through the gardens on the lake front. The air was cool. The water of the lake played in the moonlight. Far up on the hillsides watchfires were burning.

They talked of love, which Ignatieff disparaged. "I simply don't believe in it," he said. "Love is a distraction. One must be free to travel here and there, to pick up and leave at any time, to brave risks, to be jailed, to die. Bourgeois marriage with its conventions is a prison as constraining as any of the Tsar's."

Anutya nodded her head vigorously in agreement with her husband's words.

They told Flora that though they were active revolutionists they felt quite free in Geneva and declared they were not under the surveillance of the police. Flora did not believe them, though she noticed no detectives following them or posted near the Ignatieff's flat-house. Sometimes the police are not clumsy, she thought.

When Flora left for Paris and London Ignatieff walked her to the railway station to see her off. On the platform when they cried the last call for departure, he embraced her tightly and became emotional. "Comrade Flora," he said in a strained voice, "you are off for England, a country of blessed freedom, where you do work that cannot be done in Russia. The struggle is everywhere and takes all shapes. I commend you with my heart."

His earnest face was close to hers. His breath stank.

———

Flora arrived in London by the Paris mail from Calais and Dover and alit in the dusky gloom of Charing Cross Station. Lijak emerged out of the dense crowd to greet her, and they embraced warmly. Seeing him cheered her immensely.

"You look very well," he said, pulling away but still gripping her elbows. "Your letters were a great comfort, but it's so good to see you again. I missed you very much."

"And I you."

He coughed. "Geneva went well?"

"Yes. I've a packet from Russia. Rather thick."

"Good. And Ignatieff? What are his plans?"

"To stay. He talked of coming to London but was vague. I think he will not."

"Ah."

After Lijak engaged a porter to fetch Flora's baggage they took an exit staircase down to the street and hired a cab. On the way to Hammersmith Flora first talked animatedly of Florence and Italy and of her travels about the country, and of *Ribeiro*, which, she said (and as Lijak knew from her letters), had progressed well and would be enormously enriched by her researches. She then fell silent and closed her eyes, resting her head on Lijak's shoulder. He thought she was dozing and let her be.

She was not dozing, she was thinking: I have returned. McKenzie and I will meet. What then shall I do?

In The Grove, helped by the cabdriver (Sarah had gone for the day), they bustled Flora's baggage into their house: her precious boxes of notes for *Ribeiro* and her two trunks. These contained, in addition to her clothes, knickknacks from Italy for her Mama and sisters and friends; an edition of Petrarch dated 1753 for Lijak, which she had got cheap at a stall near the Cathedral; and a portrait photograph of herself in her calico dress, a memento of her time in the city.

Lijak sat on Flora's bed as she undressed and put on her nightgown. When she lay down, they embraced tenderly and kissed good night. Stroking her cheek, Lijak told her once again how happy he was to see her. Exhausted, she fell into a slumber in his arms.

Immediately she did, Lijak walked softly to their workroom, which was adjacent to their bedroom, and tore open the packet Flora had brought from Geneva. In it he found five manuscripts, each from respected writers, and a letter. This last, written sloppily on a single sheet of thick grey paper, bore a Moscow return address and a date three weeks in the past. It began:

My dear Alyosha,

We are enjoying our stay here immensely. Nadia has become betrothed to an up-and-coming secretary in the Ministry of Foreign Affairs, a match we approve whole-heartedly. News from the estate at Zhalsko, however, is not joyful. Some of the timberland…

The letter rambled further in this commonplace way, and Lijak quickly gave off reading it. Instead, he spread it flat on the bare wooden surface of their worktable, carefully smoothing it level. From a collection of chemical reagents of various sizes and colours that stood on his end of the table he took a vial of clear fluid and, using a watercolorist's brush, gently painted the paper with the fluid, covering all the inked message. As he did, the letters began to fade from view, only to be replaced by others, which appeared slowly and unevenly on the page, as if arriving out of a mist. This new letter, written in the same hand but more legibly, was from a comrade in St Petersburg and carried the same date. Addressed to "Vanya" - Ivan "Vanya" Kelchevsky, Lijak's old alias - it read:

Dear Vanya,

We have the worst news. We have just learnt that our comrade Boris Fedorovich Chernikov, who had been exiled to a labor camp at Onor on Sakhalin Island, has been slain. He had been assigned to a crew working to construct a road from Onor to Rykovskaya. By order of commanding General V. I. Kuznetsov, he had been treated with greater than usual cruelty (savage beatings and starvation). When he could work no longer the work inspector finished him off with a revolver bullet. Might you give an account of Borya's death in *Free Russia*? We embrace you from afar.

Kostya and the others

Boris - "Borya" - Fedorovich Chernikov had been a student in the Faculty of Law at Moscow University and was known to Lijak only by name. He had been a member of the regenerated People's Will Party, a terrorist organization, which had languished during the preceding decade, but which had begun again to operate. Chernikov had been tried and convicted of bank robbery and sentenced to ten years forced labour on Sakhalin Island in the Far East. He was thought hot-tempered, and it was said that during an interrogation he had struck General Kuznetsov.

"Kostya" - Konstantine Ilyich Semyenoff – was a veteran of the Struggle and an old friend of Lijak's. He was living in great peril in St Petersburg, seldom leaving his flat. Flight to the West, however, was inconceivable to him. His friends knew he would stay and fight until he was killed.

"Russia," Lijak thought, "what an abyss of sorrow!"

Yet, in truth, Lijak was losing heart for the struggle in Russia, and his life in exile was changing. Through his work for the Russian Free Press Fund, and quite by accident, Lijak was becoming a bookseller, though at this time his battered valise was his only shop.

From the early 1890s on, Lijak had travelled from London by boat train, hauling trunk-loads of Fund publications to drop with booksellers friendly to the Cause in Paris, Geneva, Vienna, and other cities on the Continent. These colleagues would turn the books over to Russian comrades, who would smuggle them by various routes into the realms of the Tsar. Shipments were occasionally seized by the Tsar's police, but most got through. In Russia the works were distributed and sold through local underground networks.

It happened that through Constance Garnett Lijak had got to know her father-in-law, Richard Garnett, who was Keeper of Printed Books at the British Museum. Richard Garnett, Lijak learnt, was keen on building the Museum's collection of early works, especially incunabula, books printed in Europe before 1501.

In Garnett Lijak saw opportunity. Whilst browsing in the shops of his bookseller friends on the Continent Lijak had come across quantities of incunabula and other rare works. These he began purchasing and supplying to Garnett at steep mark-ups. He also began spending time in the Reading Room of the Museum, where he had a reader's ticket – Sergei Stepniak had been his character reference – educating himself in the lore of manuscripts and old books.

At the same time, through Garnett and some other English members of the S.F.R.F., Lijak was becoming acquainted with the community of wealthy bibliophiles in England. He was learning their tastes in rare books – from bibles to erotica – and was finding ways to satisfy those tastes. Since few contemporary English booksellers made buying trips to the Continent, Lijak was almost alone in supplying English customers from sources in Europe and was able to set his own prices. By the spring of 1895, his career was in the ascendant and he was planning to open a real shop.

In the morning Lijak would show the letter and manuscripts to Flora, then take them to the Iffley Road offices of *Free Russia*. A note on Boris Chernikov's death and its circumstances would appear in the next issue of the paper. As to the manuscripts, Nikolai Chaikovsky and Leonid Shishko, and possibly Sergei Stepniak, would quickly edit them and see them into print. Lijak would help with the work, then haul the printed pamphlets to the Continent. He would, of course, use his time abroad to search for and buy rare books.

In his drowsy languor before sleep Lijak gazed affectionately upon his wife, who was turned his direction, palms together beneath her cheek.

We have been wed now for three years, he thought. These years have been full of work and struggle for the Cause, years of close companionship. They have been joyful years for me and, I believe, for you as well. Yes, our marriage is... incomplete, but, my beloved Flora, I have never once regretted taking you into my heart.

OZZIE

The gray, one-page image, still warm from her printer, lies on Ozzie's keyboard, where she has placed it to view.

The image is a scan of Flora Bowles and Wilfrid Lijak's wedding certificate. Their marriage was "solemnized," as the certificate puts it, in the Registrar Office of the Civil Parish of Hammersmith, County of London. The Registrar who officiated, one Matthew Harding, entered into the document, in his beautiful, late-Victorian hand, their names and addresses, Flora's in Hampstead, Lijak's in Hammersmith, and the date, 21 August 1892, on which the ceremony took place. Two witnesses, Frederick Rewick and James McClellan, signed their names at the bottom.

Mark had sent the scan in the late evening:

TO: azad.hosseini@gu.edu
FROM: mark.morehead27@gmail.com
SUBJ: Lijak Marriage cert

Hi Ozzie,

Have you seen this? Just got it from the English Public Records Office. Thought I'd pass it on to a friend who it might help write a paper.

Mark

When Ozzie saw what Mark's attachment was, she thought: Mark didn't really need this for his own work, he got it for me. More than a kindness. Getting it took some work. And some thought. Is Mark in love? Am I? Maybe a little?

She replied:

TO: mark.morehead27@gmail.com
FROM: azad.hosseini@gu.edu
SUBJ: Lijak Marriage cert

Dear Mark,

Thank you so much. No, I haven't seen this. Very interesting. Kind of you to send it. We'll see about a paper. Maybe!

Ozzie

No one has seen this document, Ozzie thinks, since Matthew Harding filled it in on that day in August of 1892. It's been buried for a century and a quarter in some file in London. Yet as I touch this copy, laser-printed in America just now, it is so tangible, so real that it brings the participants in that day's ceremony into my room: Flora and Lijak, Matthew Harding, Rewick and McClellan, they're all present here, called from the dead.

Ozzie tries to imagine that Registrar Office in Hammersmith. Walls lined with thick ledgers perhaps? Clerks at their desks, like Bob Cratchit, filling in forms under jets of burning gas? And the ceremony – what was that like? Did the Lijaks invite guests? Did they go off on a honeymoon? They felt love, she thinks. They had that.

A cloudless, hot day, also in August, at The Pond. The sun beats down on the guests, who are seated in two sets of folding chairs, Ozzie's people on the left, Tom's on the right, naturally. Baba, who has flown in from Los Angeles, is sitting alone in a back row. Behind Ozzie and Tom and the minister rises a wooden latticed arch that Grace has had constructed by a local carpenter. Grace herself has woven roses through the arch's latticework. Beyond, the pond lies blue-green and indolent under the sun. The minister, from the local Congregational Church, is a hefty woman

of middle age. Though White, she is wearing a kente cloth that
drapes around her neck and runs down to her waist. A string trio,
hired by Grace, is playing an arrangement of Bach's Air on the G
String. Tom is wearing a dark blue pinstriped suit and must be
steaming in it.

Not like the night before, when at Ozzie's suggestion they
went skinny-dipping in the pond.

Two impatient conspirators, they waited for family to fall
asleep, then slipped from bedroom to kitchen, not waking the
Welles's blond retriever Christina and black, white-socked cat
Adolphus, the two companionably asleep in front of the fireplace
in the large main room. They eased out the kitchen door, not
allowing – carefully, carefully – the screen-door with its rusted
spring pull to bang shut. They treaded in silence down the slope
from house to pond and dock.

Undressing. White bodies. Lovers in the Garden, innocent
of everything but desire. Easing silently into the warmish water
wearing nothing but moonlight. Swimming, as if that were the
point, to the small hump of an island not far from the dock. Kiss-
ing. Fondling one another's bodies. Tom's erection on Ozzie's belly, bending upward when they embrace. Pulling away from the
island, swimming back to the dock. Climbing the wooden ladder,
Ozzie first, unselfconsciously bare-assed.

Honeymoon in a rented cabin on Cape Cod just south of Well-
fleet, hidden in a piney forest on the bay side. Visiting the beach
on the Atlantic side. Ocean water too rough to enter. So, sitting in
two light aluminum lawn chairs Tom had thought to bring along
– Tom ever practical – watching the glittering, pounding water,
watching each other.

Over the wind and the crashing of the surf, Tom shouting,
Seals! and pointing out to sea, to their right.

And yes, two dark heads just above the bright waves, the an-
imals swimming parallel to the shore, out there, but not far out
there, drifting south in the current. Entrancing.

Everything ends.

———

At the picture window in her living area Ozzie raises the slats of the old-fashioned Venetian blinds and gives herself a view out into the city. Below lies the small triangle of Bryce Park, its budding trees dark and skeletal against the park's illuminated green expanse. No pedestrians are out; traffic is sparse. A police car, its blue roof-lights glowing, silently prowls north.

Ozzie exhales, hands resting on the sill. *Live or Die* is out the door. It's with Ted Greene in Ann Arbor, and Ozzie can only wait. She doesn't like that, waiting, she never has. She needs to work.

Cut the gloom, she thinks. Snap out of it. Move. Come on, come on, come on. This marriage certificate is the beginning.

Find Flora.

CHAPTER VII

"I Was Mad."

3, Iffley Road
Hammersmith
London

28 August, '92

... And now on a personal note – I have married and share
the news with you as a friend. My wife is a member of the
S.F.R.F. Committee, née Miss Bowles, a person dedicated
to the Cause. She speaks Russian well. As secretary of *Free
Russia*, she admires you for your steadfastness and your work
for the Cause. I am sure she will be writing you frequently. I
embrace you.

Kelchevsky

PS I have adopted a pseudonym and am called Wilfrid Lijak.

(The last paragraph and postscript of a letter that Lijak sent La-
zar Goldenberg in New York. Goldenberg, born in Russia in
1846 into an Orthodox Jewish family, emigrated to London in
1880 and was a founder there of the Hebrew Socialist Union,
an influential organisation in the Jewish labour movement in
Britain. In 1887 he emigrated to New York, where he established the American branch of the Society of Friends of Russian Freedom and brought out the American edition of *Free
Russia*. Goldenberg later returned to London and died there in
1916. He had known Lijak as Ivan Kelchevsky.)

—

Lijak and Flora announced their marriage, which was not unexpected, to comrades in late August of 1892. Lijak's comments to Goldenberg are typical; Flora sent out similar notes, hers praising Wilfrid. The ceremony, brief and non-religious, took place in a London Civil Registrar's office.

Decades later, in early March 1930, as Lijak lay terminally ill with lung cancer in the Baker-Craig Sanatorium in downtown Charleston, South Carolina, he and Flora reminisced about the day.

"Do you remember how hot it was?" Flora asked in Russian.

"Yes. Hot. Bright."

"And you wore that borrowed jacket."

"Yes. Shishko's. Tight. Very uncomfortable. Also hot."

"And a necktie... a very becoming necktie. A lovely, satiny mauve."

"Yes."

"And I wore a corsage of lilies. Do you recall? You bought it for me in King Street. From that tiny florist's shop. I thought it an extravagance."

Lijak smiled at the memory and pressed her hand, feebly. Otherwise, he lay motionless.

A faint odour of incontinence hung in the air.

In January Lijak had been told by a young physician in New York that he had only a few months to live. "Poor boy," Lijak remarked to Flora after receiving the prognosis. "How he hated to tell me that!"

Flora made arrangements with the Baker-Craig on the advice of a close friend, the eminent physician and bibliophile, Dr Andrew – "Andy" – LePage of Los Angeles, and, accompanied by Alice Neff, took Lijak to Charleston to get him some relief from

the New York winter. Flora and Alice had taken a room in the
nearby Hotel St John, but spent most of their time with Lijak, one
often spelling the other, who would remain nearby. By March
Lijak's disease had reduced him to choking and gasping, his skin
grey and damp, his eyes naked without his glasses and terribly
vulnerable.

Gazing on her husband's drawn face Flora recalled the portrait
photograph she had had taken of him only three years before,
on the occasion of his sixty-second birthday, in which he posed
resting his right arm on the back of a chair and holding his sil-
ver-tipped walking stick − a birthday gift from her − and Panama
hat in his left hand. He wore his linen suit for the sitting (Moffatt
Studio, Madison Avenue; Moffatt himself did the work) and in
the finished photograph looked handsome and vigorous. For the
occasion she had also given him a box of chocolates and written
him a birthday song. The photograph was framed in silver; it rested atop a cherry-wood bookcase in their small sitting room in the
Commodore Hotel. Flora adored the portrait; she considered it as
much a gift to herself as to him.

Lijak coughed, and a line of spittle began to run from the left side
of his mouth down his jaw. Flora dabbed at it with a Kleenex.
"Shtein wanted to attend," she said.

Lijak hacked a small laugh. "Yes. In a better jacket. I said no."

"And Stepniak."

"Yes. Stepniak. Do you recall? − we met there, Pet. Stepniak's.
His house."

"Yes. So long ago. In Hampstead."

"Hampstead."

He smiled. "But I saw you. That afternoon. For the second
time."

"Yes."

It was early in October 1890. The Stepniaks were holding Saturday afternoon at-homes then, which Flora often attended. That

afternoon she had just joined the other guests in the parlour when a handsome though threadbare young man entered the room and was introduced all round as Ivan Kelchevsky (later he would reveal his true name). After conversing with his hosts and other guests, he approached Flora and said in Russian, "I think I have seen you somewhere before. Were you in Warsaw in the Easter Week of 1887?"

His question startled her. She had indeed been in Warsaw then, en route to St Petersburg to spend a year with Sergei Step-niak's sister-in-law Praskovia Karaulova and her children. Flora said, "Why, yes, I was."

He then asked, "Did you ever stand in the Square near the Alexandrovsky Citadel?"

Startled again, she answered, "Yes." She had visited Citadel Square, and though three years had passed, she remembered distinctly the vast fortress of orange-red brick, the willow trees and elms about the place, even the sweet scent of budding leaves on that Easter Day, when she had stood contemplating the fortress, almost overcome with pity thinking of its inmates.

He now said excitedly, "You were dressed completely in black, were you not?"

She nodded in silent wonder, her eyes searching his, for at that time she habitually wore mourning.

"I remember you, dear lady. I was a prisoner in the Citadel then, and from my cell I saw a young woman who looked exactly like you, and I have never forgotten her face."

Flora could only gaze at him.

Lijak, a Pole born in Russian Lithuania, had joined the Polish revolutionary socialist party Proletariat after graduating with a degree in chemistry from the University of Moscow. One of his tasks for the party was to aid in the counterfeiting of Russian currency. In the spring of 1887, he was arrested by the Tsarist police in Kovno, Lithuania, and taken as a prisoner to the Citadel in Warsaw, where he saw Flora from his cell window. A year later, by order of the Tsar and without trial, he was exiled to the city of Irkutsk in Siberia. There he made the acquaintance of Sergei Stepniak's brother-in-law, Vasiliy Andreyevich Karaulov, a fellow revolutionist, who urged Lijak, a young man with no wife or children, to escape and flee to London to work with Stepniak. Karaulov gave Lijak a scrap of paper on which he had written Stepniak's address in Hampstead in the northern suburbs of London.

Aided by a network of revolutionist sympathisers known as *ukryvateli* – "concealers" – who helped with funds, lodging, and forged papers, Lijak did escape Siberia and crossed the immensity of Russia to St Petersburg. From there he made his way to Hamburg, Germany, again with help along the way from sympathisers, where he bought third-class passage on a small Danish freighter bound for London. On the Hamburg docks he smelt the moist air, which, though far up-river, had the tang of salt in it. It seemed to him a promise of England.

Before boarding, he spent the last of his funds on a loaf of rye bread and some pickled herring. The first night of the voyage a storm arose and blew the vessel off course toward the coast of Norway. In the heavy winds and heaving waters half the deck cargo was lost; Lijak, who had never been to sea, was terrified that the ship would founder and that he would drown. The ship made port safely at Grimstad in Norway, however, and once repairs were made the Danish captain set out in calmer seas for London. On 25 September 1890, in thickening dusk, the captain anchored his vessel off Wapping, where Lijak stepped ashore, dirty, starving, and penniless.

Of London Lijak knew nothing. Hoping to find his way somehow to Hampstead and the home of Sergei Stepniak, he wandered up from the river into the great murmuring, pulsing city. He climbed over slimy East End pavements in the light of rare flickering gas-lamps, up Vaughan Way to Dock Street, to Leman Street, to Whitechapel.

At the Whitechapel end of Commercial Street, a youth who

might have been a student, a Jew, Lijak thought – he was dark and bearded and had a sharp nose – accosted him and said in Russian, "You look as if you're a political man – are you from Siberia? I'm a friend."

Lijak looked the youth over, hesitating, then nodded uneasily and replied, "Yes. I want to find this man." He showed the youth Karaulov's scrap of paper. The youth read it in the light of a streetlamp. "Fine," he said. "I know him. I'll take you there."

Lijak shifted in his bed. He asked, "May I. Have water?" Alice Neff, seated beside Flora, quickly got up and took a glass and drinking straw from the bedside tray and held it to his mouth. He thanked her, and in English said to Flora, "Forty years. Pet. Since we met. Stepniak's parlour."

Lijak's face saddened. He expelled a breath and said, "Ah, Stepniak. So tragic. His end."

"Yes. Horrid," Flora said.

On the morning of 23 December 1895, Sergei Stepniak, the greatest publicist of his age for revolution in Russia, the assassin of General Mezentzev, was struck by a steam locomotive at the North London Railway crossing at Bedford Park. He had left his home – the Stepniaks had moved to Bedford Park from Hampstead – and was walking to Feliks Volkhovsky's home in Shepherd's Bush for an editorial meeting with Volkhovsky and Nikolai Chaikovsky. There was no bridge over the rails at the crossing nor any gateway leading onto the line, merely a stile over which one had to climb. The only warning of danger was a notice board that read "Beware of the Trains."

The engine caught Stepniak by his heel, dragged him under, and passed over his large body, leaving it a bloody, mangled pile of limbs. When the train stopped, Stepniak's corpse was beneath the second carriage. A bricklayer working nearby who knew Stepniak saw him die and ran to tell Stepniak's wife, Fanny. The bricklayer said Stepniak had been reading a book.

When she heard this Flora would think, How very like him. He'd always been unworldly and simply hadn't paid attention to the sign. Flora imagined Stepniak deep in thought, trudging along, nose in his book, unaware of the everyday things about him. Later a friend remarked to her that when in prison Stepniak had learnt the trick of shutting out the sounds of others in order to stay sane amidst the cacophony of a crowded cell. Her friend thought perhaps Stepniak had been using that trick while wandering across the track.

The Saturday after Stepniak died his body was cremated at Woking, a town some twenty miles west of London by rail and the location of the only crematorium in Britain at the time. A train from the London Necropolis Company carried his body from Waterloo Station, where a thousand or so of working men and women, many of them Russian Jews from the East End, had stood in the dismal English weather – dark sky, occasional sleety rain – to pay respect.

Flora and Wilfrid attended, he wearing a black armband. They shared a black umbrella. In the high-vaulted entrance to the departure platform speeches were made in Russian, English, German, Armenian, and Yiddish. Kropotkin spoke on behalf of the Russian Socialists, first in Russian, then in English. He was clearly much affected by Stepniak's death and, perhaps realising that he himself was on the brink of old age, he lamented Stepniak as a son cruelly snatched away in the prime of his life and the fullness of his vigor. He called Stepniak a faithful and valiant soldier in the fight for the freedom of his people and the liberation of all the oppressed of the world. The exiled Edward Bernstein spoke for the German Socialists. William Morris, ghost-like with his froth of steel-grey hair, frizzy beard, and old man's high-pitched voice, called for Russian and English workers to join hands building Socialism in both lands. Outside, along Waterloo Road, an indifferent London went about its noisy business.

———

It was on a warm and sunny afternoon in July, 1892 that Flora agreed to marry Lijak. He had asked her twice before, pressing her ardently, but both times she demurred, saying she could not wed, that she valued her freedom too much. The first time Lijak asked her, stroking her hand tentatively and hesitatingly, they were sitting alone in the Iffley Road bookshop. She looked Lijak in the eyes and said, "Oh, Wilfrid, I cannot be constrained by domesticity. Motherhood would tear me away from my work, which is writing and political reform. I should be a bad mother as I've no maternal instincts and I should be intensely unhappy." But she did not withdraw her hand.

The afternoon she finally agreed to marry Lijak they had been walking in Ravenscourt Park. It was here in a secluded area by the pond at its southern end that Flora and Lijak had seated themselves on a wrought-iron bench and it was here that Lijak for the third time urged her to marry him.

"I love you so much, my dear Flora," he said softly in Russian, almost whispering. "Life without you would be senseless for me. Yet don't think of me, think of us. We have had such wonderful hours together. We read, we talk, we work. We are compatible in all ways including our love of freedom. I believe that from the day I first saw you in Citadel Square we were destined for one another." He then took her right hand in both of his, gazed searchingly into her eyes, and said, "I would die for you, darling Flora. I feel I survived exile for your sake. Do not disappoint me."

She replied, "I love you and I shall marry you if you wish. But as I have said, there can be no question of children. If you can accept a marriage under these conditions, then I shall agree."

"I have thought carefully about this, dearest Flora. And, yes, I accept and honour your wishes." He kissed her hand and embraced her warmly. Then, holding her face between his two hands, he kissed her lips, which were soft and sensuous.

On their next walk, Lijak gave Flora a small volume with a dark blue cover entitled *A Wife's Handbook, With Hints on the Management of the Baby Etc., by H. A. Allbutt.*

"There is a page, dear Flora, which I have marked – see" - Lijak showed her where he had inserted a fringed leather bookmark. "Do read it – especially there." The page Lijak had bookmarked was in a chapter devoted to contraception and contained the following passage:

Dr Mensinga, of Flensburg, has invented a protective pessary, worn by the woman, which will, properly adjusted, be a real preventive of conception.

The chapter went on to discuss rubber sheaths and the proper technique of douching.

When she saw the book's title, Flora looked away and put the volume in her purse, hastily. She would read it, she told him.

In preparation for their marriage Lijak acquired a pessary of the sort Allbutt had described, cone-shaped and made of rubber, and for five shillings a number of rubber condoms – "French safes" in the vernacular – from a barber's shop, Jepson's in Frith Street, Soho, a short walk from where, three years later, he would open a bookshop. The light blue paper packets containing the condoms were printed in black with the likeness of a bearded man in the uniform of the British Navy. Jepson, like other barbers of the time, in addition to cutting hair and trimming beards, sold patent medicines and medical wares of various kinds. His briskest business was in sexual appliances.

On their wedding day, 21 August 1892, Lijak in his borrowed jacket and mauve necktie and Flora bearing her corsage of lilies, were married by one Matthew Harding, Civil Registrar, Hammersmith.

"I do solemnly declare," Flora read from a small, printed card, "that I know not of any lawful impediment why I, Flora Bowles, may not be joined in matrimony..." and here she looked into Wilfrid's eyes and said, "to Wilfrid Michael Lijak." She paused, then resumed her reading. "I call upon these persons here present that I, Flora Bowles, do take thee, Wilfrid Michael Lijak, to be my lawful wedded husband."

Wilfrid read the same formulas, in his thick Polish accent, lowering his voice and uttering her name slowly and distinctly when he came to pronounce it. Witnessing the ceremony were two employees of the Registrar's office, Frederick Rewick and James McClellan. Both had donned jackets for the occasion. The latter, McClellan, showed signs of drink. No friends or family were present. After the ceremony Lijak and Flora retired to the modest rooms Lijak had taken in Carthew Road, Hammersmith.

With the marriage came the marital act, and its repellent, invariable sequence: The ineffectual wooing. The shame of nakedness. The assault. The grunting and pounding. The final heave. The mess.

And the fears: of a pregnancy not wanted, despite all precautions that might be taken (pessary, condoms, douche); of the travail of birth and its dangers; of a child Flora was sure she could never love.

All this – her distaste for sexual intercourse and her fear of its consequences – Flora had anticipated and had determined to endure for love. What she had not anticipated was the recurrence of something like a dream, but that was not a dream. She thought it had left her, but it had not and would not for her entire life.

Her dream that was not a dream was this: a child called Flora is lying in bed at night in a dark, chilly room. She is not alone. A presence, just visible in the faint moonlight seeping past the curtains, has entered and is hovering about. The presence is breathing distinctly and rapidly, his smile as hard as his eyes. The presence is... and here she would stop thinking of the presence. She could never name that presence.

Whenever she had her dream that was not a dream, she heard

a small voice crying, "Don't hurt Flora, don't hurt Flora." She could not think for long of that dream nor hear that child's voice, nor could she think of the dark pond filled with crazed, writhing black fish, scaleless, revolting dwellers of the slime, that were part of that same dream. The recollection of those creatures and their loathsome fish odour made her shudder, always. They meant too much.

Flora's lack of sexual passion and her evident disgust with the sexual act profoundly discouraged Lijak, and after a time the couple ceased sex relations, though they remained deeply fond of one another. During the course of their marriage, they would spend long periods, sometimes well over a year, apart, Wilfrid travelling in America or on the Continent, Flora in France, Cornwall, Ireland, Italy. Flora assumed that during these periods Wilfrid would go his own way sexually, whatever that way might be. Neither spoke of the matter; they had their understandings.

In Charleston, the dying Lijak pressed Flora's hand again. "I loved you. So much," he whispered. "Always." And after a pause for rest: "I would like. My last sight. To be your face."

"Oh, my dear Wilfrid!"

Then he said, "When you left me. That time. So worried."

"Left you?" She stiffened and gripped his hand, wondering what he meant, thinking his mind might be fabricating things, then remembered, stunned to her soul.

"Oh, yes. It was so cold that year."

"Yes. Cold. And I feared. You would never. Return."

When Lijak said this, a vision came to Flora, vanishingly brief, yet intense, of a tall man striding through Washington Square in falling snow and biting cold, his arms swinging, his face set. Fused with this vision was another, of wild, passionate love in a thin-walled hotel room on the south coast of England.

Flora said, "I was mad."

Lijak said, "I was so happy. When I saw. You had come back."

Saying so was Lijak's way of conveying to Flora, once again and finally, his forgiveness – for her flight and disappearance in the frigid winter of 1918 (the behaviour she called her "madness") and for... William McKenzie.

Fatigued, Lijak shut his eyes and as so often happened now that he was heavily sedated with morphine, he drifted elsewhere.

Alice Neff, in tears, seated beside Flora in the darkened room, was well aware of what had just been transacted. She put her hand tenderly on Flora's, which remained gripping Lijak's. He died next day.

The headlines of his obituary in *The New York Times* read:

W. M. Lijak Dies;
While a Student in Russia Arrested
For political Activities and
Exiled to Siberia.
Was Authority on Medieval Manuscripts,
Of Which He Had Large Collection.
Discovered "Lost" Bacon Work.

PART TWO

OZZIE

Wednesday, 9 January 1918. I finished the choral parts of "Jerusalem" at 2 a.m. today & am exhausted. I must now rework the overture, a daunting task. I hope I am up to it. I fear I am not.

Monday, 14 January 1918. A new girl, Alice Neff, has been hired on at the office. She is from Buffalo. She is a slender thing with large, serious eyes. She is very competent.

Wednesday, 16 January 1918. The weather has been frigid & there is a coal shortage as well. The U.S. Fuel Commissioner for New York has decreed that heating be shut off in commercial buildings not only over weekends but now also in the evenings. What next? We hope this will not affect Wilfrid's office affairs.

Tuesday, 22 January 1918. I resumed work on the Bacon Cipher, on which I have expended so much effort. I saw Mr Sims at the NYPL & showed him Photostats of some of the plants. He could not identify any of the species. He suggested I show my Photostats to an herbalist of his acquaintance, a Madame Roy. I shall see her tomorrow. I hope that she

Ozzie is seated alone at a long blond wooden table in the Performing Arts Reading Room of the Library of Congress. The room is silent save for the rustle of paper and the clucking of laptop keys. Somewhere in the distance a copier is churning.

The notebook Ozzie is holding in her hands has a mottled gray cover of rough cardboard and bears the title, penned in brown ink, "American Diary, 1918." The first page bears the same title penned in the same brown ink. Four entries from January 1918, one of them partial, fill its reverse.

Inserted just here is a single sheet of lined paper folded into thirds on which, written in pencil in Flora's hand, are two lines of lyrics and their musical accompaniment:

Oh, where have you been, Billy Boy, Billy Boy?
Oh, where have you been, charming Billy?

Many of the following pages – perhaps half the notebook – have been ripped out.

Then what? There is no "then what." All the remaining pages are blank. When Ozzie saw this her heart emptied.

Ozzie had e-mailed the Library and made an appointment to view the Flora B. Lijak Collection. At the Reading Room desk she was greeted by a plump, cheery woman in middle age, the Music Reference Librarian, who gestured to a book-cart behind her desk loaded with eleven flat cardboard boxes. "These," she said, "are the Lijak Collection. You may take one box at a time to your table. This is so the contents of the boxes don't get mixed. As you work be sure you put the materials back in the box in the same order you took them out. When you're done with one box, just bring it back here, and we'll give you another. You may photograph or scan the materials. We'll make photocopies for you. Twenty cents a page.

"Also, a word on the Collection. Alice Neff, Flora's companion, inherited these materials from Flora and left them to the Library when she died. Alice, I mean. She'd put them in order. When her estate sent them to us, we pretty much followed her lead in preserving and cataloguing them. I should tell you, though, that we were reluctant to take the Collection. Frankly, Flora Lijak wasn't a very good musician. And not much of a composer either – her work just doesn't have value as music, and we'd never have taken this material based on its quality. But she was revered as a literary hero in the Soviet Union, like Jack London, and she was an important figure in political agitation in England and Russia, so we decided the material has what we call 'association value' – that is, in itself it isn't worth much, but considering who she was – her prominence as a revolutionist and as a writer – in the end we accepted the bequest. Anyway, good luck, and if you have any questions do let us know."

The Diary – Ozzie had had such hopes for it. It might have been a view, perhaps a deep one, into the life of a forgotten but powerful woman writer, a record of her struggles, her fears, her loves. Instead, the "Diary" contains only those four short entries! Who ripped the others out? Flora? Alice? Somebody else? And why?

Maddening.

Ozzie collects herself, then thinks: Still, Flora wrote this, this scrap of a diary. It isn't much but it isn't useless either. I now know that:

- Flora was living with Lijak in New York in early 1918.
- Alice Neff got hired on by Lijak sometime in January, like mid-month, of that year.
- Flora was working hard on those crazy plant drawings in the Manuscript.
- Flora consulted a man named Sims, who must have been a plant guy at the New York Public Library. Sims recommended that Flora see a Madame Roy downtown.

Ozzie has started with the last box, Box 11, "Personal Items, Miscellany," because the Library's Finding Aid listed a "Diary" among its contents. Box 11 contains three other items, each, like the Diary, protected in a ziplock bag: one is a cardboard box holding a five-by-seven inch portrait photograph of Wilfrid Lijak; another is a small spiral notebook with an orange cover, on which is written in ink in Flora's hand, "The Bacon Cipher"; the third is a spiral notebook, this one about six inches wide and eight inches long. It is labeled "Saltaire Tunes, September 4-8, 1937" in ink in Alice's hand. It has red covers.

Lijak's portrait is an elegant black-and-white photograph in a silvery frame, carefully posed and oh-so-casual. Lijak is seated facing the camera on a straight-backed wooden chair, which is turned right-side-to-the-viewer. Lijak's arm is riding the chair back. Though well into middle age, he's handsome and prosperous looking. He's clean-shaven save for a neatly trimmed mustache. He's wearing a light-colored, lightweight suit, a white shirt with French cuffs, a dark necktie and coordinated pocket handkerchief. In his left hand he's holding a silver-capped walking stick and a Panama hat; in his right, which dangles easily from the chair back, a lighted cigarette. He's wearing wire-rimmed glasses and is looking directly into the camera, coolly, assessingly, so different from that wary, fearful young man of the 1890s. The photograph was taken in New York (printed in italic at its base is, "Moffatt Studio, 751 Madison Avenue"). On its back is a penciled note in Flora's hand, "Love to Wilfrid on his Birthday, 21 October 1927."

The orange notebook contains Flora's jottings on the plant illustrations of the Manuscript. It is undated. This is the notebook Mark talked of. Mark thought Flora was trying to decode the Manuscript by guessing the identities of its plants and then somehow matching their names to the weird script. And never succeeding.

Flora's entries are few and terse:

Plants: fertility. Growth.
*Folio 43v, datura? Very likely. Almost certain. Mr. Sims concurs.
Folio 59v, Taro?
Folio 61r, Sunflower?
*Folio 57v, lords-and-ladies? Very likely.
Folio 58r, Heuchera? Hellebore?
Folio 42v, impatiens?

And more of the same for six or seven pages.

Futility.

The red notebook, "Saltaire Tunes," contains seven short songs transcribed in pencil in Flora's hand onto printed music sheets; a postcard; and a picture of a young girl running on a country lane.

The songs are simple, befitting their lyrics: "Now we see the ocean, Blue as blue can be…"

The postcard shows a party of four middle-aged women standing on a boardwalk in front of what looks like a row of beach houses. They are wearing summer dresses and wide-brimmed hats. On its right lower edge the postcard is entitled, "Broadway Saltaire, Fire Island, N.Y." The cancellation date on its one-cent leaf-green Benjamin Franklin stamp is September 10, 1937.

The message on the postcard's reverse reads: "Dear Pani Lijaka, I like your song very, very much. Mommie sang it to me in Polish and English. I am going to take it to kindergarten and ask Miss Thorn to teach it to all the children. How is Miss Neff? How are you? It is very rainy here today, worse than last Monday." The message is written in ink in an adult hand but is signed "ANIA" in pencil in a child's.

The picture of the running girl is printed in outline in black ink and is colored in – messily – in crayon. Ania has signed it at the bottom in the same child's hand as on the postcard. The girl, seen from her left, is running along a country lane holding a pig under her right arm and, in her left hand, what looks like a musical instrument, some kind of rustic black woodwind. Thanks to Ania, the girl has yellow hair, a pink blouse (with its ruff collar), and blue trousers. The sky is the same color as her trousers. Flowers of various colors sprout in the foreground and in the surrounding green fields. The country lane is orange.

These colors, Ozzie thinks, were left here by the small hand of a child named Ania, who was Polish and who will otherwise be unknown to me. In 1937 Ania was in kindergarten so she was probably born in 1932. Now she's an old, old woman or more likely is gone from us, whoever she was. Here she is, though, in this quiet Reading Room, complaining about her rainy day.

After scanning the contents of Box 11, Ozzie returns the box to the desk and begins to work through the others.

The Collection, as Mark said, consists almost entirely of Flora's music, score after score of it, box after box – piano pieces, chamber music, vast choral works, including "Jerusalem," which was written for one-hundred-person chorus and full orchestra. The Collection begins with a tone poem completed in 1910 entitled "Whitsuntide" and ends with a "Liberation Quartet" for strings, dated April 1945.

In all this, boxes 1 through 10, Ozzie finds no evidence that Flora's works were performed anywhere except at Sacred Heart College for Women - no concert programs from outside venues, no press clippings, no correspondence with conductors or performers: thirty-five years of music cloistered at Sacred Heart College and now silent.

Ozzie thinks of the old woman in the video. Her sweet face. A life lived.

Heart-breaking.

Flora's and Ania's are not the only spirits that hover about the Reading Room. Alice Neff's is here too. It was Alice, who out of devotion to Flora, assembled, sorted, and slipped into manila envelopes Flora's musical compositions and a few of her personal items.

Alice labeled those envelopes in her tight, precise hand, certain that they were destined for the Library of Congress and posterity. She would never learn what the Library thought of Flora – "not a good musician... not much of a composer... association value..." It doesn't matter. Here, thanks to Alice, repose Flora's works and artifacts from her life, never to be scattered or lost.

Apart from Alice's short appearance in the video of the visiting Russians, Ozzie has turned up only one image of her, a photograph taken in 1924 to accompany a newspaper story. In September of that year a New York paper profiled Alice – "Something More Than a Secretary." By then she had made a name for herself by producing a large catalogue of medieval manuscripts found in libraries across the United States. The paper's photograph shows a plain woman staring without emotion at the camera. She is wearing glasses that have round black frames. She has a blunt pageboy haircut.

Ozzie opens the folder "Neff" on her laptop and brings up the small amount of information she's been able to find on Alice, entirely from Web genealogical sites:

- Born New York City 1/12/1894.
- Parents German immigrants, Bernhard and Margareta Neff.
- Two siblings, younger, Emilia, Carl.
- 1900, 1910 Censuses report all five living in Buffalo.

The dates and addresses on Alice's correspondence with the publishers of Flora's music – in Boxes 7 and 10 – show that at some point after Lijak's death in 1930, Ozzie can't tell when, Alice and Flora moved together into an apartment complex called Tudor City at the end of 42nd Street on the East Side of Manhattan (the first letter to Alice at that address, from G. Schirmer, Inc., is dated March 23, 1933); from there, in 1939, they moved to another complex, the London Terrace Towers, in Chelsea, on the West side of town. Here they lived for two decades and here Flora died in 1960, then, at some later date, probably here too, Alice.

Ozzie thinks: That autumn visit to Fire Island, a well-known gay resort area – did they frequent the place? They knew at least one other woman there, Ania's "Mommie," whose name we do not know.

Old black and white newspaper illustrations are so drab, Ozzie thinks, they can lead you to believe that the past and the people living there were drab too, that they and their surroundings were just black and white and gray. But that's so wrong. Those people weren't decaying newsprint or fragile, ancient documents in dusty boxes. They lived as we live. They saw color, felt one another's flesh, smelled and tasted one another's bodies, were swept away, some of them, in torrents of passion.

When they first met in 1918 Flora was fifty-three and Alice twenty-four. At some point, they became lovers.

At the desk Ozzie asks to see the correspondence surrounding Alice's bequest to the Library. In time a young man emerges from a back office and brings to Ozzie's table a legal-size manila folder containing a few letters and other documents (interoffice notes, records of telephone calls and the like). It turns out that Alice's sister, Emily Seitz, of Buffalo (the Emilia of the censuses of 1900 and 1910), was executrix of Alice's estate. One of Emily's letters to the Library, its typewritten characters still slightly sunken into the paper, establishes that Alice died while residing at the London Terrace Towers in New York on September 24, 1961.

Barely a year after Flora.

Ozzie ponders this. With her companion – lover – of so many decades gone, was Alice seized with grief, did she feel no reason to live further? Did she sit on a sofa in their apartment crying, "Come back... Come back..."? Maybe she lived in order to put together the Flora B. Lijak Collection, and that was long enough.

Back home, Ozzie does a search for likely members of the Neff and Seitz families in Buffalo. She finds names, phone numbers, and street addresses. She sends an identical letter to five of the names explaining who she is, who Alice Neff was, that she – Ozzie – is researching a woman named Flora Lijak with whom Alice lived for decades ("I'd be very interested in any letters or papers Alice Neff may have left that would shed light on her working life and her relationship with the Lijaks."). She puts up a query on several Victorian and Feminist Literature list-serves:

I'd like information on the life of Flora Bowles Lijak, the author of Ribeiro. Please reply to azad.hosseini@gu.edu.

… and sends the same query to the *New York Review*. Messages in bottles, she thinks. Flung into the ocean. They'll drift on the waves.

Flora's orange notebook sends Ozzie back to the Weisert Web site and its high-res images of the Manuscript's plants.

These drawings, she thinks, this time paging with more care through the folios, are so precisely done, so – what other word? – so observed, yet each plant is wholly imagined. One specimen has star-shaped leaves of seven lobes overtopped with clusters of bristly, dark-green capsules. Another has two opposed disk-like heads, both chrome-yellow, that resemble twinned sunflowers. A third is an amber spike that rises on a slender green stem, arcing and hovering over a set of cones studded with what look like seeds. Who drew these things? What was the point?

Ozzie strays from the plants – the Manuscript pulls you in so – to the astrological section, lingering on the Manuscript's crudely drawn but recognizable signs of the Zodiac: Aries. Taurus. Gemini…

Arrayed around the signs, seated in tubs in concentric circles, are naked women, each holding a star in her hand or grasping a cord tethering a star that floats above her head. Thirty or thirty-one such women surround each sign, one woman and one star for each day of its month: Cancer. Leo. Virgo…

Virgo, Ozzie notices, unlike all the other women of the Lijak, is not naked. Virgo is clothed in a full-length gown of cornflower-blue, the color of the Virgin. Under her gown, Virgo's right breast thrusts up and forward: The Virgin Mother. Like her naked sisters, Virgo holds a cord tethering a star.

After the stars and the signs of the Zodiac come the bathing women. These hold no stars but recline in sinuous conduits or stand knee-deep in funnel-shaped tubs. Some wade in groups through watery pools, coordinated like aquatic teams.

So many women, Ozzie thinks. Male figures occur, yes - like Sagittarius with his crossbow – but males are rare and unobtrusive and are always clothed. Women preponderate, all of them save Virgo naked.

Covering almost every folio is the densely-written, unreadable script – Mark's "Lijakese." The strings of characters remind Ozzie of the work of a street crazy she encountered downtown her first winter in Washington, an old man, hatless, with dirty, white, wispy hair, who was wearing a woolen army overcoat and boots. He was sitting on the frigid concrete pavement in the Post Office peristyle on 12th Street near the entrance to the Federal Triangle Metro Station. His back against a stone column, his legs splayed, he was writing slowly and carefully in a notebook that had - she remembers this detail - a stiff, dark green cover marbled with white. The old man, absorbed in his work, seemed not to feel the cold.

Ozzie detoured his way to get a glance at what he was writing. Peering over his shoulder, slightly on the oblique and ready to get moving if he turned and noticed her, she saw that what he was writing with such care were numbers - no words, just numbers - page after page of them, printed precisely in thick, red ink, some short, some extravagantly long.

The Lijak Manuscript, could it be the work of an obsessed crazy? A madman - or madwoman - who simply poured out symbols and images that meant nothing?

No. Ozzie feels it. There is something here. But what?

For a time, she looks away from her flat-screen and the bathing women, then begins to take notes:

Document purports to speak. Doesn't, not to us – can't read it. Hidden world.

What meanings, secrets is it trying to convey? Who were its creators? What were their thoughts, dreams?

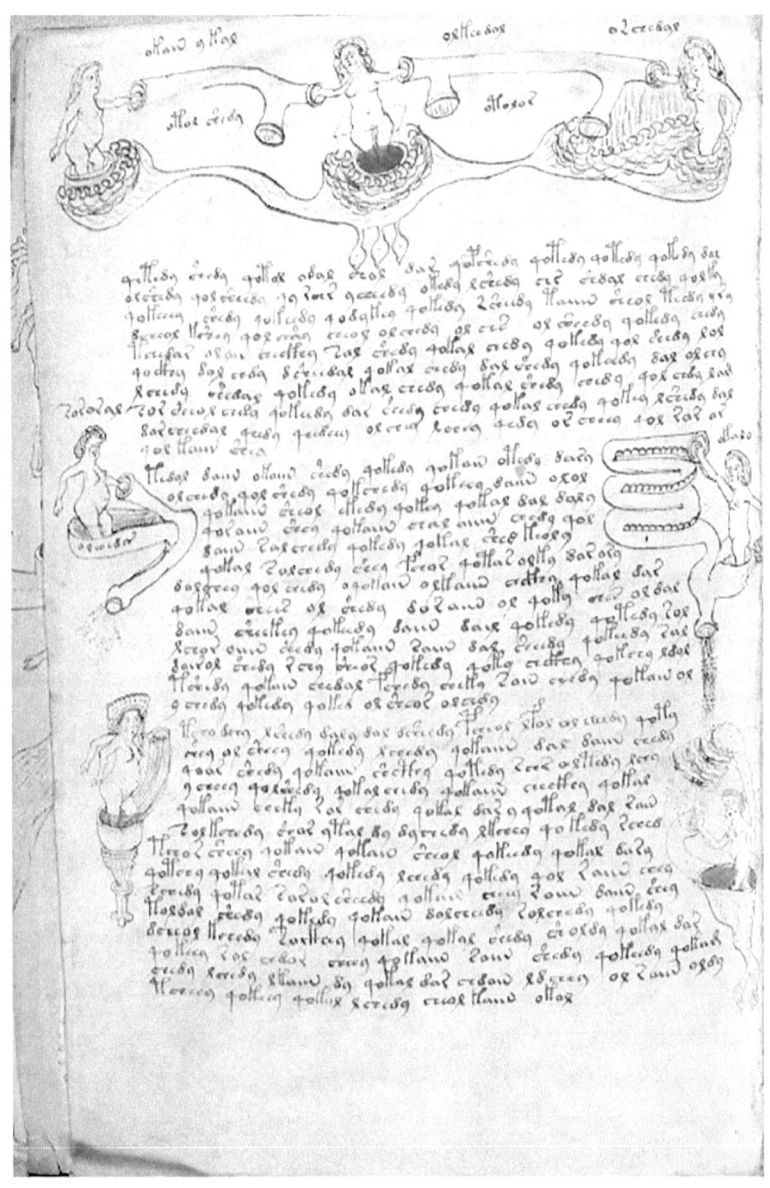

Naked women, protruding bellies, pools of green fluid, so much fluid.

Channels = birth canals?

Suns moons lunar circles (obvious fertility symbols) – – –

Also, the plants. Half the codex. Same: Fertility. Flora knew this, remarked on it in her notes.

Celebration of women? Women's power? Did a woman or women write, illustrate?

Manual of female lore?

Magical power? Enchantment?

Witchcraft?

CHAPTER VIII

"I Have Found a Happiness I Had Not Dreamt Possible."

This is how Flora Lijak and William McKenzie became lovers. On 3 August 1895, Flora left Italy for England, travelling home by way of Geneva, where she received a packet of revolutionary pamphlets and an encrypted letter, all smuggled from Russia. These she delivered to her husband when she arrived home on 9 August. Within days the Russian Free Press Fund had printed up the pamphlets in quantity, and Lijak was dispatched to the Continent with two large trunks of them to be dispersed amongst sympathisers who would smuggle them into Russia.

In her husband's absence, Flora worked tirelessly on *Ribeiro*. She arranged her notes; she sketched her characters; she plotted; she wrote; she discarded; she rewrote.

As in Florence, however, thoughts of McKenzie constantly entered her mind and would not leave. She had kept the letter she received from him in Florence ("I shall miss you so. I love you dearly and always will.") and had carried it back to England. She longed to see him yet feared the consequences of doing so and chose not to let him know she had returned. She knew, though, that they must encounter one another and soon, at a lecture or a concert or in someone's home. And so arose the fearful question, What then?

On a Sunday, the first after Lijak had left, Flora felt a need to get away from her work. It was a fine morning, cool for August, the sky clear, only a pink haze hovering over the city. She would make an outing. She would go to the Regent's Park, walk about, view the crowds, and listen to the speakers (on Sundays there were always speakers). The Zoo unfortunately would be closed, but no matter.

She took the Underground to Portland Road Station and emerged from the fug of the Underground into daylight and fresh air. In the park she strolled up Broad Walk, savouring the reds and whites and yellows of the roses and the bright green of the grass all about her and looking, perhaps wistfully, at the young couples out for a Sunday walk, who seemed happy and innocent and content. She bought a sweet bun for a penny.

When she came to the White Fountain, she saw Herbert Nicholson, the Anarchist, standing on a box ebulliently bantering with a small crowd of men, half of whom looked like detectives. As she drew near someone yelled something about the workhouse, probably that Nicholson should be confined in one. Nicholson laughed and replied, "Oh, aye, the workhouse, but if a man's hungry and he can't get work, he still must have bread, and he should take it. And if he be sent to prison for the taking, then that's society's crime. And shame."

There was sympathetic whistling here.

Someone shouted, "If a man's hungry he should take a loaf and not be sent to prison."

Hear-hears ran around the crowd and more whistling was heard.

Someone yelled, "Ah, you're just a lazy, thieving Anarchist, you are!"

"I'm a man! And all men must have bread!" Nicholson roared back, punching his right fist into his left palm.

Applause was heard here. Another listener, tiring of the subject of bread, yelled, "And will you allow interest?"

"Interest? Of course not! Interest - there's your thievery!"

There was more give-and-take shouting like this, mostly good-natured.

Nearby, Olivia and Helen Rossetti were pacing about, selling copies of THE TORCH, the Anarchist journal they edited and printed in the second story of a shed over fetid Ossulston Street (horse droppings, urine of various origins, butchers' offal, clam shells, oyster shells, the remains of rotten vegetables, and straw, all mixed in the mire and trampled under).

Olivia and Helen and their younger brother Arthur had begun producing THE TORCH two years before in the basement of their home in St Edmond's Terrace, not far from the Park, but their father, William Rossetti, a civil servant and brother of the poetess Christina Rossetti and the artist and poet Dante Gabriel Rossetti, after enduring his children's revolutionary activities for a year, had ejected them.

Olivia, hugging copies of THE TORCH, was talking with a respectably dressed young man, trying to persuade him of the merits of the Anarchist Cause, but he seemed dubious.

Flora was approaching Helen to say hello when of a sudden she saw, standing opposite across the walk, alone, William McKenzie. He saw her at the same time and started, then turned to face her directly, fixing his eyes on hers. She returned his stare. Later she said it had been a whipcrack, catching sight of him there, after which all became clarity.

He approached her; she stood coolly in place.

"You're back," he said over the shouting of the Anarchists and anti-Anarchists.

"Yes."

"Did you get my letter?"

"Yes."

"You didn't answer."

"I could not."

"I meant what I said."

"I know."

He took her hand, drawing it to his chest, guiding her touch over his heart. "We're meant to be one, my dear Flora. We will be."

She retracted her hand, but lingeringly and never taking her eyes from his.

"We must not be seen like this."

"Then let's go somewhere else. And not be seen."

He had sat on his bed. She had stood before him, dress undone to her waist. She loosened her linen slip-bodice, pulled it back, exposing her breasts, and moved to him. She put her arms about him and very gently kissed his face. He brought her to recline. She heard boots dropping, then clothes. Outside, children had been playing, their piping cries floating through McKenzie's open window. She had not calculated there might be a child. She had not calculated.

McKenzie, naked, lay back, eyes half-closed. When she dared look on him, her breath caught. An opportunity she had never had presented itself: she studied his large shoulders and rippling chest, his flat stomach, his male parts: David, she thought, the slayer of giants, not standing now with sling and stone, but in repose, after love. Toward this naked warrior she felt an ineffable tenderness.

She did not think of the future. McKenzie's future was McKenzie's, hers hers. McKenzie would go where the winds of the Cause took him, and that was as it would be. She saw herself in no future with him, only a fiery present.

Leaving McKenzie's room, they walked up Needham Lane, past the drunken idlers (McKenzie's acquaintances), through the slops and waste water emptied from the second stories of McKenzie's tenement and his neighbours', along the brick wall against which costers' barrows had been backed (each with a wheel pulled off to prevent its theft), past the stables, past the oilmonger's, past the tobacconist's, and finally through the stone archway that led out to the Commercial Road. McKenzie then stole his arm about

Flora's waist and leant his head on hers.

"You are my beloved," he said softly. It was then that he began calling her "Goddess" and "Divine Fire."

When they had got to Whitechapel Station, he was about to enter with her, but she demurred. "No, no, it's all right, I shall be fine."

"I love you, my dear Flora."

"And I you."

Over the further three weeks and three days that Lijak remained on the Continent, Flora and McKenzie saw each other almost daily. McKenzie came to The Grove in the evenings after Sarah had left (he often saw a police spy lurking on the pavement opposite) but never stayed the night. Less frequently, Flora came to him in Mile End. (Her visits were noted and remembered in his observant neighbourhood.) To prevent conception they carefully took precautions, all those that were available at the time.

Neither Flora nor McKenzie believed in destiny, but their accidental meeting in the Regent's Park that Sunday morning gave each the sense that their love had been fated.

One evening when McKenzie had come to The Grove and he and Flora were sitting together in the parlour, she said, "I've a song for you. It's an old English ballad."

Flora sat at the piano and played and sang the English folk song "My Boy Billy":

Where have you been all this day, my boy Billy?
Where have you been all this day, pretty Billy? tell me.

She repeated the lines, then played the answering tune:

I have been all this day,

Courting with a lady gay,
But she is too young to be taken from her mother,
But she is too young to be taken from her mother.

McKenzie recognised the song from its American variant, which he had learnt from his mother. At night when Nell McKenzie would tuck Billy and his brother Frank into bed, she would, sometimes, lean over Billy and sing this song:

Oh, where have you been, Billy Boy, Billy Boy?
Oh, where have you been, charming Billy?
I have been to seek a wife,
She's the joy of my life,
But she's a young thing and cannot leave her mother.

McKenzie's mother Nell had a sweet soprano voice. The memory of her singing to him made him ache.

McKenzie tried to hum, then whistle the American version of the tune for Flora (he hadn't his mother's gift for song). Flora followed him with one finger, quickly working out the tune to McKenzie's approval. She added chords and played it out, singing the American words, as McKenzie rested his arm on the piano lid and smiled down on her.

"You're my 'charming Billy'," she said, and that is when she started calling him, "Billy Boy" or simply "Billy," a name she used with him ever after.

The next afternoon Flora's sister Evelyn paid a call at The Grove. Evie, her dearest and closest confidante, knew the nature of Flora's marriage to Lijak, which saddened her. Now Flora was burning to tell her of "Billy". As they embraced and kissed in the entrance hall, Flora said, "Sis, we must take a walk."

Directly they were out the door Flora turned toward Evie and said, "I've a lover."

Evie's eyes widened. "Oh, dear Flora!" she cried, first bringing her hands to her face, then quickly grasping both of Flora's. "Do I know him?"

"By reputation. He is the American journalist I met at our Anglo-Russian soirée in the spring. I wrote to you of him. You've forgotten."

"Is he handsome?"

"Very."

"You are happy?"

"I am. I have found a happiness I had not dreamt possible."

"Oh, Flora, then I am so terribly happy for you! Shall I meet him?"

"Yes, of course, if you wish."

"I do!"

Billy became their conspiracy.

In 1899 Evelyn Bowles will elope to Tokyo with a married man named Charles Merton. There, Merton, who had a degree in mathematics from Cambridge, will teach mechanical engineering in the Imperial University. In 1901 Merton and Evelyn will move to New Haven, Connecticut, where Merton will teach physics at Yale University, then, in 1903, to Washington, D.C., where he will work in the U.S. Patent Office. In the winter of 1907, Merton will die of a heart attack, collapsing face-down in a snow-drift just outside his and Evelyn's rented rowhouse in East Capitol Street. Ten months later, deeply despondent over Merton's death and nearly penniless, Evelyn will kill herself in a boarding house on Capitol Hill by running a rubber tube from a gaslight fixture to her mouth.

Today, however, she beamed on her sister, and once even threw her head back to laugh to the sky and exult.

Sunday a week, Flora and Billy made a holiday. Flora packed a lunch, and together they travelled to Hampstead Heath by train and omnibus. At the north edge of the Heath, they sat on the grass and viewed in the distance the eastern parts of London. Because of the superb weather, the crowds – in the summer of 1895 some fifty-thousand persons might visit the Heath on a fine day – were thick and exuberant. Children ran about. Dogs barked. Cricket bats tapped. Close-by, to their left, a pretty, rosy-cheeked girl and handsome boy of the working classes were seated on a blanket eating fresh tomatoes. Close-by to their right, a large, noisy family were shouting and flying kites, even the mother in her high-laced boots.

Flora said, "Billy Boy, the world is too much with us. Let's get away. Come on, follow me." Flora led Billy to a secluded footpath she knew which led over to the Finchley Road. Blackberries were ripening on either side, and they picked and ate them as they walked. In a few minutes they came to a field enclosed by a wood-en paling and punctuated with hayricks. The nearer hayricks, still damp from a rain, gave off a thick, sweet smell. Here in the shade of a chestnut tree they picnicked on Flora's sandwiches of buttered bread and ham and on the eggs and apples she had packed.

After eating they lay in silence. Presently Flora asked, "Can love last, Billy Boy?"

"Yes."

"Can ours?"

"Yes."

They were silent a moment, then, Billy, not looking at Flora, said, "How time rushes."

"Yes."

Flora moved her hand toward Billy's. He caught her gesture in the corner of his eye and joined his hand to hers. Both were thinking of Lijak's return. Neither mentioned it.

———

That night, after Billy had left and Flora lay just on the borders of sleep, she felt wonderment. The realisation that she loved Billy fully and in every sense was like an exotic chord, previously unimagined, that rang in her depths. Then she dreamt (or was it wished?) that Lijak had died. She came awake in horror, asking herself, What am I doing? What have I become? And if my husband learns of Billy, of our affair – what then? What anguish will he feel? Or shame? She told herself that she must end this business with Billy before Wilfrid returned, but when she reflected on what she would lose by doing so, she could not bear the thought.

OZZIE

You're smiling.

Thinking.

About what?

A girl. And her mother. I saw them out running together. They were having a good time. They bumped hips once. That's all.

Hunh... Hey, gee, what's... what's this? ... Hey, Oz, what's...?

Nothing.

You shouldn't feel... Sorry, what's...?

No, no, no, no, I'm okay, it isn't anything. I'm okay. Really. No, no... no, I feel good. It's happiness.

She wiped her tears with her hands and shifted the sheet and blanket back over them. It was chilly in his room.

Mark had called Ozzie at her office. She thanked him again for the Lijaks' marriage certificate. She mentioned viewing the Flora B. Lijak Collection at the Library.

Not a lot there. And it's hard to piece together what is there. In fact, you can't. I mean, okay, there's all her musical compositions but not a lot of other stuff. The Diary sounded promising, but it's disappointing. Just a few entries.

Yeah. See her notes on the Manuscript? The plants?

Yes. Not much substance. Just guesses.

Yeah.

So, I took another look at the Manuscript, a closer look. When you think about the imagery – the plants, the astral stuff,

176

and especially the naked ladies? In their pools and streams and all that? – it looks like – I don't know, it's not feminist, they didn't have feminism back then, whenever the thing was composed, but let's call it "female-ist" - woman-centered. And sexual. Maybe witchcraft. That'd be my guess anyway.

Witchcraft?

Benign witchcraft.

Good witches?

Right. Like Glinda in the *Wizard of Oz*.

Hunh. Have to think about that.

You're not buying it.

Not sure. But if it's witchcraft there'll have to be two witches. Two...?

The Lijak's written in two different dialects. They're called Lijak A and Lijak B. You can tell the difference in the words that are used – if they're words. We've known this since the 1940s. The difference runs all through the work. So, two dialects. Also, the Lijak is written in two different hands. And the difference in hands and the difference in dialects coincide.

God, you people sure have picked this thing over. Two dialects, two hands. So maybe we've got a coven? Of two?

Could be. The Lijak Club at the Fort, I'll tell them your witch theory.

Pause.

Anyhow, I was wondering if you'd feel like taking another walk sometime.

Yes. Sure.

She'd been thinking of him. She'd seen da Silva, her OB-GYN, and had gone on the pill again. When writing the prescription, da Silva had given her a look of fond approval.

How about the Mall? Saturday afternoon?

Fine.

If it rains, we could go to a museum or something.

Sounds good.

———

Saturday afternoon was warm and overcast, but it didn't rain. They walked from the Lincoln Memorial, past the ponds and bridges and gardens, to the Monument, then crossed 14th Street to the part of the Mall where the museums start. Here – they were just passing the Smithsonian's red stone Castle and the deep blue-bronze statue of Joseph Henry – Mark offered to cook dinner.

She thought he'd say something like that, that that's how he'd work it.

She said sure.

Mark's apartment was on the fifth floor of a large, flimsy, six-story building close-in in Arlington. It was a one-bedroom with a living area and, near the kitchen, a small dining space. Two picture windows gave a view of the apartment parking lot and of Langston Boulevard climbing into Virginia. On the horizon, silhouetted against the sunset, were more apartment buildings.

Mark lived sparely: in the living area were a couch that looked new, a stereo, and under the window two low bookcases; in the dining area a Shaker-style, drop-leaf dining table and four straight-backed chairs.

He kept his apartment neat, as she had expected. Nothing was strewn around. Magazines and newspapers lay in tidy piles on what he called his "coffee locker," a battered black footlocker he'd placed in front of his couch, on which his name and an old address were written in blue paint. He kept his bicycle just inside the door.

In the zone between the living and dining areas sat a large rectangular wicker basket containing books (*But Not The Hippopotamus, Thomas The Tank Coloring Book*) and toys (Junior Monopoly, Monster-Sized Dinosaur) for Ollie. On the windowsill in the dining area sat a planter – Ollie's seeds project. You watch them sprout, Mark said, watch the green shoots grow, then they bloom into – hey! boom! snap dragons!

Mark cooked Chinese – spicy diced chicken breast and rice. When, to begin, he threw grated ginger and dried Szechuan peppers into his wok they sizzled explosively in the searing peanut oil, throwing off a cloud of choking, cough-inducing fumes that filled his apartment, making Mark and Ozzie laugh together, tears in their eyes, as Mark cranked open the casement windows to let in air.

Afterward, sitting on the couch, they talked, sipping Chablis left over from dinner. Then, after a silence, he touched his hand to hers.

She smiled at him.

They kissed. Chastely at first. Then, not. Then, warmth, rising. Then, hand in hand to his bedroom. Then, clothes, his, dropped on the floor, hers in the one chair.

Then, waves.

Next morning, he called.

Hi. It's me. I just wanted to say I had a wonderful time.

So'd I. Hey, come over sometime. See how I live.

They settled on Wednesday night. She cooked, he stayed the night. They made love before sleep and again in the morning.

And so, they began to share their lives. Wednesday nights he stayed at her place, Saturday nights she stayed at his.

On a brilliant Saturday afternoon, they took Ollie, who did not stiffen when Ozzie hugged him, in fact hugged back, to Rock Creek Park and chased minnows at Peirce Mill. Mark pointed to the herring ladder beside old man Peirce's dam and told Ollie that the ladder allowed herring – little fish – to swim up-stream and lay eggs. Ollie was disappointed that there were no herring, but Mark told him it wasn't time for them yet. A little later maybe, he said, glancing at Ozzie, we'll come back. Maybe we'll see the herring.

On another Saturday Mark and Ozzie – just the two of them – hiked Sugarloaf Mountain, a forested monadnock just south of Frederick, Maryland. On the sheer north side of the mountain they found a ledge where they sat and gazed on the Monocacy River below and toward Frederick, half hidden in its valley. At just their altitude a hawk circled, catching the updrafts, tilting on its wings, then suddenly plummeted from sight, leaving the vast sky empty.

Ozzie gave Mark an electronic pass that let him enter and park in her apartment building's underground garage. At his apartment she left a brocade satchel containing a bathrobe, a toothbrush, toothpaste, a Tampax cylinder, perfume spray (Amarige – a gift from Tom), and a pair of panties. Eyeing the satchel, he told her that his apartment had been sterile, nothing of the feminine there, but now there is – that satchel with its silvery floral pattern is just enough to hint at a feminine presence. He told her that when they lie in one another's arms she leaves the imprint of her right ear on his chest. She told him that she hears his heart. It's what she used to tell Tom: I hear your heart. Now she was telling Mark. She knew that in doing this she was not betraying Tom. She realized then that she had fallen deeply, crashingly in love.

Grace calls.

"Hey, Mom."

"Hi, Oz. Just checking in. How's it going?"

Ozzie will not talk of her fear, diminished in intensity now but ever-present, that she will lose her job.

"Hey, okay. How're you doing?"

"Oh, swamped as usual. I've got two new cases, one child custody, one stalking. I thought they'd be easy but no, no, no, they're turning out to be a lot of work. Warren's busy too. He's on call at night right now plus hospital rounds. They rotate at his practice. But we still manage to see each other."

"Mom, is this going somewhere?"

"I'd like it to. I think. Not sure."

"Not sure it's going somewhere or not sure you'd like it to?"

Ozzie hears Grace's breath on the phone. A laugh? Nerves?

Just Grace breathing?

"Little of both, I guess." Another breath. "Not sure."

It's time.

"Mom, I've got some news – I'm dating a guy."

There's a delay here, as if the signal had to bounce off the moon, then: "Oh, wow! That's wonderful, Oz! Oh, I'm so happy for you! Who is he?"

Ozzie tells her about Mark, Ollie, not about Anne, not much anyway. How they met, how long it's been going on.

"So, you really like the guy?"

"Yeah. Yeah, I really do."

I hear his heart.

CHAPTER IX

"This," She Said, "Shall be Our Bower."

Pastens Rd.
Limpsfield

10 September '95

Dear Bulochka,

We shall vacate our cottage on the 15th. We have been here too long this summer, and I am accomplishing nothing. I have hired the place through the month, however. Would you and Lijak wish to come down and stay some days? The neighbourhood is beautiful, and I believe you could work. Or if not work, then you and he could rest a bit and refresh yourselves. Do let me know.

Stepniak

Sergei and Fanny Stepniak had taken a tiny cottage for the summer at Limpsfield, a village near Oxted in Surrey, an hour by train south of London. Amongst the intellectual and aesthetic circles of the period Limpsfield and its environs were fashionable places to reside. (So many Russian exiles and their English friends lived there, summers or year-round, the town had come to be known as "Dostoyevsky Corner.") When hiring his cottage Stepniak had told friends he wanted "the simple life" so that he could be remote from the city and rest from lecturing and his social duties and think and write, but it turned out he did not like being remote from the city and found it impossible to work in Limpsfield. He longed for London.

Stepniak's offer arrived only two days after Lijak had returned from travel on the Continent and one day after he had had a blazing row with Feliks Volkhovsky, Leonid Shishko, and Nikolai Chaikovsky.

The row was this: at a tense meeting in the Iffley Road offices, Volkhovsky, Shishko, and Chaikovsky confronted Lijak and accused him of misusing monies of the Russian Free Press Fund. Volkhovsky, in cold, quiet anger, his unblinking eyes fixed on Lijak's, spoke for the group: "Mikhail Leonich, you returned only yesterday after more than a month on the Continent. Fund business did not require so much time. We believe you are extending your stays abroad for your own benefit and you are using Fund monies to do so. We also believe that you are 'borrowing' surreptitiously from the Fund to buy the books you sell to wealthy Englishmen. This is improper and unacceptable, even if you pay the monies back." When Volkhovsky said this, Shishko and Chaikovsky nodded grimly.

For a moment Lijak sat speechless and gasping, then cried, "Feliks Vadimovich, this is disgusting! And insulting! The accounts are open, for God's sake. Anyone can look."

"Don't be ridiculous," Volkhovsky said, his eyes never leaving Lijak's. "As you are treasurer and you manage the cash and as you also keep the books no one can tell whether you are lending yourself from the monies of the Fund. What you say is silly. And insulting. You are lending to yourself from the Fund's accounts. You must end the practice."

"I'm... The practice? The practice? There is no practice to end! As to the items I purchase abroad, my God, you know Flora and my circumstances! You are aware she and I have at times gone without food because we had so little income. Feliks Vadimovich, you are revolting!"

Volkhovsky replied, "You are not fully trust-worthy, Mikhail

Leonich. And you are head-strong and wilful. We intend to find someone else to deliver Fund publications to the Continent."

At this Lijak stormed from the offices determined that he would never speak again to Volkhovsky, Shishko, or Chaikovsky. He had long been contemplating leaving the Fund and ceasing his work at *Free Russia* to devote all his time to his growing trade in rare books. Now, with aspersions cast on his honour, he decided to leave the Movement immediately and forever.

Lijak angrily recounted all this to Flora as soon as he returned home, pacing their parlour, red-faced, his rage surging. "My God, I have worked tirelessly for the Cause. I've given my life to it and have suffered for it beyond measure, in prison and in exile. I've crisscrossed Europe repeatedly to ensure that our publications reach Russia. I've worked hard and honestly as treasurer of the Fund. No monies have been stolen. All the books are regular. Yet now these so-called 'comrades' of mine are treating me as a thief! I cannot express the humiliation! I am not a thief, I am not a thief!" He collapsed into a chair, panting.

Flora tried to console her husband with kind words, standing behind him, massaging his shoulders. After a time, he seemed to come round. She had known, of course. She thought, Yes, you have dipped into the monies of the Fund. You have not told me of this, but I know that you must have done. I am sure, too, that you have repaid the Fund and that the accounts are square. And, yes, we did starve, or come close to it, and the income from your book sales saved us. Your behaviour was understandable and excusable. You are leaving the Movement? Well, so am I. I am resolved to be a writer and to earn my way in life through my literary work. I shall resign my position at *Free Russia*, though I will retain my friendships there. I love you still as I always have, but I have found a new love of a different order and intensity, and I must be true to that love as well. My dearest Wilfrid, we may part.

———

The following day, when Stepniak's invitation arrived, Lijak told Flora he was tired and depressed, particularly after the row with Volkhovsky and the others, and had not been sleeping well. He wanted simply to be at home. Flora replied that she would relish a few days in the country, and he assented to her going without him. Flora wrote Stepniak accepting his offer and explaining that Lijak would not be accompanying her. Then she wrote and posted this:

12 September 1895

149, The Grove

Billy Boy, I have been invited to spend a week or so (to the end of the month) at the Stepniaks' cottage at Limpsfield. They are returning to London before they had planned. I shall arrive at Limpsfield the 19th & they will depart the 20th. Wilfrid will remain in London. The cottage is in Pastens Road, s.e. of the town. The carriage drivers at Oxted Station know it. I should receive a certain guest most warmly. The 21st?

Flora

To which Billy replied:

September 12

I'll be there.

On Tuesday, 19 September, Flora caught the 12:21 train from London Bridge and arrived at Oxted at 1:15 in the afternoon. She hired a trap to the Stepniaks' cottage, which she found in a beech-tree lane next an apple orchard and overlooking a meadow. Two cherry trees flanked the entrance path. When she knocked at the door, she found Fanny alone inside, peeling and slicing potatoes for dinner. Stepniak came in presently (he had been out gathering wood for the stove and fire), brandishing a huge axe and looking like a medieval warrior. He embraced Flora and all three sat and talked.

Fanny said, "When first we arrived, we had nothing whatever – no furniture, not the least utensil. We were able to borrow some things from kindly neighbours, but for a time we had to eat off paper using sticks. Seryozha white-washed the interior, but when he did, he white-washed himself as well! Completely! – and I had to wrap him in my shawl while I laundered his clothes!"

Stepniak said, "Edward and Marjorie Pease are here." (The Peases sat on the General Committee of the Society of Friends of Russian Freedom.) "As are Edward and Constance Garnett. You'll find dozens of the Arts and Crafts sort in cottages roundabout. They paint, they poetize, they weave. One of them, a man named Carpenter" - Stepniak laughed and bulged his eyes - "makes sandals! Marvelous company! Well, Fanny has worked too hard this summer." When Fanny shook her head demurring (though not vigorously) he said affectionately, "Yes, yes, yes, you have, and you know it. And I'm unproductive, and we are both bored, so we are off."

Early next morning Stepniak walked to Oxted and procured a carriage to transport himself, Fanny, and luggage to the station. Flora rode with them to see them off, then walked back through Limpsfield, where she bought bread, butter, cheese, eggs, sugar, and tea (the Stepniaks had left their larder all but empty).

That night, anticipating her lover, thinking of his touch, Flora lay awake. Beyond her window and its decaying lace curtain a bright full moon glided horizontally across the empty sky. Before it disappeared from her view, she fell asleep.

Billy came down next afternoon, and for seven days he and Flora played at country life. Flora first showed Billy the cottage: the cozy sitting room on the ground floor with its one small, latticed window and yellow curtain; the fireplace corner and the two comfortable armchairs facing it; the simple wooden dining table on which sat a wrought iron oil lamp; the scullery. In the upstairs room, where the night before Flora had watched the moon pass, she brushed Billy's face with her fingertips. They kissed and made love then and there.

That evening they sat side by side in the two chairs before a popping, hissing fire built from the wood that Stepniak had cut. In the flickering light Billy said, "I don't think you know how beautiful you are." He took her hand and kissed the fingertips that earlier had brushed his face. He and Flora continued holding hands, watching the dance of the flames.

She said, "I think of you constantly, wherever I am, whatever I'm doing." Then with despair, "Oh, Billy, I love you so."

He said softly, "We live in the today, don't we, Goddess? We forget our yesterdays and we don't think about our tomorrows." He turned his face to her. "What about our tomorrows?"

"I don't know, Billy, I don't know."

Do not ruin our time, she thought.

Next day they woke to the churring of a ringdove. Late to rise, they breakfasted on the cheese, bread, eggs, and tea that Flora had bought, then went for a cross-country walk. They passed a copse where woodcutters were chopping and singing at their work. They crossed a hayfield, which was newly in stubble, then climbed a grassy ridge. At the summit there was a wind, and Flora was glad she had a chin-stay for her straw hat. In the distance a wagon drawn by two horses lumbered toward the far rise. Coming opposite was a lone cyclist (it was Mrs Pease, in bloomers, venturing forth in the rutted lane). They saw no other human activity.

Continuing across the fields they got as far as Westerham, where they lunched at The Green Man. Billy had a pint of ale and Flora a lemon squash.

Returning by road, they came to the common known as

Limpsfield Chart, on which sheep were silently grazing. Here they turned south and entered a public wood of sweet chestnut, hazel, silver birch, and oak. The wood, purposed long before by some Oxted notable for the hunting of deer, had escaped the plough. Somewhere on the other side lay their cottage, and they decided to cross through. Though there were no paths, and leaves were thick on the ground, the walking was easy. They came to a mossy brook and by it a growth of underwood and bush that formed a small covert. Flora looked about, then did something extraordinary: she gripped Billy's right hand, hard, in the two of hers, her eyes glistening, and dropped to the long grass, bringing him down with her.

"This," she said, "shall be our bower."

OZZIE

Rita Kronenberg. "The Paris Agentura: The Tsarist Secret Police in Europe." CIA Studies in Intelligence. Stepniak… Wilfrid Lijak… *Free Russia*… Okhrana… Download PDF.

In the dark of her office nook, staring into the cold glow of her flat-screen, Ozzie notices a hit she hasn't seen before. The link takes her to a document published in-house by CIA in 1977. It has just been declassified and put up on the Web by something called "The CIA Center for the Study of Intelligence." Its author is Rita Kronenberg.

Her breath catching, Ozzie scrolls quickly through the document, which details the operations in Europe in the 1890s of the Tsarist secret police, known as the Okhrana. Flora, achingly, tantalizingly, is mentioned once:

> In all major European capitals, Okhrana operatives made free use of retired police officers and others as informants. In London, individuals such as Sergei Stepniak-Kravchinsky, Felix Volkhovsky, Ivan Serov as well as Wilfrid and Flora Lijak of the Free Russia group came under such surveillance. All were subjects of written reports.

On the Web Ozzie turns up four Rita Kronenbergs, two of them dead, none of them, living or dead, likelies for this Rita Kronenberg.

As she's searching for Rita, Mark calls, as he does every evening now.

"Mark, I can't believe it, I've found this thing, this article – about Russians spying on Flora? Some kind of CIA thing? It talks about the Tsarist secret police and about 'reports' they wrote. Like on Flora and Lijak? And their friends?"

"Wow. Hey, cool."

"Right. Well, those reports must exist somewhere. Got to. And I really, really want to know what they say."

"Hunh. What's the title again?"

Ozzie tells him.

"Hang on."

She hears keys clicking in the background. "Hang on, hang on... Okay... Hang on... Right. Got it. The article. Okay. Russian secret police. Okay... just declassified, okay, okay, it's old enough, so they declassified it and printed it in *Studies in Intelligence*. That's a journal they produce. Open to the public. And they put it up on the Web."

"Mark, this thing's about Russian secret police in the nineteenth century. Tsarist stuff. Why'd they classify it in the first place?"

"CIA employs historians. They write up intelligence history for their spies, who are supposed to learn from it. Some do, some don't. Point is, they don't want outsiders knowing what they care about. They even classify newspaper articles so people won't know what they're reading."

"This article dates from the '70s – and they're just declassifying it?"

"CIA. It's who they are."

"You're probably worse." Meaning NSA.

"Yeah, we are, actually. Unnh... Oz, can I call you back? Might take a few minutes but I'll get back."

"She's in Bethesda. Your Rita." He gives Ozzie an address and phone number and says, "She's way old. In her nineties. Only, her name's not Rita Kronenberg, it's Esther Kominsky. Rita Kronenberg's an alias."

"Alias? How'd you find that out?"

"I talked to a friend."

So easy. Ozzie feels a quantum of disquiet at this, but says, "Well, hey, thanks."

"Going to get in touch?"

"Sure. I mean I'm going to try. She's so old, I don't know..."

"Right. She may be pretty feeble. Unnh, if she's alert, she might want to know how you found her, and you'll have to have a story."

"What?"

"They declassified her article but not her identity – her identity's secret. Still. She might not want to talk with you."

"Oh, God."

"I'd give her a call and tell her the truth. Tell her that her article's just been declassified and that you saw it on the Web – if she understands what the Web is. And if she... if she gives you trouble, tell her that you know someone in the quote 'intelligence community' and that he told you who she is. You can also say that Russian scholars outside the government – academics, think-tank types – know her work and have a pretty good idea who 'Rita Kronenberg' was. Or is."

"Is that true?"

"Yes. Really. She probably knows all this anyway."

"All this?"

"That people know who she is."

Why is this conversation bothering me?

Mark says, 'Hey, I miss you."

"I miss you."

Whoever you are.

"'Night, Oz. Good luck with 'Rita.' Let me know."

"Hey, sure, thanks. 'Night."

Punching off, Ozzie breathes out through her mouth.

Oh, Mark, with those exquisite eyes and those sensuous, caressing lips, you are kind and sweet and decent, but finding Esther was terribly easy for you. You're NSA. Do you know too much? You're not an experiment, are you? I love you. Dearly. Don't be an experiment.

"I feel as the Sibyl of Cumae must have felt – so very, very old. Cumae was a town on the Italian coast, and the Sibyl was a prophetess who lived in a cave nearby. People came to consult her. Over the years she grew old in the darkness of her cave, but she never died, she just withered away, until finally she was only a voice. That's me now, just a voice. But I don't foretell the future. I tell the past. Or used to. Now I'm the past."

Esther Kominsky is spectral, like Flora Lijak in her last days: Esther's gray hair is pulled back and up in a disorderly bun, her skin, like Flora's, looks terribly woundable, her body fragile and bent with age.

Ozzie called the number Mark had given her. Someone picked up. After a short silence Ozzie heard a feeble, Yes?

Ms. Kominsky?

There was more silence, then another feeble, Yes?

Hi, Ms. Kominsky. My name's Ozzie Hosseini. You don't know me, but I teach English at Georgetown University. I was doing some research the other day and I ran across an article you wrote a long time ago that mentioned a person I'm interested in. The article – maybe you remember it, it was called "The Paris Agentura"? – am I pronouncing that right? It was about the Russian secret police in Paris in the 1890s and it mentioned a woman I'm researching, a woman writer named Flora Lijak. I wondered if we could talk about it? Your article?

Pause.

Article?

This is going to be so hard.

For an instant, Ozzie pictured Moo Moo lying in her nursing home outside Hartford, soundless as a stone and as inert, eyes open, watching the light shift on the ceiling of her room.

Yes, Ms. Kominsky, an article you wrote in the 1970s. It's about...

An article?

Esther finally understood.

Ah. Yes. Yes, I did that. Wrote that. An article. Several articles. They were my field. Russians. Rachkovsky, the rest. Yes. But how did you find me?

Ozzie told her the truth.

After a moment's quiet, Esther said, So long ago. My work. You're at Georgetown?

Yes. I teach English.

English? And you want to know about the Paris Okhrana?

Yes. According to your article they did reports on dissidents. I'm interested in a person named Flora Lijak. She...

You must come visit.

Esther and Ozzie are sitting in Esther's apartment — Esther lives in a retirement colony off Rockville Pike in North Bethesda — having tea and cookies. These have been served by Julia, Esther's home care companion, a tall, boney Black woman with a quick smile who appears to be somewhere in her fifties. Julia's gone to the kitchen to prepare Esther's dinner.

Esther has already asked Ozzie about her name and Ozzie has explained it ("My father's Persian..."). Now Esther's telling Ozzie of her own life. She speaks slowly, but, as Ozzie notes, in complete sentences that form into paragraphs.

"I was born at seven in the morning on the seventh day of the seventh month of the year. Do all those sevens mean anything? No. Silly coincidences. The Sibyl of Cumae, by the way, was the seventh sibyl of the ancient world — they had ten — which particularly endears her to me. But I was born in Detroit, which has nothing at all to do with sibyls.

"We were from Russia. My father's father's name was Shmuil Sinyavsky. He'd been drafted into the army as a young man. He was a common soldier. My father liked to say that his father peeled potatoes for the Tsar. Later my grandfather Shmuil kept a tavern off in some provincial town. He had red hair, and my father didn't like him. That's all I know about him. My father and my mother married and left Russia. This was before World War I and the Revolution and all the upheavals. They were lucky to get out when they did. They arrived in New York at Ellis Island, then went on to Detroit, which they thought was the Wild West. My mother had a brother there who owned a haberdashery. My father joined the business. He became a partner.

"My mother had five children, all girls. Two of us were born in Russia, three of us here. I was the youngest, like your Flora Lijak. In Detroit we grew up speaking Russian. There were a lot of differences between my father and my uncle, business differences. They had tremendous fights, but that's all over now. Everyone's gone. My sisters, they're gone, all of them. So is Bernard."

Esther smiles at Ozzie's questioning look.

"Come with me." Esther grapples with the arm of her couch as if to free herself from a trap, but with Ozzie's help manages to rise. Slowly, using her aluminum cane with its tripod foot, she leads Ozzie to two photographs hanging on the wall opposite. One is a formal portrait of a middle-aged couple, a man standing behind a seated woman. The man is resting his right hand on the woman's shoulder. They look contented. He is wearing a dark suit, she a dark dress and a silvery pendant broach. He has a broad, friendly face. The woman is a younger Esther. Esther would be in her sixties in this portrait. She is sharp-eyed and handsome, her hair still dark and carefully combed into place. The colors of the print, probably severe to begin with, have faded and have gone to earth tones.

"Bernard Kominsky. My husband."

Not my "late husband," Ozzie notes. Esther says, "My husband." As if he still is. Like Tom.

"Anniversary photograph. Friends called him 'Bernie,' but I always called him Bernard."

"Did you have children?"

"Children? No, no, no. Some people shouldn't have children.

Can't give them time or attention. Or if they do, they lose their minds at it. Literally. I have no regrets."

No regrets. Ozzie wonders at that. Where are you going, little one, little one...? Will she — Ozzie — tell someone someday that she has no regrets? And will it be true?

Esther says, "Bernard was a Soviet specialist. His field was Economics. He was well-thought of. He taught at Chicago for two years, then joined CIA and came down here. We met at Langley. I had been a Russian translator in the War. I was with SIS - Signals Intelligence Service then, but I went over to CIA when it was created. At SIS I knew William Friedman. He had a great mind. He was the greatest cryptologist ever. I knew Elizebeth, too. His wife. We got invited to their parties. Their invitations were always cryptograms — you had to solve them! Very amusing. They were wonderful talkers. Friedman tried to decrypt your Lijak Manuscript. He spoke of it. It stumped him and his team at SIS. Even they couldn't break it. Beautiful thing, the Lijak, but unbreakable."

Hanging next to the anniversary portrait is a black-and-white photograph of a younger though much-aged Esther, striding barefoot along a beach, alone, beach grass and sedge in the foreground, ocean behind. She's wearing a loose, summery cotton dress, and is leaning forward, hands locked behind her, eyes intent on some sight in the distance.

Esther raps the photograph with the nail of her reversed index finger. "Assateague. I walk on the beach there. Or I did. I go still but I creep. A nephew who lives in the area drives me down. He took this picture. Years ago. His children are grown. Now I'm his child. The ocean — I find the surf, the unceasing wind, the blue horizon that stretches forever, I find this all so alluring. The ocean answers one's moods, speaks to one. Lulls one." She arcs her neck to smile up to Ozzie. "Eternal peace."

"Now, let me show you my library." She leads Ozzie into a large room, the walls of which are covered with shelving, floor to ceiling, save for a line of pictures – Soviet-era black-and-white portraits of Marx, Lenin, Trotsky, and Stalin, all the same size in identical black frames - high up on one wall. In the center of the room two low bookshelves stand back-to-back, full.

"So many books, Esther!"

"Yes."

Many of the books are in Russian, French, and German. In the far corner under a floor lamp sits a single easy chair.

"I live here. In the past. My past. Theirs." She gestures with her eyebrows at Marx and the others. "Sometimes when I'm alone in here I think they are watching me. Now I think they're listening. To us.

"My books are my old friends. In the evenings I sit among them. I take them out and peruse them. I love their covers, their textures, I love the feel of their pages. We go far back, some of us, even to my childhood. Those old volumes are falling apart. Like me. This place – the administration, awful - didn't want me to keep my library. They said I didn't need a library because they had their own. Well, they do, but it's all large-print silly best-sellers you don't want to read, silly magazines. I insisted on putting in shelves and filing cabinets. I made it a condition of taking my apartment. They harrumphed about 'rules,' but gave in. These" – she attempts a sweeping gesture at her books – "have meaning for me. Not just their contents – their history too, even the way they are arranged on the shelves. They are my life. They'll dissipate when I do. My nephew will call in the second-hand book dealers, but they won't want these things. Most of my old friends will be pulped or buried in a landfill. Come, let's go back to the couch."

Esther leans toward Ozzie. "I've reviewed the article that interested you. I can't tell you anything at all about Flora Lijak or her husband, but I can tell you about the Russians who spied on them.

"The Russians had no Okhrana station in London, believe it or not. They ran all their London operations out of Paris. They had two rooms at 97 rue de Grenelle. Fancy address, but nonde-script building, down the street from the big embassy. I've seen it. I went there in the sixties and seventies, when I was working on my articles. Just to feel the place. In the 1890s Rachkovsky ran it. Pyotr Ivanovich Rachkovsky, top Okhrana officer in Europe. A schemer. He didn't like his picture taken so we have only the one photograph of him. He has a wide face and he's wearing a bowler. The Okhrana spied on everyone – Stepniak and the Nihilists, the Anarchists, the Communists, the Jewish labor people. The Okhrana had informants everywhere. Rachkovsky had lots of British on his payroll. Police, politicians, the press.

"Rachkovsky kept records on all these people. So did his successors. In 1917, with the Revolution, the last Tsarist ambassador to France, Maklakov, closed the mission and sealed its secret files – there were crates and crates of them. Well, the new government in Russia, Kerensky and his people, wanted to prosecute Tsarist police officials, including Okhrana officials, for their misdeeds. Maklakov was willing to cooperate with Kerensky – he had no use for the Okhrana, disliked them in fact – and he was about to send the files to Moscow, but before he could, Lenin and the Bolsheviks took over and threw Kerensky out, and Maklakov decided to send the files to the U.S. instead. It's a long story, but they went first to Washington, then to Stanford, to the Hoover Institution. Wonderful place, the Hoover, I spent such happy hours there! Stanford has a big bell tower – not ivory, real world, limestone. So, the Okhrana files sit at the Hoover. Open to the public, to anyone."

"Esther, you mentioned the Lijaks in your article. You must have seen a report on them."

"Yes. Some document. I must have. Yes."

She pauses. "I knew the Okhrana Collection once. You have no Russian?"

"No."

Esther stares away from Ozzie. "Well. Let me think."

CHAPTER X

Free Love

When Flora returned from Limpsfield she learnt that Sergei and Fanny Stepniak had resumed holding their Saturday afternoon at-homes in Bedford Park and sent a note to that effect to Billy suggesting they meet there.

Both attended the Stepniaks' next. Lijak refused to go, thinking Volkhovsky, Chaikovsky, or Shishko, all of whom he now loathed, might be there. They were not, but amongst the callers that afternoon were Fisher Unwin, other luminaries of the Society of Friends of Russian Freedom, the Kropotkins, Ivan Serov in his mismatched suit, and a few trade unionists.

Also attending were the Socialist Edward Aveling and his mistress Eleanor "Tussy" Marx, Karl Marx's daughter. (In three years, Aveling will desert Eleanor for a younger woman, and Eleanor, devastated, will poison herself with cyanide.)

Billy's sudden appearance amongst these (he had never attended an at-home before), taking tea, chatting affably with all, seemed to surprise no one.

That afternoon someone happened to ask Stepniak his views on Free Love (a group had gathered about him, as usual, to ask him questions and ponder his answers). Stepniak replied, "I believe in personal freedom as much as political freedom. Individuals should love whom they wish, whatever their marital situation." Flora and Billy were amongst the group surrounding Stepniak. Each felt the truth of Stepniak's remark; neither reacted to it overtly.

Olive Garnett, who was standing at Stepniak's side, said, "I disagree. Troth is troth. Love to be meaningful must be a union of two souls for life. It is then at its most spiritual and its most perfect and beautiful."

At this Stepniak simply inclined his great bearded head and smiled benignantly, as if to say, "Believe as you wish, but I am right."

Stepniak felt an especial cordiality toward Olive, who was eighteen and had milky skin and lush hair. Olive was trying to become a writer, and Stepniak, who was a gifted pamphleteer and novelist, encouraged and coached her at her work. It was thought that Olive was in love with Stepniak, but that her principles (or her fears of the sexual) kept her love that of a disciple.

As to Free Love, what Stepniak the assassin would have done had Fanny taken a lover is not known because she never did. Nor did he: the Stepniaks led a mutually faithful married life in Bedford Park, till his death at the rail crossing.

Whilst the group standing around Stepniak chattered of Love and Troth, Flora stood silent. She, too, had once disagreed vehemently with Stepniak's views, but now understood them. Love, absolute love, had changed her and had altered forever the way she thought about such things. With Billy her moral universe had upended itself.

From time to time, as the group talked, she glanced at Billy, she hoped not with obvious fondness.

When Billy noticed Flora alone at the tea table, he approached her and said under his breath, "Come visit me. Soon. I've got something important to tell you."

Flora responded quietly, "I shall. Monday afternoon?"

Billy nodded. Shortly after, he thanked Fanny Stepniak and left the gathering without looking back.

OZZIE

Ozzie?

Hi, Esther, how are you?

Oh, I'm fine. How are you?

Just fine.

Ozzie, I wanted to tell you, I've looked through my old notes on the Okhrana Collection and I've found a document that contains information on your Flora.

Oh, wow, wonderful! Thanks so much!

Yes. Now, it doesn't have much on her but it's interesting and it's got some gossip about her private life. She had a lover, apparently. I thought you would be interested.

Esther removes from a manila folder two dark, blurry pages – old photocopies – of a document typed in Russian and places them on her coffee table alongside a tea setting and a basket of cookies.

"This is a report sent out from the Paris Agentura to headquarters in St. Petersburg in the fall of 1895. It describes persons associated with the Society of Friends of Russian Freedom, including Flora Lijak and her husband. The report was signed off on by Rachkovsky, but that's the way they always did it. Someone else most certainly prepared it, an aide perhaps. This" – she removes another document from her manila folder, two more pages, neatly typed in English – "is my translation of the report. I made it years back for my article on the Paris Agentura and filed it away. And now here it is again."

Esther pushes her translation toward Ozzie. It begins:

Subject: Principal members, Society of Friends of Russian Freedom.
Date: September 19, 1895.
Sources: POLYPHEMUS, Imperial Archives.

"You see a 'POLYPHEMUS' listed there as a source. POLYPHEMUS is the cryptonym of a person."

"Source? Meaning a spy?"

"Yes. Someone in Rachkovsky's pay. Someone who apparently knew the S.F.R.F. well. If I ever knew who it was, I don't now. And I haven't been able to find notes in my files on him. Or her."

The report consists of short biographical sketches of the S.F.R.F. leadership – Feliks Volkhovsky, Sergei Stepniak, Nikolai Chaikovsky, Wilfrid Lijak, the others. And Flora:

> Lijak, F.B. Secretary of Society. Translator, editor of revolutionary organ Free Russia. Wife of U.M. Lijak. Lives with husband. English, born 1865 in Cork, Ireland. Resident St. Petersburg 1887-89. Smuggler of subversive literature out of and into the Empire. Known to have romantic liaison with American anarcho-communist William McKenzie.

Ozzie calls the Hoover Institution and just catches the young woman who curates the Okhrana Collection before she leaves her office for the afternoon. Ozzie explains. She asks if there might be other records at the Hoover that mention the Lijaks or the William McKenzie named in Rachkovsky's report as Flora's lover. And do we know who POLYPHEMUS was?

The young woman is sympathetic but is leaving for an exercise class. She gives Ozzie her e-mail address and asks for a scan of the Rachkovsky report. She promises she'll have a look at the Collection tomorrow and see what she can find.

At home Ozzie sends the young woman scans of Esther's documents and orders a large bouquet of pink lilies delivered to Esther's apartment; then, working into the evening, she searches every source on the Web she can think of – genealogical sites,

shipping records, U.S. and British censuses of various dates, newspaper archives, rare old publications put up on Anarchist sites —
but finds no one who could have been Flora's William McKenzie.

Next day the young woman from the Hoover responds with an
e-mail, which arrives in the evening:

TO: azad.hosseini@gu.edu
FROM: jyama@stanford.edu
SUBJ: McKenzie, Lijak

Dear Professor Hosseini:

Thank you for the scan. I have looked at records from the relevant
years (1890-1900) of the Okhrana Collection. Regrettably, I
can find nothing further pertaining to the Lijaks or to William
McKenzie.

Of the lists of Okhrana sources I've been able to locate for this
period one does mention a POLYPHEMUS. He is described as "a
well-connected English journalist of impeccable reputation who
operates in London." Per usual Okhrana practice, he is not named.

I hope this is of some help. Best of luck to you on your project and
do let me know if I can be of further assistance.

June Yamazaki

Tea and cookies, spies and lovers. Ozzie daydreams for a time.
Then it strikes her: she hurriedly navigates to her scan of that
fragile sheet of lined paper with its dog-eared right corner and its
penciled arrangement of two lines of "Billy Boy."
    It's him, Ozzie thinks. Hidden away in the Hoover Institution
and, yes, very likely, in the Library of Congress, Flora's shadowy
lover William McKenzie has a presence, just.
    The thought pleases her: text is memory.
    He was real. He lived, was flesh, like Flora and Alice. And
Flora loved him.

CHAPTER XI

"I'm Going Abroad. I Don't Know for How Long."

Monday afternoon next, as she had promised, Flora came to Billy's room. Entering Needham Lane under the now familiar stone archway, she passed through the barefoot, noisy children pattering in the slops, passed the idle women sitting on the kerb, gossiping. These, of course, recognized her and, as ever, eyed her up and down. "'Er Lydyship," she heard one say to the others' smothered merriment.

Greek chorus, Flora thought. Hags.

After she and Billy had embraced, he took her hand and led her to his table, where he sat her across from him, retaining her hand in his. "I've got some news," he said. "I'm going abroad. I don't know for how long. Maybe a few weeks. Paris, probably some other places."

"When do you leave?" she asked evenly.

"A week from Friday."

"And the purpose?"

"I'm going to meet with some people."

"For your book?" She knew it was not for his book.

"Well... in the end maybe. For now, no."

"For Anarchism."

"You could say that."

"And there's danger."

He laughed. "No, no. Please hush about that. I'll be fine."

"And you can't tell me more?"

"I have to look out for others so I can't say more than I've said
– you know these games better than I do. But listen, Flore, I'll be
fine – don't worry!"

Flora preferred to believe Billy, but she did not. He was going
into danger, and the thought chilled her.

That evening in Hammersmith Flora wrote to her sister Evelyn
that they must meet as soon as possible. Evelyn came to The Grove
next afternoon, worried, since Flora had explained nothing in her
note. As they embraced and kissed in the entrance hall, Flora said,
"Sis, we must take a walk."

"Another walk?"

Flora smiled.

As they strolled together down The Grove (The Limpet was
not in sight), Flora said, "McKenzie's going to the Continent for
a short visit. I shall accompany him as far as Newhaven and stay
the night there."

It took Evelyn no time to divine her sister's intent. "Well, we'll
tell… We'll say that you'll be visiting me that day in Highgate and
staying the night. You will have your bag packed and we shall leave
together. What day?"

"Friday a week."

"Done."

"Oh, Sis, you're such a true friend!"

Flora took Evelyn's hand in hers and swung it happily as they
walked.

Evelyn said, "Sis, I still haven't met this American."

"You shall. I promise. As soon as he returns."

OZZIE

Twerp, I'll be in New York May 2-3.

Great! Why?

Research. Want to get together evening May 2?

Sure. Dinner?

Okay. That restaurant on prince street?

Great. Time?

7:30?

Cool. See you!

———

Ozzie is being led to the Weisert Rare Manuscript Facility in the basement of Butler Library by someone's assistant, a slim, sallow young woman in black, with silky, electric blue hair. Her nose ring is a blue double band. She says little, though she manages small, tight smiles. Her name is Théa (pronounced TAY-uh).

Ozzie has decided it's time to view the Lijak, not its digital avatar, but the real thing, and scout out the neighborhoods in New York where Flora and Alice lived and where Lijak had his showroom. She wants to see and feel these places – like Esther Kominsky tracking down the old Okhrana headquarters in Paris, where Pyotr Rachkovsky spun his webs. Later she'll see David and Buzz.

Théa gives Ozzie a pair of thin, disposable white cotton gloves, de rigueur hand-wear for archival work, but not making much sense to Ozzie since, as she has been given to understand, only Théa will be handling the codex.

Also: No purses, bags, daypacks, fanny packs, sharp objects, drinks, cell phones, cameras, tablets, or other electronics in here. Ozzie has duly deposited her purse (with cell) in a small metal locker provided for the purpose.

Théa has taken a key – an actual metal key – and unlocked the door to "The Cage," a sanctum constructed of heavy, black steel mesh (Columbia's ancient infrastructure) and has preceded Ozzie inside. The Cage, which follows the contours of Butler Library's basement, is a grim, claustrophobic maze of closely spaced metal shelving piled with dusty documents – manuscripts, leather-bound codices, ancient printed books – and with numbered cardboard boxes of various sizes and shapes. A constant, faint current of cool air passes through. The lighting is dim.

Théa leads Ozzie to a cramped nook in which sit an easel covered in green flannel and two straight-backed chairs. On the easel rests a mouse-gray volume recognizable even from a distance: the Lijak.

The Chief Curator of the Weisert explained in an e-mail when Ozzie first requested to see it that the Lijak Manuscript, Weisert MS 408, is kept in its own box and is taken from that box and so displayed for visitors, that, given the nature of the artifact, Ozzie would be a "restricted visitor," one who, when in The Cage, would be accompanied by an employee of the Weisert and could look at but not touch the volume and could take notes using only the pencil and lined paper supplied by the Weisert.

The Curator turned out to be an expensively clothed woman of spikey, moussed hair, who wore sunglasses. The woman welcomed Ozzie minimally and explained once again the rules governing the viewing of the manuscript, then said, "Théa will stay with you as long as you like."

Théa escorts Ozzie to the chairs and motions her to sit, taking the seat beside her.

"Théa, let me just look for a sec."

This is it, Ozzie thinks. Flora held this volume in her hands. So did Lijak. So did Alice. And so did... fifteenth century witches?

The codex: its vellum cover is gray and has a faint pinkish sheen. It's the skin of a calf or sheep, the animal's pores just visible. Seven hundred years ago this skin breathed and perspired.

On the tray to the right of the volume rests a card with an inscription penned on it:

A Great Cypher Codex of Roger Bacon of the XIIIth Century
Once Belonging to the Emperor Rudolph II of Bohemia
Brought to that Country in 1595
And Presented to
The Emperor by John Dee of England,
Emissary of Queen Elizabeth I

The inscription is in Flora's hand.

Ozzie hadn't expected this. For a moment she sits quietly, gazing on the card. Flora, she thinks, you're here now too, with us, with Théa and me.

"Okay, let's start. Théa, would you open to the first folio please?"

The young woman gently turns back the cover of the codex – the vellum crackles faintly and gives off a musty odor – and holds it with both her gloved hands. Folio 1 recto: the first of the plants, a scattering of green leaves not unlike laurel overwritten by text in the Lijak's fantastic script. The script is smaller and more delicate than Ozzie had expected, and the brown ink in which it is written is lighter.

As Ozzie silently nods like a concert pianist to an assistant, Théa, breathing softly through her mouth, pages through the folios, plant by imaginary plant, each distinct from the last, the limbs, the sprigs, the branches of each one painstakingly delineated.

Petals, calyces, leaves, roots. Phallic stamens, vulval bracts —
these pages pulse with sexuality. At a few — the large green bulb
from which shoots a stem topped by a blue blossom, the pale-yel-
low pan-shaped bloom studded with what look like black seeds
and surrounded by florets — Théa hesitates and seems reluctant to
turn the folio, seems to want to stay.

Ozzie regards her.

"Have you shown this before?"

Théa nods.

"A lot of times?"

"No, unfortunately. Only a few visitors want to see it."

Théa's eyes meet Ozzie's. Hers are filmy. She has a pretty,
heart-shaped little face. And she is oh so weird.

"So, you know the Manuscript," Ozzie says, "its background
and all that?"

"Yes."

"What do you think of it?"

"I love it," she whispers, deflecting her eyes.

"Why?"

"Because it's beautiful."

"Beautiful. How?"

Théa's eyes return to Ozzie's. "It's a timeless world. We can
enter it and make of it what we want. And feel."

"And you like that?"

"Yes."

"There are a lot of people out there who spend long hours
trying to crack this, read its language." Some of them have beautiful eyes and caressing lips.

"I hope they don't."

"Why is that?"

"Then we wouldn't be able to imagine what it is."

"What do you imagine it is?"

"It's a Garden of Delights. Of Joy. For women. Overseen by
the turning heavens."

Ozzie notices that Théa has slender, milk-white wrists. Did

the two authors of this codex have such wrists?

After the plants come the suns and moons, the signs of the Zodiac – Pisces, Aries, Taurus, the rest – and circling each sign, the naked women holding their stars.

As Théa is leaving the Zodiacal section Ozzie suddenly recalls one sign, realizing now its oddness. "Théa, wait! Wait, wait, wait! Théa, would you please go back to Gemini? The Zodiac sign? Gemini? I want to see something."

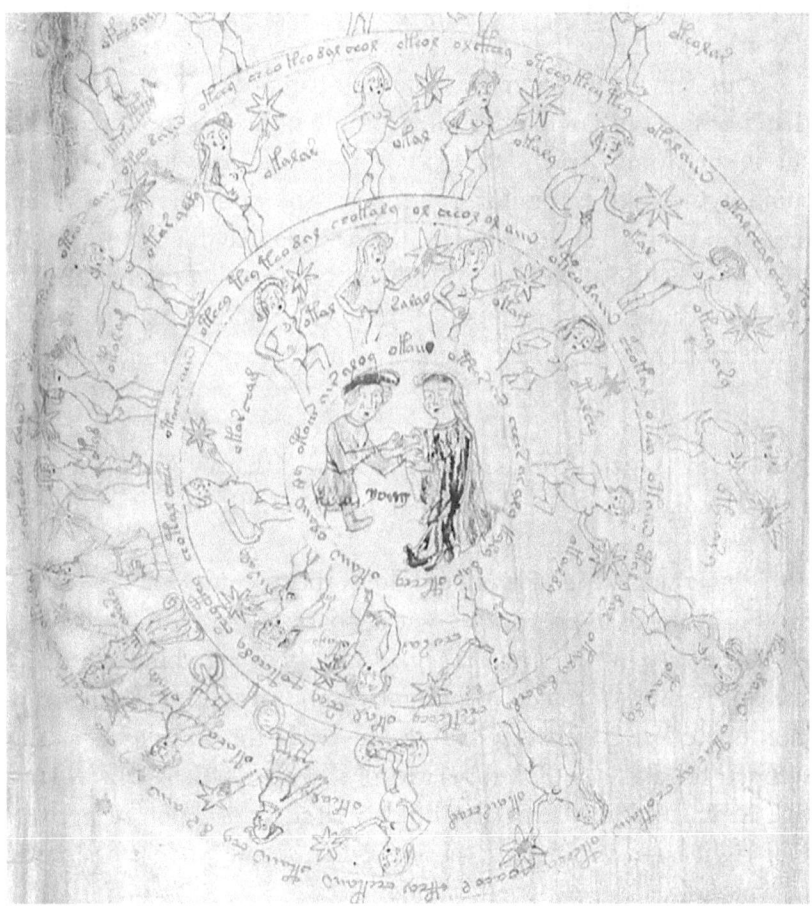

Théa complies, leafing backward, and there, yes, at folio 72 recto is Gemini, the twins Castor and Pollux. But in this bizarre document Gemini is composed of a male and a female! One of the twins is a woman! Female partner in Gemini? Unheard of, got to be.

Like Virgo, the female partner is gowned in cornflower blue. Her male twin, pictured on the left, is wearing a long green tunic, green hat, and green boots, the only figure in the Lijak so clad.

The Green Man, a vegetation symbol.

His blue-gowned female partner wears a white train that flows down her back from her head to her heels. The hands of each twin, extended left to left, right to right, touch but do not grasp the other's.

This female member of Gemini, attired like Virgo, is larger than her male partner and is foregrounded: though they are twins, she is the dominant. At this discovery Ozzie feels a thrill in her spine, which she savors for a moment. She nods then, and Théa pages on to the bathing women, the solitaries laving themselves in tubs and channels, the groups frolicking in green and blue pools.

This thing, Ozzie thinks, is all fertility and sexuality, Théa's Garden of Delights, for women, which Ozzie now understands.

At the desk Ozzie returns her temp ID and thanks Théa (the Curator has disappeared). Théa says good-bye softly, her eyes directly on Ozzie's.

This strange young woman knows the Secret.

From the Weisert's subterranean spaces Ozzie surfaces by cement staircase into Columbia's quad and the warm, blue-skied day she left behind. Crowds of students, some of whom seem barely clothed, loll on blankets spread on the grass. Beyond them, up the stepped terrace, sits Columbia's lovely bronze statue Alma Mater. She is wreathed in laurel and holds a large Bible open in her lap. Her right hand steadies a long, lance-like scepter, her left is raised in welcome. Or is it benediction?

From Columbia Ozzie takes a local subway to 96th Street, then the shrieking, brain-rattling Number 3 down to Times Square. She emerges into the crowds on 42nd Street and walks over to Bryant Park. On the north side of the street, rising over the park, is the Aeolian Building, where, on the top floor, the 16th, Lijak had his showroom. To get photo documentation of the slender, soaring structure she backs into the park, halting on the walk in front of the Bryant Park Grill and its planters full of pink tulips, and takes a series of pictures – wide-angle views of the pale limestone building and its beautiful lines, telephoto shots of its upper reaches and the row of five large windows that run across the very top, Lijak's old bailiwick.

Retracing her steps, she crosses 42nd Street to enter and explore the building, but security won't let her past the reception area. So, she takes shots of the lobby, knowing it can't be as it was in Lijak's day. The circular reception desk came long after his time, and the marble walling looks as if it had been installed in a renovation. To her right, though, two pairs of dark, burnished brass elevator doors catch her attention. She approaches them to get shots. They are decorated with square panels of a symmetrical vegetal design interspersed with smaller, rectangular panels. These depict two dog-headed dragons that flank and seem to guard bowls of fruit.

Art Deco. Could have been here in the twenties, she thinks. Flora, Alice, Lijak could have waited at these doors, paying little attention to them, thinking whatever thoughts they thought. Ozzie will find some architectural historian. She'll learn about those doors.

A guard asks her to leave.

She walks east to Tudor City, a complex of apartment buildings at the end of 42nd Street, constructed on a granite escarpment hanging over 1st Avenue and the East River. Here, sometime after Lijak died in 1930, Flora and Alice began their life together. They lived in the large building, Prospect Tower – 45 Prospect

Place at the time, 45 Tudor City 2 Place now – on the north side of 42nd Street. Ozzie gets shots of the green entrance canopy and the stone carving to the left of the door (an arch under which two small, spiraled columns flank a guardian griffin and shield, and under them an inscription in mock Tudor characters that names the developer, Fred F. French, and date of construction, Anno Domini 1927).

Across Tudor City Place Ozzie finds a small, quiet park: benches, shade trees, ivy, hosta, thickly planted flower beds. At the park's very center, where two flagstoned paths cross at right angles, stands a four-sided fountain of weathered brown limestone, waist-high, decorated with a lion's head on each of its sides. Dry now, the fountain is planted with English ivy.

Did they know this fountain, Flora and Alice? Did it flow when they were here? On summer evenings did they sit in this park and converse?

Ozzie buses to Chelsea, on the West Side, to survey another red-brick apartment complex, the London Terrace Towers. Flora and Alice moved here from Tudor City in 1939 and here lived out their lives. The Towers occupy a full city block, from 9th to 10th Avenues and 23rd to 24th Streets.

Here in 1959 the delegation from the Bolshoi Ballet piled out of their cab and performed for a British news crew, craning their necks to stare up the face of the building. In apartment 260 in this building, the beautiful ballerina presented Flora with a card and bouquet on her 95th birthday, and an ancient Flora blew a kiss to the camera.

Ozzie thinks: Flora and Alice and the Russians, five persons, came together here for a small birthday celebration, which was caught on that newsreel and, digitized now, is viewable to anyone anywhere in the world, forever.

Ozzie takes shots of the building's 24th Street exterior.

———

Crowded Houston Street, 8:00 p.m. Bars, kids, lights, noise. Ozzie's on her way to meet David and Buzz at a café in SoHo around the corner from their Mott Street loft. Crossing Mulberry Street Ozzie pulls her phone from her purse to text David and let him know she's down here – and to make sure he is – and she sees, she hadn't heard it announce itself – a text in from Mark a few minutes back.

> Hey, Annie. Sweet one. You. Annie. Love you.

Funny, she thinks, which thought is instantly overwritten.

She halts and stands breathless on Houston, traffic roaring in her ears, young people jostling her. She stares at the screen, at its black letters. Her stomach clenches like a fist. She gulps for air, gazing at, not seeing, the little message:

> Hey, Annie. Sweet one. You. Annie. Love you.

How much time goes by? A minute? An epoch?

Breathing softly now, she turns into Mulberry to escape the noise on Houston. She brings his number up on her phone.

There it is.

His number.

Yes?

No?

Yes: She plunges and taps her screen. She brings her phone to her left ear, covering her right with her hand to dampen the street noise.

She hears rings. His voice breaks in. "Hey, Oz."

"Mark, I got this text?"

"Sorry?"

"Text. Uh, I got this text? Like, just a couple minutes ago... from you?"

A pause. He makes a sound. Then: "Oh. Oh, oh, Oz."

"Yeah. I mean, I got it. And…"

And what to say? She has nothing prepared, no script. She's breathing rapidly now. Peripherally she notices some guy in a black cowboy hat and black dungarees passing her, giving her ass the eye, then gone. A blur.

"If it's you… I mean, if it's the way things are, with you and her, with Anne, I mean it's okay, it's okay. It's your life."

No, it isn't okay, it sucks.

He exhales something like a sigh. "It happens."

"What happens?"

Mark gives out another sigh. "Last night… I was there. Long ago we were hot. Memories came back. I wanted to tell her… I don't know, tell her something. Oz, it doesn't…"

"You guys make love?"

No answer. Meaning, Yes.

Meaning, Yes, yes, yes, yes.

"I didn't think it would go that way."

Didn't? Think? Go? Way?

Her eyes are focusing on nothing.

"Mark, she's alcoholic. And you…"

Ozzie's nodding her head: And you.

Silence on both ends.

"Has this happened before? Like before last night?"

More silence, then, "Oz…"

"Do you want to get back with her?"

Silence, then, "I don't know."

After giving out a desolate puff of breath, Ozzie taps the red End Call icon and punches off her cell. Her screen goes black.

Anne, Azadeh. Probably close, maybe right together on his contact list. Hit the wrong name. So, is this his way of breaking it off? Of saying good-bye? No. Freud's dead. Better: NSA guy screws up signal.

A laugh. A laugh.

They go back. Will did. Who I'd fallen for.

Mark…

Oh, Mark, Mark, even you…

Ozzie stands there in Houston, letting her purse dangle, oblivious to the dead phone still in her left hand. She punches it back on and ignoring a just-missed call from Mark calls David. As expected, David doesn't answer.

This call is being routed to a mailbox.

"Hi, David. Something's come up. Can't make it tonight. Don't worry, not a big deal, a friend is in some trouble, and I have to uh… give her some support. Big deal for her and kind of for me. So, I have to head home. I love you, Twerp. Love to Buzz. Bye."

The Uber car – she can't face the subway – is a quiet, black chamber. She silences her cell.

The driver looks Middle Eastern. He's young, chunky, mustached, has a nice face and a nice manner. She thinks he's probably not Persian. Persians are too good for this line of work. An Arab.

She notices now a medallion hanging from the rearview mirror that reads "Allah" in Arabic, whose written form she can recognize.

God. Trust in God. If there isn't anybody else.

The driver heads up Lafayette to Fourth to Park, where he will turn on 34th Street and head for 12th Avenue and the West Side Highway – he has asked permission to do that, and she has given it – and up to her neighborhood. Yes, a little indirect, but fastest, probably cheapest in the end.

The car is new and clean. The lights on the dash are a low, tranquilizing green.

Back to D.C.

She checks her bus company's Web site.

Yes, good, she thinks, they've got space tomorrow on their 10:30 run from Penn Station. She reserves a seat.

Sigh no more, ladies, sigh no more,
Men were deceivers ever;

One foot in sea and one on shore,
To one thing constant never...

Constant never... Constant never... Ta dah ta dah... what?

Then sigh not so...

Yes. Right.

Then sigh not so,
But let them go,
And be ye blithe and bonny,
Converting all your sounds of woe,
Into hey nonny nonny.

Yes. Blithe and bonny.
They go back.
Let them go.
She erases Mark's voicemail message unheard. She shuts off her phone.

I know, I know, I know I'll get over this, Ozzie thinks, her body bent forward, handbag between her knees.

The cab is up on the West Side Highway now, New Jersey on her left, the lights over there pretty as stars.

CHAPTER XII

"Not Much Time."

When they boarded the train for Newhaven in the early afternoon Billy did not give their luggage to the porter, but carried it himself, Flora's, a small leather satchel that locked, his, a large, thick woolen bag. Billy tried joshing with the porter, who thought Billy was being mean and not wanting to give a tip and took the joshing sourly, refusing to look Billy in the eye. Flora was certain Billy did not want others handling that woolen bag. She surmised he was carrying something in it. A message. Money. A weapon. Something.

At Newhaven they climbed a steep footbridge over the railway tracks to the London & Paris Hotel, where they registered as Mr and Mrs Long. (Billy had telegraphed ahead for the room.) Again, declining help from the porters, Billy carried their luggage himself. Their room turned out to be on the harbour side of the hotel and looked onto the wharf and across the harbour to the town. It was from this wharf that Billy would take the steam-packet to Dieppe in the morning.

Billy drew the curtain on the window and closed and locked the door. Without a word, he pulled one of the room's two small beds against the other and turned to Flora. She rushed to his arms.

—

They lay naked on their sides, each studying the other. In silence Billy caressed Flora's hair, she touched his lips with her fingers and brought her hand to his cheek.

I cannot lose you, she thought.

"Billy, you must write or telegraph, I implore you."

"From wherever I can, Flore. I promise."

"It is dangerous, isn't it?"

"I'll be back, Flore. It's not like that."

"Do you promise 'It's not like that'?"

"Flore, there's risk in everything we do."

"And so you must write to me."

Flora rolled from Billy, reached to the pile of her clothing lying by the beds, and took from it her straw hat. The hat was banded with a wide blue silk ribbon that tied in back in a butterfly knot, its two ends trailing down. She pulled the ribbon from her hat and laid it on his chest. "The colour of this ribbon is the blue of corn-flower," she said softly. "Did you know, in our rural districts young men in love pick cornflower and wear it as a token of their troth? If the cornflower fades it means that their love is unrequited." She placed her hand on his heart and said, "This ribbon will never fade, Billy Boy. Keep it. Take it with you. And bring it back."

"I will," he said. "I'll carry it with me, I swear. And bring it back."

Later, after a light tea in the hotel saloon they whiled away the time before supper by hiring a cab to see whatever sights Ne-whaven might offer. Their driver told them there was a fort on the south promontory worth a look and that from the commons above the chalk cliffs the view was very fine. So, they drove up to the fort and its great ramparts, which were impressive, though the artillery had been drawn in and the embrasures closed.

At the driver's urging they left the cab and walked from the road over tall grass, dry and sere now, avoiding gorse and wild blackberry bushes and rabbit-burrows (not altogether successfully

– Flora's boot caught twice), to the cliff-side to view the Channel, which lay before them serene and blue.

"Can't see France," Billy yelled over the wind.

"France is too far away to be seen from here."

"There's a haze over there. Maybe that's France."

"We'll say it is."

"Yes. We'll say we saw France, but it was indistinct."

The wind was strong and constant, the Channel featureless. Far from shore two black ships steamed slowly west.

Billy yelled, "Well, let's not let this guy gyp us anymore, let's go back."

As they passed through town, Billy halted the cab at a flower stall to buy Flora a nosegay of pastel chrysanthemums.

"Take these as my pledge of troth. Like cornflower. You have to keep them."

"Preserve them?"

"Yes. Press them in a book. If you do, they won't fade."

"Then I shall. I shall keep them for you, and you must see them after they've been pressed." Billy smiled his agreement.

When they returned to the hotel they washed in their room and went down to supper, then strolled along the wharf in the dusky autumn light. Among the three vessels moored there the largest was the *Tamise*, the single-decked packet that would take Billy to France in the morning. It had arrived from Dieppe that afternoon. Arms linked, they walked to the end of the wharf, admiring the yellow lights of the town across the harbour which were beginning to come on.

Their intimacies that night aroused in Flora passions of a kind she had not experienced before, and she cried aloud, again and again, "Oh, yes, love, oh, yes, yes... Oh, love, love, yes... You. You. Oh, you!"

In the bright morning Billy shook Flora from slumber in his brisk American way: "Breakfast, sleepyhead. Time to rise!" He had washed, shaven, and dressed. How had he done all that without her waking?

"Not much time," he said. His ferry would leave at 9:30.

His phrase, "Not much time," uttered casually as he stowed his shaving kit in his bag, caught her up with its frightening implications. For the whole of her life, to its very end, she will remember Billy saying, "Not much time."

At breakfast, for which they were almost late, she felt eyes on them: the hotel's walls were thin, and the room doors fastened lightly. The glances they received in the saloon bothered her not one whit.

Breakfast over, Billy, dapper in his light travelling suit (her blue band peeked up from his jacket pocket), proceeded with Flora to the wharf. When they halted at the barrier, Billy turned to her and they clasped arms.

She said, "Oh, Billy, Billy, for heaven's sake, do be careful!"

He winked. "Tell you something, Flore – one, there's no such thing as heaven except right here and I mean here" – he gave her arms a knowing squeeze – "and two, I'll be careful. Always am."

"One does worry so!"

"Well, 'one' shouldn't. This 'one' doesn't, anyhow. Come on, cheer up, Flore, I'll be back soon enough."

"'Soon enough.' And will you think of me?" She tried to sound teasing as she said this, as if the question weren't absurd.

He laughed and nodded, stroking her cheek with the back of his hand.

"Billy Boy, I do love you."

"You're my dear heart, Flore. I love you too – you know that – and I'll miss you terribly."

They kissed, more passionately than was usual in public places in those days, then Billy said simply, "See you, Flore," picked up his bag, and boarded the packet for Dieppe. She watched him push his way through the other passengers to the railing amidships, where he tipped his boater to her and where he remained, smiling at her.

The whistle blew, the gangplank was drawn up clatteringly, and the hawsers cast off. The whistle blew again, and the *Tamise*, its propellers churning and frothing the water, maneuvered away from the wharf. Billy waved a last goodbye and left the railing.

Flora remained at the barrier with a few others, watching the *Tamise* slip out the harbour entrance and steam south over the green blue of the Channel, growing ever smaller until it passed from view and like a dream was gone.

OZZIE

An e-mail from Mark. Subject line: I LOVE YOU.

Oh God.

It's Sunday night. Ozzie, back from New York, has just checked her mail.

Can't look at you, she thinks, just go away. But you will not just go away. You will sit in my Inbox until I do something with you.

What? Open? Delete?

Ozzie mouses over the Sender Name, Mark Morehead, and his familiar photo appears. His face, puffy, slightly off-center, was a selfie, he had told her, taken with his webcam.

Mark. Your so kind face. And a preposterous distortion of your beautiful eyes.

She opens his e-mail.

TO: azad.hosseini@gu.edu
FROM: mark.morehead27@gmail.com
SUBJ: I love you

Dear Ozzie,

I can explain it I suppose, though I can't justify it. I know that. How did it happen? We got to talking. We both felt something, I'm not sure what. We were happy once together, so I think that was it. We have old memories of good times, happy times, and that is very seductive when you have that. It happened as a result of memories and I wish so much it had not. But the fact is of course it did. Still, I can't go back to her and I won't. She wants the marriage over now too or so she says. I think she means it. Or maybe she's just

222

resigned to it. Maybe that's it. But that doesn't matter because I know that for my sake and for my son's sake Anne and I have to separate forever. Dear Ozzie, I'm so, so sorry about this. Believe me even if you didn't know I'd be sorry and guilty. I don't know how to say what I feel. I have no one but you and I have lost you. I love you.

No signature.

Now what? Think. Can't.

I love this man.

Derp.

Ozzie doesn't click Reply. She sends his e-mail to her Spam Folder. She stares and waits.

I love you. Crazy to make it such an issue. Crazy.

She clicks on Spam.

There it is. There you are. Are you Spam?

She stares at her screen, mouses over his name again, gets his image again, and for a moment leaves her cursor there.

She clicks on the little box by his e-mail and a checkmark appears with the choice: "Not Spam" or "Delete Forever".

Which?

She thinks: I hear your heart.

She thinks: Anne is alcoholic. Anne, who as an adolescent was chased around the house by a knife–wielding father. Anne, who is losing everything important in her life because she is ill. And you... You go and...

She sits composing herself. He'll have to return the parking pass. I'll call. But that's all we'll talk about - the parking pass. No: have to retrieve my satchel. We'll talk about that too. He can bring it here with the parking pass. To the lobby. Or maybe we'll meet somewhere else. Neutral territory. Yes. Good idea.

Not. Replace the pass, replace the satchel.

She clicks the little box, the choice disappears. She clicks the box again, and there it is again, her choice: "Not Spam" or "De-

lete Forever".
   She thinks of Mark's hurt.
   She thinks: Find someone without hurt.
   She thinks: Who's without hurt?
   Stop, stop weeping.

   Delete Forever.

POSTLUDE:

Washington Square, 1918

"This I Will Keep of You."

This is the story of Flora Lijak's madness, her singular behaviour after she had seen her long-dead lover Billy McKenzie in Washington Square.

A little after 6:00 that evening, Lijak and Flora closed Lijak Rare Books and Prints (Alice Neff had already left) and walked, as they customarily did, to their hotel, the Waldorf-Astoria, where they occupied a suite. As they walked down Fifth Avenue through the crowds, past the warm lights of display windows (dodging vans and taxis at cross-streets), Lijak made happy conversation about the shipment of books recently arrived from London and the talents of Miss Neff. (Lijak's irritation that Alice had not delayed the wealthy Dr Neubrander until he – Lijak – could return to the office had evaporated.)

"She knows Latin very well and reads it easily! And she is so careful, such a precise transcriber!" He went on to repeat some amusing things the manager of the London shop, Herbert Garland, had written about a visiting American customer (who bought no books).

Flora was taciturn, responding in monosyllables and nods. Her mind was on Billy. As she and Lijak walked she thought, Oh, Billy, I adored you. Had you come back to me from your journey, what course would our lives have taken? For a few weeks at the end of a long-ago summer you brought me the joy of love, never knowing that in doing so you were exorcising a demon or that when you left me the demon would return and that I would not love again.

During dinner, Flora spoke little and was distant. Once Lijak thought he saw her eyes welling. Something obviously was quite wrong with his wife, but he could not imagine what. When appropriate, when she was in a better state, he would try to learn what was troubling her. Toward bedtime, however, she seemed improved, and Lijak concluded that she had simply been suffering a temporary dark mood.

That night Flora slept badly and had horrific dreams. In one she is walking with a man. His shape is vague, his face cannot be seen. He is wearing a dark suit, brown, she thinks. He seems to be someone she knows, but she cannot name him. She asks him, "Are there such things as giant squid?" She knows there are, she has read of them and has seen engravings in the press of such monsters attacking men in boats, wrapping their cupped tentacles around the unfortunate sailors, pulling them underwater, drowning them, consuming them. As soon as she asks her question the man plummets into the sea, which has been present the while but not visible. The sea is all wave and green spray, roiling under a gale. She, a calm, complaisant observer, watches as the monster, the squid, which has been lurking under the waves, seizes the man, pulls him to its beak, and crushes him. He bursts with blood. She woke then and realised that the man in her dream had been her Uncle Charles.

At breakfast Lijak noticed his wife had reddened eyes and began again to worry. Something truly was the matter.

He said, "Pet, you seem not well. I saw it yesterday and again this morning. I'm most concerned. Shall we call Dr Paxton?"

"Oh, no, no, it's simply a weakness. It will pass. If it doesn't, then perhaps we might call in a doctor, but don't worry, Wilfie, it's probably a cold or a grippe coming on – really." She smiled when she said this, but Lijak sensed she was putting up a front. That morning when he left, alone, for Lijak Rare Books and Prints he felt deep unease. His wife was suffering, but she would not or could not tell him why.

When Lijak had gone, Flora wrote a note for him and left it, as they often left communications for one another, on the small cherry-wood telephone table at the entrance to their sitting room. It read:

My Dearest,

I must be away for some time. I must concentrate on important work & I need to be alone for that. Do know that I am well & that I love you & that when I return I shall explain.

Flora

She would leave and find a room, a refuge, where no one knew her and where she could think and work. She, once a novelist, would write again – to arrange her memories and make sense of them and to give an account of the two most intense experiences of her life: the predations she had suffered at the hands of her Uncle Charles and the brief, incandescent love affair she had had with William McKenzie. She did not chide herself for acting impulsively or irrationally. I am doing what I must, she thought. Though I've no notes or records, only my recalcitrant brain, I must proceed.

She packed a small suitcase with warm clothing, an extra pair of boots, and pen, pencils, ink, paper, and the Diary she had begun keeping. She waited till the banks were open, then put on her cloche hat and thick blue woolen coat and went to the branch of the Manufacturers Trust Bank in 3rd Avenue. There she withdrew a small amount from their joint account, enough in her estimate to last her a week or two, which she thought would be sufficient. Leaving the bank, she felt light and unrestrained, almost giddy. The world had become... odd, its outlines less distinct, its colours less hued.

She took the Lexington Avenue subway south, exited at 8th Street, and went directly to Washington Square, where the day before she had seen her lover. Entering the park from the east, she walked under the statue of Garibaldi, paused briefly at the central fountain, then turned south. When she reached the edge of the park, she did not stop as she had done the day before, but continued, roaming aimlessly the streets below the park.

At some point she came upon Byrne's Hotel, in Sullivan Street, in a neighbourhood of red-brick tenements and small shops. The area seemed populated by Italians. (Near the corner was a church serving them, the Shrine of St Anthony of Padua.) No one would bother her here. No one would even find her.

The room Flora took was small and sparely furnished but would do for her needs. It contained a bed, a mirrored dresser, a water basin, a table and straight-backed chair, and, under the window, which was flanked by dusty, faded beige curtains, a small easy chair with padded arms and back. A gas lamp hung by the door; on the adjacent wall sat a squat black gas heater. One paid for the gas by dropping coins into a meter-box. At the rear of the room was a window onto a narrow air shaft, which she opened despite the chill just to look. From somewhere below floated a pungent odour, which she could not identify, but later thought was that of burning opium.

The weather, as it had been the day before, was bitterly cold, and a wind was up, furtively entering through the rotted frame of the room's one window, causing drafts that chilled her. The cold of the days and nights she spent in Byrne's Hotel Flora would ever after remember.

Flora thought the balding desk clerk at the hotel had looked at her peculiarly. He seemed to want to ask questions but refrained. He asked her to pay a week's rent, seven dollars, in advance. She did. He gave her her room key and told her there were bathrooms with tubs and hot water on the first and third floors. He told her that her room, number 44, was on the fourth floor. She felt his eyes upon her as she climbed the stairs.

In her room, to calm herself, Flora stretched out on the bed, which was not uncomfortable, and closed her eyes. Next door must have been a family for she heard the sounds, mercifully muffled, of children playing and crying, and of adult talk, perhaps argument, the words of which she could not make out. Lying on her bed in the chilly room she felt terribly alone.

When she had collected herself, she rose and hung her cloche and coat on a hook by the door. She unpacked her suitcase; she lay her clothing in the dresser. She changed the places of the table and the armchair, tugging the chair aside and moving the table to the window. The table would be her desk. She arranged her writing materials in neat order before her. She put a few loose sheets of lined paper in the centre, lay her Diary to the right, and just below it her pen, pencils, and bottle of ink.

She sat and began to write.

It was from Nikolai Chaikovsky that Flora learnt McKenzie's fate. A week or so after McKenzie had sailed for France, she and Chaikovsky met at Chaikovsky's request in the Iffley Road offices to polish a translation for *Free Russia*. As soon as Chaikovsky arrived he said, "Have you heard? Appalling news from Paris. Our Ivan Serov has been arrested there and the American McKenzie – you knew him, Kropotkin's friend – McKenzie has been shot dead."

Flora sat still, her throat closed, her body benumbed. Yes, she thought. It would be like this.

"A comrade in Paris, David Stirn, just sent word," Chaikovsky said. "He got the news from an informant in the Parisian police. McKenzie was in Paris to make an attempt on the life of General Kuznetsov. You recall this Kuznetsov. He was responsible for the murder of Boris Chernikov in a labour camp on Sakhalin Island – you wrote that piece on him for *Free Russia*."

Flora did recall.

"It seems word got out that General Kuznetsov had been assigned to the Paris embassy. Well, Serov, Stirn, some others decided to take advantage of Kuznetsov's presence in France. They held a trial in Geneva in Salomon Ignatieff's apartment and voted to punish Kuznetsov with death. They would carry out the sentence in Paris – await their chance and shoot Kuznetsov down in the street.

"Ignatieff volunteered for the task, but Serov warned that Ignatieff, the rest of them, were all well known to the authorities in Paris and Geneva and might be arrested before they could accomplish the deed. Serov told the others that it might be possible to recruit a person not closely connected to the group and unlikely to be under suspicion who would carry out the sentence.

"Serov had McKenzie in mind. McKenzie was completely unknown to revolutionary circles in Russia or elsewhere, but Serov had got to know him here in London. Serov mentioned him to the group. He described McKenzie as 'an Internationalist' and 'a true comrade.' The group approved Serov's suggestion and asked him to approach McKenzie. After returning here, Serov sounded McKenzie – cautiously, I'm sure, it was Serov's way – but when McKenzie understood what was being proposed he enthusiastically agreed."

You told me you wanted to move History, Flora thought, to destroy the Capitalists and build a better world. You told me of your father Lockie, who drowned himself, and of your mother Nell, who sang you to sleep.

"The plan was, McKenzie and Serov would travel separately to Paris and meet there. Serov would act as liaison between McKenzie and the Geneva group. He would see that McKenzie got a weapon – a revolver belonging to Ignatieff, which Stirn would bring from Geneva.

"But the plan failed. Somehow the Okhrana knew of McKenzie and Serov – a spy here in London according to Stirn's informant, we don't know who. The authorities in France were alerted. Both Serov and McKenzie were followed in Paris. Armed detectives confronted McKenzie in the street near the Russian embassy. He resisted. They shot McKenzie dead. He is buried in some cemetery plot in the east of the city. Among paupers."

Flora thought: I gave you a blue ribbon that would never fade. As my love for you would not. Were you carrying it when...

"Serov was arrested in Paris, the Ignatieffs – Salomon and Anutya – were arrested in Geneva, and they have all been transported to Russia. We do not know their fate. Stirn got away. I don't know where he is."

When Chaikovsky looked up Flora was gone.

In The Grove, Flora told Lijak that her sister Evelyn was suffering terribly from an influenza and that she must go to Highgate to nurse her. He was understanding. Flora stayed with Evelyn six days, heart-broken and inconsolable. Evelyn wept with her, embracing her and stroking her hair, telling Flora how she loved her and how badly she felt for her.

Later, when grief relaxed and allowed her to think, Flora realised that Chaikovsky had chosen carefully when and where to tell her of Billy's death, in the Iffley Road offices when no one would be about, and that he did so for a purpose: privacy.

She understood then that they – Chaikovsky, everyone – must have known of her affair with Billy, everyone including her loving husband. She recalled, in fathomless guilt, the kind and understanding look on Lijak's face when she lied to him about her sister's illness.

In the days that followed she managed to throw herself into work on *Ribeiro*. She continued translating for *Free Russia*. In time she seemed to recover.

Until yesterday, when she saw McKenzie and went mad.

For twelve days in Byrne's Hotel Flora tried to write of Billy and Charles. She failed. She took many notes, but because her memories were tangled and blurred these were brief, sometimes only a few words ("Soirée. Fanny Stepniak. Hodgson", "Mile End, small boys", "Spotty beaten", "Jack", "Checked coverlet", "Limps-field") and try as she would, she could not elaborate on them or connect them into narrative. She sometimes sat at her writing table for hours, producing nothing.

For respite and to refresh her mind she wandered the streets paying little attention to where she was going.

Hoping that her lover would appear to her again, she frequented Washington Square and sat in the cold on a bench (the same bench always), but he never did.

Once, returning to Byrne's from a walk, she tumbled into the slush in Houston Street and struck her face straight on, cutting her lip and lacerating her forehead. Unsettled, though not in great pain, she bought bandages and tincture of iodine from a druggist in Sullivan Street and applied them in her hotel room. She seemed not to be seriously injured; she suffered no infection.

During her stay at Byrne's, she did succeed in making short entries in her Diary. These are some:

Tuesday, 29 January. I have not written today. I shall try tomorrow.

Thursday, 31 January. Today I passed Mme Roy's shop. I dared not enter. The scent of tobacco from the nearby warehouse was strong but not pleasurable.

Friday, 1 February. Last night I dreamt of Charles again. We were moving through a great house. He was leading me by the hand. Aunt Elizabeth accompanied us. Many other children were there in many rooms. Not Jack or Edna or Esther.

Her last entry was this:

Tuesday, 5 February. I have tried to write of Charles Bowles my rapist and destroyer of my childhood & of William McKenzie my lover. I have found doing so beyond my power. I cannot think & my strength is done.

After writing this she sat for a time, desolate. Then, with gathering resolution, she collected and threw into the dustbin all the notes she had written in Byrne's save for one loose sheet of paper on which she had pencilled the first lines of the song "Billy Boy" and their accompanying tune. She had thought the arrangement very like the one she had worked out years before with Billy in The Grove.

"This I will keep of you," she thought.

She then tore away all the pages in the Diary containing entries she had written at Byrne's. Nothing remained from the time she had spent there but that scrap of song, which she folded and inserted into the little notebook.

The evening Flora returned to the Waldorf-Astoria, the clerks at the desk and the loafing pageboys looked at her as peculiarly as had the clerk at Byrne's. One of the page boys offered to carry her suitcase, but she waved him off. The lift attendant, Eddie, who was simple, was notably quiet on the ascent to the 12th floor (he usually remarked on the weather). Silence was his way of pretending nothing queer had happened. Other passengers in the lift seemed to give her distance.

When Lijak opened the door of their suite and saw her in the hall, he gasped and, uncharacteristically, stood frozen, hand on the doorknob.

I must look a sight, she thought. How stupid.

She did. She was hollow-eyed and gaunt (she had eaten only irregularly). Her face showed cuts from her fall. She had not bathed.

Lijak whispered, "My God, Pet, oh, Pet, I have been so worried!"

In truth, Lijak had been beside himself. When he found Flora's note, he immediately alerted the police and called them every day she was gone. He mentioned her absence discreetly to the manager of the Waldorf-Astoria, who showed great concern (but also fretted to himself about the press and the reputation of his hotel).

As she stood in the hall Flora did not tell her husband, "I saw a man in Washington Square who had been my lover long ago but who had died. You knew him. William McKenzie."

Lijak did not reply in shock, "Your lover...? Who had...?"

She did not interject, "I went quite mad. Ancient grief and even more ancient dread returned to afflict me. It is with these that I have wrestled in the days that I have been away."

Neither she nor Lijak said any of this. What she told her husband was, "I tried to write of important matters. I could not. I botched it."

Lijak finally came to his senses and rushed into the hall to embrace her. His left arm about her, supporting her (she was close to collapse), he led her into their suite.

After she had bathed and eaten and fallen asleep, Lijak sat alone pondering Flora's condition. Travel would be good, he thought, a trip to Florida perhaps, or to the West. A psychotherapist, of course. Dr Neubrander may know of someone.

As he held her in his arms while she was falling asleep, she repeated faintly, "Oh, Wilfie, I botched it."

CODA

Flora will recover. In the early spring of 1918 (she will take no trip to Florida or the West nor consult a psychotherapist) she will sail to France, where she will join a Quaker organization performing war relief work. In 1922 she will return to New York to live with her husband in the Commodore Hotel, to which he had moved, next to the Grand Central Terminal. She will become Professor of Music Theory at Sacred Heart College in Manhattan. She will teach; she will compose. Wilfrid will die in 1930. Thereafter, Flora will live with the final love of her life, Alice Neff.

Yet not a day will go by when she does not think of McKenzie. She will picture him in his youth and his innocence and his melancholy beauty, and from time to time she will visit Washington Square to relive the moment she last saw him.

OZZIE

It's a bright, easy Sunday afternoon, the first day of June. Ozzie, in jeans and tank top, walks briskly down lower Fifth Avenue. When she crosses into Washington Square she discovers, astonishingly in this city of astonishments, parked in the open space under the great arch, a shiny, black baby grand piano and seated at it a young woman. The young woman has short, springy red hair. She's wearing buttonhole glasses. She's playing what sounds like Bach.

The pianist's black day pack is leaning on the left front leg of the piano. A water bottle and tuning instrument lie on the pavement by her right foot. She's wearing heavy, dark gray, laced, kick-ass boots – how can she pedal wearing those things? – and has a small audience, now including Ozzie. Face dreamy, eyes closed, the pianist throws her red head back, rocks and sways, lost in Bach's baroque sequences.

The Square on this marvelous day is packed. The crowd, mostly young, is happy. Couples – lovers – stroll hand-in-hand. Girls in hijabs pass girls in short-shorts and halters and platform sneakers. Young, slim male couples with high-and-tight haircuts wander through. There are baby buggies, reeling toddlers, chess players, mimes. Under the Garibaldi statue a young black man is pounding a drum set, whipping his thick wild dreads in circles. Across from him, sitting on the stepped terrace, a middle-aged white man wearing a two-foot-tall gray conical hat adorned with odd symbols – they look occult, but Ozzie doesn't recognize them – is holding a yellow sign that reads in blue letters, "Tarot Readings Performed by Tyler." He awaits customers. Down the central walk a young woman in wine-colored jeans is playing bagpipes, marching in place, and skirling out some bloodthirsty Scottish tune. In the Square's central circle – its fountain has been turned off – three young black men in long, loose white Tees and shiny black warm-up pants are dancing with arms and legs to hip-hop from a large boom box. They've gotten volunteers from onlookers to come down with them into the circle and learn the moves.

The circle.

Flora passed here carrying her drawings portfolio, and...

Lovers and madmen have such seething brains,
Such shaping fantasies, that apprehend
More than cool reason ever comprehends.
The lunatic, the lover, and the poet
Are of imagination all compact...

The break came in early May:

Professor Azadeh Hosseini
Department of English
Georgetown University
Washington, DC 20057

Dear Professor Hosseini,

My cousin Harold Neff passed on your letter inquiring about Alice Neff to me. Alice Neff was my Aunt, the sister of my Mother, Emily Seitz (Mrs. Frederick Seitz). I knew Aunt Alice only somewhat. We visited her once in New York and she came here sometimes for visits. I am not very good at computers but if you would like to talk I would be happy to speak with you. My telephone number is (516) 334-4933. Call any time. Take care,

Joanne Seitz

Joanne Seitz was a chatty, friendly woman. She had lived in Buffalo all her life and had never married. She remembered Alice and

Alice's friend, the very old woman Alice lived with and took care of. Joanne hadn't remembered the old woman's name until she saw Ozzie's letter.

I was taken to their apartment. It was my first time in New York City, so I remember it. It would have been in the fifties and I would have been ten or twelve, something like that. Aunt Flora was bent over. She walked with a cane. I remember that. It didn't register with me at the time, but she must have been in pain constantly. It was a small apartment in a large building. The living room is the only room I remember or probably ever saw. It was very light. There were flowers. I remember flowers on the table. Aunt Alice was very nice. And Aunt Flora was too. They loved children. Aunt Alice gave me ice cream. Yes, there was a picture of a man on the wall. I remember that because Aunt Alice told me that the way you tell whether a picture of someone is good or not is if the eyes follow you across the room. She said that if they do, it's a good piece of work. First time I'd heard that one. I don't think she believed it, she was too intelligent. I think she was putting me on. But his eyes, the man's eyes, did seem to follow me. Or I remember thinking that at the time. That's all I remember. Memories fade, don't they? My mother passed in 1999 and I still live in our family home. My father passed in 1950. I don't remember him very well. My mother took care of Aunt Alice's will, she was the executor. She kept some things of Aunt Alice's and I've never thrown them out. I'm not sure what it all is. Would you be interested in any of it? If I can find it? I think it's up in the attic just gathering dust.

The red, white, and blue mailer arrived in Ozzie's departmental box three days later. It contained a thickish manila envelope and a note from Joanne Seitz:

Dear Professor Hosseini:

This is the material we talked about. It is very interesting
and I hope you find some use for it. I don't remember
what Aunt Alice died of. I think it was cancer. I remember
mother went to New York to take care of Aunt Alice's
estate. I remembered after our conversation that once in
a while Mother would talk about scattering Aunt Alice's
ashes together with Aunt Flora's. Aunt Alice wanted them
scattered together at Fire Island because they spent time out
there in the summers and were very happy there. Mother
went and did it. She said she thought it might be illegal, but
she did it anyway because that was what Aunt Alice wanted
done. Mother was like that. If you need more help please
don't hesitate to get in touch. Take care,

Joanne Seitz

In addition to a copy of Alice Neff's will and a file folder
containing Emily Seitz's complicated correspondence with the Library of Congress, the envelope contained a neatly typed prose
manuscript of some two hundred pages marked with corrections
in Alice Neff's hand. It was entitled *Billy McKenzie, A Story of
Love*. In the top left corner of the first page Alice had penciled in
red: "Completed by FBL Sept. 12, 1945. To be published after
our deaths."

Leafing through the manuscript, her heart tightening, pounding, Ozzie found stories – of Flora glimpsing the apparition of
her dead lover in Washington Square, of an Anglo-Russian soirée
where she had met him, of an assassination in St. Petersburg, of
a child raped repeatedly at the age of twelve, of the adult Flora
Bowles's love for and marriage to the Polish exile Wilfrid Michael Lijak, of the creation of her masterwork, *Ribeiro*. Running
through the whole, linking its parts, was the story of Flora's brief,
fiery love affair with the American Anarchist William McKenzie
and his death in Paris, betrayed by a spy, who Ozzie knows but

Flora did not, was the "well–connected English journalist of impeccable reputation," Richard Lane Hodgson, cryptonym POLY-
PHEMUS.

Ozzie's eyes grazed her desk, seeing: a green felt frog; blue
books from a final she had given the day before; a just-arrived
PMLA, whose transparent wrapper she had not yet forced herself
to tear open. And the last pages of *Billy McKenzie, A Story of Love*
by Flora Bowles Lijak, completed when she was eighty-one years
old.

Ozzie wondered if Emily had tried to get *Billy McKenzie* published. It wouldn't seem so. No correspondence with agents or
editors accompanied the manuscript. Why not, then? Maybe Emily didn't want the bother – it was Flora's manuscript after all, not
Alice's. Or, maybe she didn't know how. Or, possibly – it was
1961– shame at the words, "Flora will live thereafter with the final
love of her life, Alice Neff"?

No matter. What Ozzie did know was that Alice Neff and
Emily Seitz and Emily's daughter Joanne preserved this manuscript
and that she, Ozzie Hosseini, had found it.

Leaving Washington Square, Ozzie walks down Sullivan Street to
view the site once occupied by Byrne's Hotel (listed in the 1910
Directory of the City of New York). Crossing Houston Street,
she passes the Shrine Church of St. Anthony of Padua (it occupies
the corner now; Houston Street, where Flora fell in the slush, has
been widened since her day), then a butcher shop, an antique store
displaying Asian and African artifacts, an Italian take-out place, a
children's boutique, a pastry shop. The older buildings down here
are red or gray brick. All are apartment houses of five and six stories; fire escapes descend their fronts.

Byrne's Hotel has been demolished; nothing of it remains save
Flora's account. The building now bearing its address is a gray-
pink brick structure, pleasant and pretty with its false balconies of
white stone and wrought iron. Peeping over its street-side cornice

leafy branches hint of a tree garden on the roof. The building dates from the fifties.

Ozzie takes documentation shots of the site and of Sullivan Street in both directions. Far to the south, One World Trade Center soars in its beautiful, blue-gray, gleaming symmetry.

Commerce Street is a shady refuge of low brick buildings, secluded and quiet, angling away from the noise of Seventh Avenue. Somewhere toward its end Madame Roy had her herbal establishment, presiding, Flora wrote, at her specimens table in satin dress and satin turban and smoking her cigarettes. Ozzie has found no telephone or business directory listing a Roy in Commerce Street. The Madame's premises are not identifiable today.

Ozzie takes shots of all the buildings on Commerce Street where it hooks around to join Barrow Street. It was in one of these on a bitterly cold and snowy late afternoon in 1918 that Flora displayed for Madame Roy her photostats of plants from the LMs, hoping Madame Roy could help her identify them. One was almost certainly *datura*, Flora thought. Could another be Lords and Ladies? she asked. It seemed to her very likely. The images – and, Ozzie thinks, their manifest sexuality – frightened Madame Roy. She thought they were witchcraft.

Unsuccessful, Flora left Madame Roy, walked up toward Fifth Avenue to catch her bus, and, passing through the park, saw her lover.

Billy McKenzie, A Story of Love will be published by a small LGBTQ+ press in Eugene, Oregon in the early fall – it took the editors three days to accept – with introduction and notes, yet to be written, by Professor Azadeh Hosseini of Georgetown University. In the introduction, Ozzie will write what she can of the facts of Flora's life and observe that nothing occurring in the text of the novel is contradicted by those facts. She will comment on the differences between memoir and fiction (noting the ways in which memoir is its own kind of fiction) and will speculate that

Flora wrote her autobiography in novel form to distance herself from her pain.

Ozzie will point out that in writing of her romance with Billy, Flora brought him alive forever; and that by naming her uncle and describing his crimes she bore witness finally to what she had endured, silent no longer.

Text is memory.

The newly discovered novella will further strengthen Ozzie's bid for tenure, which she now seems all but certain to receive. She has a signed contract for *Live or Die* and readers' reports that are highly positive. Wally, who bumped the date of the meeting of the Department Tenure Committee into late June – "for administrative purposes"– is ecstatic.

Mojo.

He came to New North 346 and tapped at the door, which was ajar.

Come in.

When she saw who it was, she nodded. Right.

Silence.

Then: I'll leave if you want me to.

She stared at him, thinking: Do. Just go.

We said hello here.

Good place to say good-bye.

He closed the door quietly.

You're my life. I want no one else.

Mark...

She let out a breath. I don't think so.

I understand. But I'm here. I mean, I came... came to...

Pause.

Oz, I don't want to lose you. I loved you from the very start, from the first time I saw you. I don't want to say good-bye.

He stood at the door, awkward (of course) and vulnerable, not daring to advance.

Oz, I have no one but you. I love you.

His voice was that same kind, soft voice she had loved and, though not admitting it to herself, had longed to hear again, fearing she never would.

Her eyes fastened on his, and she knew in the instant, without thought, that she had been foolish, self-righteous, unforgiving. She knew as he stood there, anguish and yearning in his face, that she loved him more at that moment than she had ever loved him before.

Ozzie returns to the genial mayhem of Washington Square, to its sunshine and music, to its lovers and children and dogs and dancers. Mark is standing by the fountain, where they've arranged to meet up. Though they're in New York on a kind of honeymoon – they're not married, not yet – Ozzie had told Mark she wanted to experience alone the streets Flora Lijak wandered during those frigid days of January and February 1918, and he had understood.

When Mark sees her, he waves and waits for her, and they link arms and wander among the other lovers.

"Find what you were looking for?"

Not Byrne's Hotel, not Madame Roy's establishment. The one is gone, erased by time; the other unfindable.

"Yes," Ozzie says, and, smiling at his question, smiling at him, gives Mark's arm a tug.

Author's Note

Billy McKenzie is partly based on the lives of Ethel and Wilfrid Voynich and Anne M. Nill. I have drawn on work by: Anne Fremantle, an English scholar-journalist who befriended Ethel in the late 1940s; Yevgenia Taratuta, Ethel's Russian biographer; issues of *Free Russia*; accounts written by acquaintances of the Voyniches; Elaine Showalter's *A Literature of Their Own*; and the diaries of Olive Garnett, edited and partially published in two volumes, *Tea and Anarchy!* and *Olive and Stepniak,* by Barry C. Johnson.

My thanks go to:

Professors Jennifer Natalya Fink and M. Lindsay Kaplan of Georgetown University for lengthy and helpful interviews on life as professor of English Literature at Georgetown; and Professor Amy Appleford of Boston University for a helpful exchange of e-mails about that institution.

Karen Moses, formerly Senior Reference Specialist in the Music Division of the Library of Congress, and Tom Barrick, also of the Music Division of the Library, for cataloguing the Ethel L. Voynich Papers and making them accessible to researchers.

Pam Blevins, who kindly shared with me her large collection of newspaper articles and other materials relating to the Voyniches.

Ann Warwick, who was Vice President for Institutional Advancement, SUNY College of Optometry when I visited, for permission to tour the Aeolian Building, where the college is located, and Ann Beaton, Associate Professor for Biological Sciences at the college, for showing me around the building, particularly the 16th Floor (much changed from when Voynich had his offices there) and its view down onto Bryant Park and 42nd Street.

Anne Kumer, now at Case Western Reserve University, formerly Archivist of the Bryant Park Corporation/34th Street Partnership, who helped me visualize what the park must have looked like in 1918.

Raul Peña and Meghan Constantinou, formerly Librarians at the Grolier Club of New York, for assisting me in reviewing the Grolier's Wilfrid Voynich Collection. Ms. Constantinou very kindly supplied me with scans of the "Russian Letters," three mysterious missives handwritten in Tsarist–era Russian script, which Voynich for some reason preserved from his revolutionary days.

Trooper James D. DeAngelis of the Massachusetts State Police, for an account of how the MSP deal with the remains of those killed in traffic accidents and how next-of-kin are found and informed of the deaths of their loved ones.

Gerry Kennedy, who furnished me with a scan of the Voyniches' Registration of Marriage.

My late friend Erik Sandberg-Diment, whose home in rural Connecticut served as model for The Pond.

www.ingramcontent.com/pod-product-compliance
Lightning Source LLC
Chambersburg PA
CBHW020129120726
47903CB00007B/2180